Out of the Mountain's Shadow

Rose Alexander has had more careers than she cares to mention and is currently a secondary school English teacher. She writes in the holidays, weekends and evenings, whenever she has a chance, although with three children, a husband, a lodger and a cat, this isn't always as often as she'd like. She's a keen sewist and is on a mission to make all her own clothes.

Also by Rose Alexander

Along the Endless River
Out of the Mountain's Shadow

Rose
Alexander

OUT *of* THE
MOUNTAIN'S
Shadow

CANELO

First published in the United Kingdom in 2021 by

Canelo
31 Helen Road
Oxford OX2 0DF
United Kingdom

A CIP catalogue record for this book is available from the British Library.

Print ISBN 978 1 80032 310 0
Ebook ISBN 978 1 80032 311 7

Look for more great books at www.canelo.co

Printed and bound in Great Britain by Clays Ltd, Elcograf S.p.A.

1

Before the house belongs to the owner, it first belongs to God and the guest.

The Albanian Kanun

An Albanian who says besa once cannot in any way break his promise and cannot be unfaithful to it.

Mehmed Ferid Pasha

Prologue

Albania, 1938

The muezzin's call echoes out through the winding, baked-mud lanes of the old town, haunting and familiar. It is early morning and the minarets sparkle in the glow of the rising sun, as does the sea that is gently lapping at the harbour walls. It's the weekend and I have nothing much to do, so when the light shafting through the windows woke me, I decided to come down here, to the port, my favourite place in the whole of Durrësi. I love to see the ships come and go, flying flags from far-flung foreign lands: Turkey, North Africa, Russia.

My father, Gezim, works here. Or at least, he comes to the docks every day, and if a big boat is in and he gets lucky, he is hired. But not today. He was already home, unemployed, before I left. Another day when there won't be much more than bread to eat for dinner.

I turn my attention back to the ship in front of me, ignoring my grumbling stomach. The hold is being emptied, the creaking of the winches and the oily rattle of the sliding chains competing with the call to the faithful and the shouts of the dockers. Watching the unloading of the cargo, I imagine what is contained within those wooden crates – flour, salt, textiles, building materials.

This boat has come across the Adriatic from Bari. Italy is not far away but nevertheless, I've never been there.

The furthest I've ever been is to the Accursed Mountains. Despite their name and fearsome reputation, I love the mountains. We go there in summer, to my father's ancestral village, when it is too hot down here on the coast. Many relatives live there, with their sheep and goats and chickens. It's the children's job to take the flocks up to the grazing pastures and guard them all day, taking care to scare off any wolves that might come prowling by, looking for a decent meal. There are bears too, and wild boars with skin as thick as leather, but I am Bekim the brave; a wild animal can't scare me. In any case, I always have my slingshot at the ready and my knife: the knife that my uncle Altin gave me, sharp as diamonds and twice as precious.

I've let myself get distracted, thinking of the village, and I've missed the last of the crates settling onto the ground with an exhausted groan. There's nothing more to see now and I turn to go, but as I do so, something unusual catches my eye. A small group of people is walking down the dockside, hunched and wary, looking as if they slept in their clothes and for nowhere near long enough. The women and children carry nothing but a small leather suitcase apiece; the men have briefcases, too. It gives them a business-like air that is belied by their weary, effortful gait. They seem exhausted, and traumatised somehow, frequently casting quick glances over their shoulders as if anxious about being followed.

Their clothes are good quality, made of decent cloth and well-fitting – which is strange and unexpected considering that the other noticeable thing about them is that they look hungry. Hunger is something I recognise only too well because of the number of times I have experienced it, including right at this very moment. It is all around us, never far away, waiting to come and gnaw viciously at the belly when there is not even the end of a loaf to fill it. My mother says that we get by with the grace of God and our wits, but it seems to me that oftentimes even those things are not enough.

I can tell already that these people are not Albanian. Albanian women wear headscarves, sometimes tied and sometimes hanging loose around their heads as if they have just been thrown on temporarily to guard against the fierce midday sun. These women's heads are bare. The men are hatless and clean-shaven, dressed in suits, again completely different from my father and the men of the town who, for the most part, wear waistcoats and tall hats and sport long beards.

Flattening myself against the wall of the nearest wharf, half-hidden behind a stack of piled-up crates, I wait for this peculiar troupe to draw near. As they shuffle past, I listen carefully. They aren't saying much, seeming too tired and worn out for speech, but the words they do utter are in an unfamiliar language that I don't understand. Other than Albanian, I only know Italian, and it definitely isn't that; it sounds completely different, harsher and staccato like the irregular banging of a drum.

Mystified, I watch them pass. Who are they? Where have they come from and where are they going? I have to take my puzzlement and my unanswered questions away with me.

It is only a few days later that I get any enlightenment, and even then I have no way of knowing that these people are the first ripples on the water that presage the coming storm – and that my life and theirs will be inextricably linked for more than half a century.

Chapter One

Italy, 2019

Stepping out of the echoing terminal building, Ruth instinctively raised her hand to shield her eyes from the scorching white intensity of the brilliant light. She halted in her tracks as swarms of people buzzed past on either side of her, entering, exiting, crossing, all talking at the tops of their voices, all seemingly intent on where they were going, pushing trolleys that dripped with assorted luggage. It was simultaneously bewildering and intoxicating, but underneath it all pulsed the irregular beat of Ruth's own uncertainty. Fumbling for her sunglasses, she hastily put them on and waited, momentarily, for her head to cease throbbing.

Steeling herself, she ventured forth – and then immediately stopped again as she looked for the signage to the car rental office. She was here, in Brindisi airport in the heel of Italy, in order to restart her life. Or rethink it. Rehash it. Whatever. The whole point was to be brave and bold, to deal with the personal with the same assurance and confidence that she'd always brought to her work. But it was different, somehow. Apart from anything else, she didn't have any work anymore. For the first time in twenty-five years she was unemployed. She'd been let go, made redundant, unceremoniously cast off from her job as a newsreader for a regional TV station. However you wanted to look at it, it was pretty bleak, facing an uncertain future at forty-five years old, completely alone.

Now, if ever, was the time for courage – in her head she pronounced the word the French way, as that made it seem infinitely more galvanising – but courage was a quality that seemed to have a remarkable ability to make itself scarce just when it was most needed. Riven with self-doubt, Ruth stood, motionless and despairing, until the sharp thrust of metal against her ankle galvanised her to take evasive action.

'Scusi, scusi,' shouted an Italian child who could not have been more than ten years old and who was, inexpertly and with great difficulty, manoeuvring a trolley piled high with baggage along the concourse, clipping heels and running over the toes of innocent bystanders all along the way.

Ruth smiled and shook her head. 'It's OK,' she murmured, 'no worries.' She spoke in English for want of knowing any Italian so the child probably wouldn't have understood her, but it no longer mattered as she was already out of earshot. Squaring her shoulders and straightening her back, Ruth pulled herself together. Grasping the handle of her own unwieldy trolley, she pushed it determinedly forward. She was ridiculously conscious of being literally the only person who seemed to be travelling solo and thinking how conspicuous that made her amongst the sociable crowds around her.

The car hire man clearly thought the same.

'Just you?' he asked, with a puzzled frown. 'I saw on your booking that you were British and I expected one of your big British families so I upgraded you.' He fumbled amongst the key rack behind the counter. 'So you've got a Ford estate rather than the Clio.' He smiled brightly at Ruth as he handed over the key, a smile that slowly faded as he took in her expression. 'That's all right, isn't it? Plenty of room for your luggage!' He gestured towards the trolley, upon which lay Ruth's underwhelming belongings: a medium-sized roller case, her laptop bag and a duty-free carrier bag containing the plenteous supplies of sun cream, insect repellent and contact lens solution that Ruth had preferred to buy in Boots rather than to risk the extortionate prices of a foreign pharmacy.

Ruth forced her look of apprehension into a smile of gratitude, and dismissed the voice inside her head which was telling her, 'It'll be far too big; you'll never park it; you'll get a scratch,' and all the other myriad worries of the motorist unused to driving on the right or parking anything bigger than her own Fiat 500. Not to mention the man's certainty that all British families were large ones. Was Ruth really such an anomaly?

'It's fine! Lovely! Thank you!' she replied, covering her dread and self-consciousness with an excess of exclamations.

Settled into the driver's seat a few minutes later, she forced herself to be resolute once more.

'You've got this,' she whispered to herself. 'Nothing to worry about at all.' She steered her way out of the underground car park and into the airport's exit lane. Hot sweat trickled down her armpits and her back, despite the roaring air conditioning. Flustered, she somehow managed to navigate herself onto the *autostrada* to the south and, finally sure she was heading in the right direction, she allowed herself to relax. Her dislike of driving and lack of confidence in her own motoring skills were something she tended to keep to herself. It didn't match with the image she had spent so long carefully cultivating, that of a go-getting, capable media professional and TV personality. There was no room in the world she inhabited – had inhabited – for wimps.

Despite her misgivings, she reassured herself, she'd somehow surmounted the first hurdle and was on her way. She spent the rest of the journey vacillating between joy at the prospect of two months of rest and relaxation under the hot Italian sun, and horror at the idea of what she was going to do with herself for all that time. The longest holiday she'd had since she'd begun her first job at the age of twenty-one, having just graduated, was two weeks. Now she had four times that long. It had seemed like such a good idea when she'd been forlornly searching holiday destinations online, the perfect antidote to a mid-life crisis. And the choice to stay in one place, to give herself the headspace to really get to grips with what she was going to do with the rest of her life, had seemed necessary, important. Enjoyable, even.

Now, when all the other travellers were couples and families and groups of friends, she wondered if she should have thrown caution to the wind and joined a guided tour to South East Asia, or gone on a world cruise or something. Except that she hated organised jollity of any kind, she reminded herself, and had always regarded package holidays as something to be avoided at all costs. Nevertheless, the fact remained that, although she was fairly self-sufficient, and hadn't had a partner since a relationship breakdown five years ago, she had never before faced the prospect of spending so much time alone.

'Oh, Christ,' she muttered to herself, as she sailed past the exit for Santa Maria del Mare, having failed to notice its impending arrival entirely, 'that's all I need. Lost in

Southern Italy.' She gripped the steering wheel more tightly and attempted to change gears, before remembering that the car was an automatic. A desperate craving for a cigarette assailed her. *Perhaps just one*, a little voice in her head coaxed, *when you get there, as a reward for being so brave*, before a louder one retaliated with a forceful '*no*'.

She had given up smoking several times – well, ten at least, if she were totally honest – and each time she'd had a perfectly understandable and reasonable excuse for relapsing – the stress of work, the stress of splitting up with her ex, the stress of moving house. Now she had the most stressful thing of all to contend with: losing her job entirely. And she was absolutely adamant that she wouldn't let that be the reason for taking up smoking for the eleventh time. There would be no cigarettes on this trip.

Another turn-off hove into view and she pressed the indicator stick purposefully. The next eight weeks were going to be all about self-care – eating healthily, getting fit, quitting the fags for good this time. Alcohol, well, that was another matter. She needed at least one vice, she reasoned to herself. A nice glass of something cold and refreshing would go down a treat as soon as she got to her accommodation. She hoped there'd be ice in the freezer.

An hour later, Ruth was gratefully clutching a glass of chilled white wine offered to her by her landlady, a British woman called Caroline.

'Well, it's six thirty already,' Caroline had laughed, as she'd helped Ruth with her bags, 'and far too hot for tea.'

Ruth had tried to stop Caroline from hauling her suitcase up to the first-floor apartment because it was clear that she was heavily pregnant, but Caroline had insisted. Together with her small son, Daniel, she'd just finished showing Ruth around, having pointed out the air conditioning unit, the spare towels and linen, and the back staircase to the garden, Daniel helpfully assisting by repeating in Italian everything Caroline said, as if concerned that Ruth might not understand.

'He's so cute,' Ruth smiled, resisting the urge to tousle his curly brown hair. She'd always thought it must be annoying for a child when strange adults felt it was acceptable to invade their personal space. Not having any children herself, she always erred on the cautious side when dealing with other people's. But Daniel was the sort of little boy you wanted to clutch into your arms and give a big hug. 'Just adorable,' she added, as Daniel smirked in appreciation of being admired.

Caroline nodded, and gave a half-grin, half-grimace in response. 'Yes, he is – most of the time! But the long summer holidays, when even his nursery school is closed, and the heat, combined with the fact that this is the busiest time of year for the holiday lets and for Enzo's boat hire business means that one can have too much of a good thing.' She waited until Daniel had gone out onto the wide balcony, out of earshot, before continuing. 'Being seven months pregnant doesn't help, either,' she concluded with a sigh. 'Daniel wants to go to the beach and in the few free hours I have, I'm simply too hot and exhausted to take him. It's not going to be much of a summer for him, I'm afraid.'

Ruth took in Caroline's face, upon which was written her weariness, and then looked out to where Daniel was playing with a pretend football, swiping at it and swerving as if to avoid invisible tackles. It was clear he had all the energy – and demands – of any four-year-old. Ruth had every sympathy for her hostess; no wonder she looked exhausted.

'Well,' she said, taking another sip of her wine, 'I could help. If you trust me with him, I mean. I'm here for ages, and I'll have time on my hands, plus I love children. My nieces and nephews are all grown up now so I never get to play sandcastles or go rock pooling anymore. I'll take him to the beach every now and again if it gives you a break.'

Caroline looked at Ruth as if she could hardly believe her ears. 'Really? Do you mean it? Look, honestly... I feel bad now... I've made you feel sorry for me. I really shouldn't impose on a paying guest!'

'Really,' insisted Ruth, in her most sincere, well-modulated TV newsreader voice, the one that no one ever argued with. 'I mean it.'

'Well,' responded Caroline, in a tone of utter relief, 'if you're sure, that would be amazing.' She paused, as if searching for the right words. 'And – if it's not prying – what is it you're here for, anyway?'

Ruth gulped some more wine. 'In all honesty,' she replied slowly, her eyes searching the room as if for answers, 'I'm not sure. I really don't know. I'm just hoping that two months is going to be long enough to find out.'

Chapter Two

Santa Maria del Mare beach was small but impeccably formed, a picture-perfect golden arc of fluffy sand fringed by a row of blue-doored beach huts that nestled snugly against the old harbour wall. A few well-used fishing boats bobbed up and down on the water and on their prows and masts perched gulls, eyes darting to and fro like avian security guards.

On the first full day of her holiday, Ruth was taking possession of a turquoise-cushioned lounger under an azure umbrella at eight thirty in the morning. She was the beach boy's first customer and remained the only one for the next hour or so. For years she'd worked on the early news programme and getting up at four a.m. was in her blood, a habit she intended to work hard at breaking. For break it she must if she were to live like an Italian, dining late and staying up to the small hours. Her body clock was still firmly set to pre-dawn alarms and bedtime by nine p.m.

Spreading out her towel on the sunbed, she kicked off her sandals and sat down. Carefully and precisely, she applied sun cream and lay back, adjusting the seat to the perfect angle that would allow comfortable reading and, of course, people-watching. She looked around her. There were not many opportunities for the latter just then. Not only were all the other loungers unoccupied but also the rest of the beach was sparsely populated, just a smattering of mainly under-fives or over-eighties.

Ruth opened her book and then, immediately thinking better of it, shut her eyes. This was the life, she told herself, as the warmth of the sun suffused her veins. Nothing to do but lie here soaking up the rays and the atmosphere.

When she looked at her watch on opening her eyes, all of five minutes had elapsed. This relaxation business was harder than she thought, Ruth realised. Her gaze roved her surroundings; so much blue, the sea and the sky, the lounger and the umbrella, the beach hut doors and the awning above the cafe. I wonder why they chose blue, she mused to herself. To match nature? To blend in? They could have picked yellow, to go with the sand...

Ruth sat abruptly upright, burying her head in her hands and rubbing her eyes. What the hell was going on? Why was she spending her time analysing the colour choices of random strangers? Oh dear, she thought to herself, she needed to get a grip. Surely she wasn't so lacking in imagination that she couldn't find ways to fill her time and entertain herself with anything more profound than contemplation of the colour blue?

Swinging her legs over the side of the chair, she surveyed the water. Perhaps a swim? Or a walk around to the rocks on the other side of the beach? Could she be bothered? As she was mulling this over, a group of teenagers arrived noisily beside her and proceeded to settle themselves onto sunbeds adjacent to hers. Their bronzed and burnished bodies gleamed with youthful beauty; they were all long limbs and swishing, gleaming hair, their sultry voices filled with promise. Ruth observed them, fascinated.

I suppose I was like this once, she thought to herself. Young and hopeful, with no idea of what the future held and no inkling that it might not live up to expectations. Where had all the years gone, she wondered now. The quarter of a century that had elapsed since graduating and launching herself into the world of media seemed to have passed without her even noticing. How had she got to forty-five? How had she reached a point in life when she could look back on events and think, *ah, that was twenty-five years ago*, and not be referring to a point in early childhood? It was ridiculous, impossible. But it was true.

Like Joni Mitchell, over the years she had looked at life from both sides and she now had to conclude that she had absolutely no idea what it all meant. Not a clue. Perhaps her sojourn in the south of Italy would help her come to some conclusions. She hoped so anyway. Otherwise it might all turn out to be a total waste of time.

With a stifled sigh, Ruth slumped back down onto the sunbed. The Italian youths had quietened, fully absorbed in the fascinating content of their phones, and there was nothing to disturb the gentle peace of the beach. Sunglasses pulled down over her eyes, Ruth drifted off, lulled into a semi-doze by the soft lapping of the wavelets against the shore.

When she woke again, she felt more tired than she had before her little nap. Years of suppressed exhaustion, mental fatigue, emotional stress and living on her nerves was catching up with her, now that she was giving it the chance to. She should go swimming, get some exercise, make inroads into her fitness campaign, an idea for a novel, make a plan to find a new job.

She couldn't do any of it. A deep and profound ennui filled her soul, paralysing her limbs, plastering her to the lounger and making it impossible to move. Nothing made sense anymore. If she wasn't Ruth Randall, TV newsreader, who was she? Would she ever be anyone ever again?

On that first day, Ruth stayed on the beach until dusk. The boy in charge of the chairs and umbrellas had seemed barely to notice her at first, wordlessly taking her money with hardly a glance. But by the time evening fell, Ruth caught him staring at her curiously on several occasions. *Feels sorry for me, I bet*, Ruth thought, and why wouldn't he? A poor, lonely middle-aged woman, nothing else to do and nowhere else to go, waiting to be chucked off a sunlounger and told to go home, where once upon a time she'd have been ejected from a nightclub at closing time with a group of friends, all howling with laughter.

It wasn't just the years that had gone, Ruth realised, but the friends also. She had lost touch with most of them, so caught up in her glorious career, her ambitions, her dreams – all of which had crumbled around her, fading away the same way the sun was now sinking into the sea.

God, you are a self-pitying misery guts, Ruth chastised herself. *You need to get a grip, sort yourself out*. With that thought, she stood up purposefully, packed her beach bag and marched back to the apartment. She spent that evening on her balcony with a book and a bottle of wine, determinedly telling herself how much she was enjoying it all, the solitude, the freedom from obligations of any kind. And so passed the next few days, uneventfully and slowly, and gradually the beauty of her surroundings and the warmth of the sun did indeed begin to work their magic. The heat, the light, the long bright days all acted together to ease her fractured nerves and allow her frazzled mind and body to recover from the mauling of the last few months.

By day five of her holiday, Ruth felt rested and restored enough to make good on her promise to Caroline that she'd take Daniel out and entertain him for a bit. Reckoning that he wouldn't be interested in sunbathing she walked past the tidy rows of sunloungers, all the while gripping the little boy tightly by the hand so there was no chance of losing him. You could never be too careful with someone else's child. They made their way to the edge of the beach where there were rocks to sit on or lean against, and where the high cliff behind provided some shade from the sun.

Kicking off her flip-flops, Ruth danced around awkwardly for a few moments whilst she flung her towel to the ground to stand on. The dry sand without the cover of an umbrella was scorching, burning through the soles of her feet. This was not an issue one often had to deal with on Norfolk's windswept seashore. Not that she went to the beaches often in summer when she was at home. She preferred them in winter, when they were bleak and empty, and she could run unhindered and, for the most part, unseen – though she had to admit that she hadn't been doing that much running recently, the result of which was a slowly expanding spare tyre around her middle.

It occurred to her that she needed to get a move on with her Italian fitness campaign, especially as she'd rashly committed to taking part in a half-marathon to raise money for a local charity. The race would take place in September so she didn't have a great deal of time in which to prepare. She'd start tomorrow, she convinced herself, early in the morning before it got too hot. That, at least, would give her something to focus on.

She turned to Daniel, his little brown body bared to the sun. 'Shall we swim?' she asked him. 'Cool off a bit? And you can show me your doggy paddle.'

Daniel did not have to be asked twice. In a flash, he tore away and was halfway towards the sea before Ruth had finished speaking.

'Wait!' she called anxiously after him, as she hurriedly discarded her own clothes. Caroline had told her that Daniel could swim well but when it came to children and water, constant vigilance was key. A few years back, Ruth had covered the terrible story of a double drowning of two siblings on one stunning but hazardous Norfolk beach… but no, she mustn't sully her head with tales of disaster.

That was the problem, she mused, as she and Daniel splashed in the shallows, the water deliciously cool in contrast to the fiery heat. When you worked in news, day in day out, you got a jaundiced view of the world, hearing everything that was bad and terrible and so little that was uplifting or just plain happy. That was part of the reason she'd hatched the plan of writing a book, a cheerful, jolly one, to spread some joy around the world. But what about? She found herself devoid of ideas, realising that she'd spent so long disseminating reports of what everyone else was up to that she had nothing left for herself. People said to her that she must have plenty of material from her work, and in a way she did, if she'd wanted to write true life crime drama. But many of the stories were so unsavoury she'd never want to fictionalise them, and others were so improbable that no one would ever believe them if she did.

A face full of water launched at her from Daniel's cupped hands brought her back to her senses and she laughed out loud at the sight of his cheeky little face sniggering at his prank. Pushing all thoughts of what she should or could be doing from her mind, Ruth tried to concentrate on the moment: the warm sea, the hot sun, the delighted chuckles of her cute new friend. For now, her loneliness was banished by her companion's lively charm and never mind that, at four years old, his conversational powers were somewhat limited.

They stayed in the water until the skin on their finger-tips was puckered and crinkled. Once back on the beach, dried off and covered in sunscreen, Daniel indulged in that favourite childhood pastime of making cups of pretend salt-water tea for Ruth to drink.

'Umm, umm, lovely,' she gushed, fake sipping at the plastic cup he handed to her. 'So delicious, just what I needed.'

'You hungry?' asked the little boy. He pulled a piece of slimy green seaweed off a rock, put it into a shallow mould shaped like a turtle that made an improvised plate and handed it to her. 'Spaghetti?'

Laughing, Ruth accepted the offering. 'So kind,' she enthused, 'thank you.'

This was a game that Daniel could clearly have continued with all day, and Ruth was wondering how to move on from it when a voice interrupted their play.

'Hello, Daniel,' called a man who'd halted in his peram-bulation of the beach in front of them. 'What are you up to? Enjoying yourself?'

'Zak!' cried Daniel cheerfully, running over and flinging sand-encrusted arms around this Zak's chino-clad legs.

Ruth regarded the man, who Daniel clearly knew well. He was average height and burly, with a close-cut beard and deep-set, dark eyes, not exactly handsome, but certainly personable and attractive.

Seeing her gaze upon him, he held out his hand. 'Zak,' he greeted her.

Hastily, Ruth stood up, brushing her hands off on her swimsuit. 'Ruth,' she responded, as they shook, his big hand enveloping her much smaller one.

'A pleasure to meet you, Ruth,' Zak said, giving the 't' in her name a harder sound than a native English speaker would have done. Though the few words she'd heard him speak were impeccable, Ruth could tell English wasn't his mother tongue.

'How do you know this little one?' she asked.

'I'm a family friend of Daniel and his parents. I've known Daniel since he was born. Before, actually,' Zak explained, before raising his eyebrows enquiringly at Ruth. 'And you are...?'

'Just a guest staying in one of their apartments,' answered Ruth, quickly. She felt suddenly self-conscious, aware of the temporary nature of her affiliation with Daniel and his parents which was in stark contrast with Zak's established and on-going connection. 'I took it upon myself to offer some help with childcare – so here we are – me and my new mate!' She laughed to show what great fun it all was, in case Zak was wondering why an adult would willingly choose to spend her time with a child to whom she was unrelated. The truth was that Daniel was a marvellous tonic to Ruth's loneliness – a loneliness that she did not want to draw attention to. Nobody wants to look like a Billy no-mates, do they? Zak might pity her and that would be awful.

'He's a delightful little chap,' agreed Zak, with no appearance whatsoever that he was judging her. 'And where…?'

'*Gelato!* Can we have a *gelato*, Zak?' Daniel's pleading drowned out whatever question Zak had been about to ask.

Zak chuckled and turned to Ruth. 'What do you say? Can I treat you to a coffee and an ice-cream? If you are finished with sunning yourself on the beach, Daniel and I know the best place in town.'

Ruth scrabbled in her bag for her watch. It was eleven thirty, enough time for Daniel to have a treat without spoiling his lunch. And an espresso in a cafe definitely held more allure than another cup of briny water. 'That would be super,' she replied. 'Lead on – I always want to get the inside info from the locals about the top spots.'

On the piazza above the beach, they found a spot beneath a white sunshade. Nearby, a fan blew water-laden air in a cooling stream, and the breeze it created rattled the fronds of the dwarf palm trees that ringed the stone paved area. It was utterly idyllic; the sea stretching in an unbroken line to the horizon, the mid-morning peace reflected in the muted clinking of cups and teaspoons and uncharacteristically hushed voices. The latter Ruth put down to the fact that there seemed to be few Italians there on a weekday before the full August holiday season had begun. The volume always increased noticeably when the locals were in residence, something Ruth loved when she came for her evening aperitif. She liked being surrounded by excitable chatter and interlocutions so voluble it was often unclear whether they were amicable conversations or full-blown arguments. It filled the silence in her mind and stopped her focusing on her solitude.

But now, in the full heat of the day, it was pleasant to be surrounded by tranquillity, a calm on land mirrored by the flat calm of the water down below. Zak put in their order and, as the waiter retreated, a container ship let off its horn in the Strait of Otranto, a low boom that echoed off the cliffs.

'I wonder where it's going,' mused Ruth, looking out across the shimmering water. 'Or where it's been.'

Zak smiled. 'It looks like one of the Greek shipping lines that ply across the Mediterranean. It might be headed for Albania.'

'I suppose Albania's right across the way from here, isn't it?' agreed Ruth. 'Such a mysterious place. I feel I know very little about the country, even though it's been years now since it opened up.'

Zak gave a short, dismissive snort. 'Well, if you want information, you're with the right person. I'm actually Albanian, though I've lived in Italy for nearly three decades.'

'Gosh,' breathed Ruth, interested to hear about her new acquaintance's origins, 'I've heard it's a beautiful country.' She paused for a moment, searching her mind for where she'd got that impression from. 'Beaches, mountains. Lakes?' she concluded, somewhat doubtfully. She really was woefully ignorant of all things Albanian.

'Lake Shkodra is the biggest,' affirmed Zak, smiling. 'Though we share it with our neighbour Montenegro. But yes, you are right, Albania has natural bounty aplenty.'

'Do you go back there often?' asked Ruth.

Zak shrugged. 'Every now and again, when work allows. My parents are very old now, and my father is in ill health. So I visit whenever I can.'

Ruth nodded. 'I'm sorry about your father. But I'd love to hear more about what it was like growing up under Communism.' She paused, and then added hurriedly, aware it might be a sensitive topic, 'If you're happy to talk about it of course.'

'If you promise to tell me when I get boring!' Zak exclaimed, laughing. 'But you also need to tell me about you – where are you from, how long you are staying. What you're doing here.'

Ruth's heart sank at that last, dreaded question, the one she didn't have an answer to. Fortunately, providence intervened in the form of Zak's phone ringing, meaning she could avoid responding. Picking up the handset, he briefly scanned the screen, then declined the call.

'Unfortunately,' he said, with a regretful grimace, 'I'm going to have to go. I'm sorry to be so rude, abandoning you like this. Work, you know…' He gestured towards the phone in his hand. 'But I wondered – would you give me the great pleasure of joining me for dinner tonight? It's the Italian tradition to welcome newcomers to our country, and it would give us the opportunity to get to know each other properly, and talk without boring our little buddy here.'

He glanced at Daniel. The ice-cream had kept him occupied for a few minutes but it was nearly all gone now, some of it into his mouth but an awful lot, as far as Ruth could see, dribbling down his arms, splodged onto his knees and deposited in a slowly spreading puddle beneath his chair.

Sensing their eyes upon him, Daniel looked up. 'Look, Zak, look, Ruth,' he shrieked, sticking out a tongue stained bright blue by the bubble-gum ice-cream.

'Oh no,' gasped Ruth, in a tone of grave concern. 'Daniel, I think you must be very ill. We better take you to the doctor straightaway!'

Daniel dissolved into a paroxysm of giggles.

'Time to get him home, I think,' said Ruth to Zak, standing up. 'I've divested my duty for the day.'

Zak smiled. 'You've done well. Though why the children always want these vile flavours, I have no idea. What's wrong with vanilla, I ask you?'

Daniel did not deign to answer such a ridiculous question. After a quick clean up with the wet wipes Ruth found in the bag Caroline had given her, he leapt down from his chair, full of energy from the ice-cream sugar rush. Taking his hand, Ruth turned to Zak.

'Dinner sounds lovely,' she said. 'I'd be delighted.' She still hadn't acclimatised to Italian late-night dining habits; she wondered if it would be OK to suggest a very English eight p.m. or would he find it uncouth?

'How about we meet at eight then?' suggested Zak, as if reading her mind. 'Meet me here and then we can have an aperitif before eating.'

'Perfect,' agreed Ruth, hoping her relief wasn't too obvious.

Daniel was tugging at her hand, impatient already with just a few moments of inaction. 'I'll see you later!' she called back over her shoulder as she and Daniel headed for home.

'I'll look forward to it.'

Chapter Three

A lingering feeling of intrigue about her new acquaintance stayed with Ruth for the rest of the day. Interesting,
she thought, as she sat on her balcony later, looking
out over the fruit trees in the garden that were laden
with pomegranates, apricots and peaches. Definitely an
interesting man. She always admired people who'd left
their birthplace and established a life somewhere else. She
thought often she should have done that, wondering how
differently things would have panned out for her if she
had. New York, Sydney, Madrid… if she'd gone to one of
those places, perhaps she wouldn't be approaching middle
age single, childless, jobless. Directionless.

Sighing, she gave into yet another moment of despair,
slumping forward across the table. 'What ifs' and 'if onlys'
were no way to live, she knew that. But it was hard,
sometimes, not to rake over everything she had done, and
whether she could have done it better. She languished
like this for several minutes, until she heard Caroline and
Daniel coming out of the ground floor apartment beneath
hers. Abruptly, she sat up straight, pushing her shoulders
back. Caroline might look up and see her and wonder
what was wrong. Ruth did not want to draw attention
to herself, nor did she want anyone feeling sorry for her.
But Caroline was dragging a huge basket of wet washing
towards the line strung between two tall trees and didn't

so much as glance in Ruth's direction. Daniel gambolled off to the paddling pool and clambered purposefully into it with all his clothes on. Ruth could not suppress a smile.

Cheering up a little bit, she gave herself a strict talking to. Things really weren't so bad; lots of people had it immeasurably worse. She had much to be grateful for: her health, her mother, who was endlessly supportive, her former colleagues, who she hoped would remain in her life as friends even though she wouldn't be seeing them on a daily basis anymore. She must make sure she spent time cultivating these relationships, Ruth averred. Friendships were like houseplants: they needed care and nurture in order to thrive. Through neglect, she'd killed off enough of both in her life to know.

She could put her resolution into practice that very evening with her new acquaintance, Zak, and begin work on the art of amity even before she got back home after her holiday. At the same time, she could put on hold at least for one evening the burning question of what to do with the rest of her life and focus on the intermediate goal of just plain enjoying herself.

The rest of the day dragged. Ruth tried to read and tried to rest but was successful at neither. She went down to the garden and examined more closely the fruits she had observed from the balcony. Under the hot sun, they seemed to be swelling and ripening before her very eyes. How wonderful to be able to grow lemons and oranges as well as apples and pears, Ruth thought. Perhaps she should move out of her swish city-centre apartment when she returned to the UK, buy a house in a more rural location with a little bit of land, grow vegetables, keep chickens. The picture formed in her mind, a bucolic idyll where the sun shone just like it did here in Italy.

The loud, insistent buzzing of a bee resounding in her ear brought her to her senses. She had absolutely no interest in gardening, let alone self-sufficiency. Why bother to grow tomatoes when the farmers' market stall-holders did it so much better? And Norfolk, where the wind sliced off the North Sea for half the year, was the last place to want to be compelled to spend time outdoors. No, whatever the answer was, it definitely wasn't The Good Life.

In the apartment's tiny bathroom she showered and tried to apply make-up. She had forgotten the cardinal rule of living in a hot country, which was, of course, to keep mascara in the fridge. The brush came out of the tube coated in horrifyingly large globs of black goo. Scrutinising herself in the mirror, she contemplated whether she could go without. She'd had her eyelashes tinted before leaving and they still had some colour left in them. Blinking at herself, she decided they'd have to do. Anyway, why was she expending so much energy on getting ready for dinner with a random Albanian? It was hardly a date; it didn't matter what she looked like.

With a sigh, Ruth replaced the brush and purposefully marched to the kitchen to deposit the mascara in the fridge. Might as well be ready for a time when it was needed. She straightened up her shoulders, trying to rid herself of the sense of despondency that had settled upon her. How many times had she prepared to meet some swipe-right guy in her increasingly desperate attempts to find lasting love, only to be disappointed once more? It had been that desperation that had led her to push aside her doubts about the traitorous Simon, to ignore anything that could – and should – have sounded the warning knell.

Nothing she could do about that disaster now. Except make sure that she never fell into such a trap again.

Though why I'm even thinking about that, I have no idea, she remonstrated with herself. She was still by the fridge, the open door supporting the air conditioning to bring her body temperature down to something approaching reasonable. It really was hot. Reaching in, she pulled out the bottle of wine. A little Dutch courage. Even if it wasn't a date, it was better to be relaxed.

By the time eight p.m. came, Ruth was sauntering into the piazza, relishing the gentle breeze blowing in from the sea and grateful for the slight lowering of the mercury. The square was bustling with people dressed in their evening finery, looking effortlessly cool and sophisticated as only Europeans can. Weaving around the packed tables in search of Zak, Ruth fleetingly wondered if her plain dress was not understated as she hoped but dowdy instead, and then immediately dismissed the thought. She wasn't looking for attention, just to have a nice meal with a pleasant new acquaintance. Her clothes were unimportant.

'Ruth!'

Zak's call alerted her to where he was waiting, standing by a table on which two wine glasses filled with ice and a liquid of a vivid tangerine hue already presided.

'Over here,' he said and, with an almost imperceptible bow of his head, indicated her chair. 'I took the liberty of ordering us both an Aperol spritz. It is, in my opinion, the most pleasant way to preface a meal.'

'Lovely,' enthused Ruth, as she sat down, smiling to herself at his somewhat old-fashioned English. It sounded a bit like he'd learnt it from a 1950s textbook. She looked at the drink in front of her which glowed like a glass of child's pop. 'I'm sure it's delicious,' she went on, a tad dubiously, 'but I have to confess I've never had it before. It looks like something Daniel would choose.'

As soon as the words were out, Ruth realised they didn't really sound complimentary.

'What I mean is,' she added hastily, 'the colour – it's so bright and eye-catching and, um, well, *orange*…' She ground to a halt, sure she was only making things worse.

Zak emitted a delighted chuckle. 'Ruth, it's fine, don't worry. You are absolutely correct; its appeal may not lie in its appearance, but I can assure you it tastes good – and I can't believe you've never had it before. Give it a try. If you don't like it, we can get you something else.'

Ruth smiled at him gratefully. He hadn't taken offence at all at her crassness. She took a sip of the drink. It was bitter and herby and refreshingly bubbly.

'Gorgeous,' she affirmed, savouring the unusual flavour. She took another, less tentative and larger, sip. 'Really very, very nice,' she added. 'Even if it does resemble a cross between Lucozade and Irn-Bru.'

She glanced up from under her – un-mascared – lashes and caught Zak's eye. And suddenly they both burst out laughing.

'I've got no idea what Irn-Bru is,' chuckled Zak, 'but I'm assuming it's not what one might call a sophisticated drink.'

'You can say that again,' agreed Ruth, 'though it has its aficionados.' She contemplated the contents of her glass. 'I mean, this Aperol – it looks summery, I'll give it that. And orange is my second-favourite colour so…'

'Your second-favourite?' questioned Zak. 'And what is your first favourite, then?'

Ruth was silent. Zak regarded her for a moment. And then suddenly let out a loud guffaw. 'Oh, I fell right into that one, didn't I? You're just teasing me, aren't you? If you tell someone something's your second-favourite, they immediately ask what is your first... oh yes, I see what you did there. Very clever.'

Ruth grinned. 'Sorry, I just couldn't resist.' She swirled the ice in her drink. 'Blue is the answer, anyway.' She looked down at the beach far below them, where the azure umbrellas were folded away now. As the sun faded, the vastness of the sea was darkening to navy. Had she had too much to drink? She couldn't quite fathom the turn of the conversation, the easiness of their interaction. It was a long time since she'd felt so comfortable with someone she barely knew.

'If you're ready to move on, we should head for the restaurant.' Zak's words interrupted her thoughts. 'I booked for eight thirty and they don't look kindly on latecomers – they're always full.'

'Of course,' agreed Ruth. 'Let's go!'

Following Zak as he led her out of the thronged square, she understood why it all felt so natural and relaxed. Precisely because of what she'd been thinking earlier: this wasn't a date; no one had swiped in any direction; she had no expectations of the evening and, she was sure, neither did he, other than to pass a few hours in the pleasant company of another.

'At least you didn't offer me Pernod,' Ruth said, once they were clear of the crowds and able to walk side-by-side. 'I cannot stand aniseed.'

Zak pulled a face of disgust. 'How funny – I'm exactly the same,' he exclaimed. 'I really can't abide the taste. Nor celery, for that matter,'

Ruth's eyes widened in astonishment. 'Me neither!' she agreed vociferously. 'It's horrid.'

'Well, that's settled then,' joked Zak. 'This evening's meal will contain neither Pernod nor celery.'

They were still laughing as they arrived at the osteria, which was tucked away on a narrow walkway hewn from the sheer cliff face. Planters overflowing with lavender, rosemary and thyme fringed the terrace which benefited from spectacular views across the Adriatic, and the tables were interspersed with huge pots of night-scented nicotiana plants, whose delicate, delicious aroma wafted over the dining tables.

Ruth implored Zak to choose and order for her, explaining that she simply didn't know enough about Italian food to make the best choices.

'I'm not a gourmet,' she confessed, 'and I'm a terrible cook. So I need all the help I can get.'

Zak smiled graciously as he called the waiter over. A lengthy discussion ensued, none of which involved a menu of any kind, and soon after, dish after dish of regional specialities appeared on the table, along with a carafe of local wine. 'So,' ventured Ruth tentatively, once the waiter had left, 'tell me more about Albania, about what life was like there under Hoxha.'

Though her knowledge of Albania was hazy, she was aware of the decades the country had spent locked away from the rest of the world under the tyrannical rule of communist dictator, Enver Hoxha. She knew, too, of this man's terrible reputation on human rights, his brutal crushing of any opposition to his rule, his ever-increasing isolation as even the Soviets were forsaken as trusted allies. Stories of torture, execution and disappearances had emerged sporadically from under the tight wraps of propaganda, along with accounts of almost medieval backwardness: no cars, no telephones, no freedom.

Ruth wasn't sure how much Zak would want to talk about his own experiences of living under Communism – after all, presumably he'd left for a reason. But the opportunity to find out more was too compelling to resist. You can take the girl out of the news station, she thought wryly to herself, but you can't take the news station out of the girl. Ruth was, above all else, curious. Some may say nosy, she acknowledged. Nevertheless, finding things out had been her life for twenty-five years and, like waking up early, it wasn't something she could stop doing just like that.

'After World War II, Albania entered a very dark period for over forty years,' Zak began slowly, his strained expression and low tone of voice confirming Ruth's suspicion that his past hadn't been entirely rosy. 'All borders were closed, all channels of communication curtailed. Albanian citizens were not allowed to know anything of the outside world. Summary justice ruled. The death squad could come at any time, its victims often going to their graves never knowing the crime they were supposed to have committed.' Zak halted, casting his eyes down as he struggled to contain his emotion. Ruth felt a frisson of guilt – she really shouldn't be asking him to relive what were clearly painful memories. But on the other hand, she really wanted to know.

'Near the coast,' Zak continued, once he had composed himself again, 'it was possible – illegally, of course – to pick up Italian radio stations. My family lived in Durrësi, a port city on the Adriatic and we could get those signals. So that's what I did. I listened and I learnt, every word I could and, the moment communism was overthrown, I left. Got the first ferry out and didn't go back for many years. There was no reason to; Albania remained in a pretty dreadful state throughout the 1990s, riven by financial scandals that gave rise to widespread rioting. I spent time in the UK – that's where I learnt my English – but I always came back to Italy in the end.'

'You're brave.' Ruth pursed her lips, thinking hard. 'I don't think I would have done anything to disobey the law,' she said, referring to the clandestine radio listening. 'I'd have been far too scared.'

Zak shrugged. 'Needs must,' he replied. 'It was that or accept subjugation. Not even the threat of life imprisonment or the death penalty was enough to stop me. Not after...' his voice tailed away as if what he had been about to say was too difficult for words.

'After what?' questioned Ruth, eyeing him quizzically. It was dark now, the only illumination provided by the glittering fairy lights strung around the restaurant's canopy and a street lamp that glimmered brightly, the view beyond now one of impenetrable blackness.

Zak shook his head. 'Nothing' he said. 'Nothing at all.'

Ruth knew there was something more, but Zak was obviously not quite ready yet to divulge whatever it was.

'We have no idea, do we,' she pondered. The story had gripped her so much she hadn't even craved a post-prandial cigarette, and that was definitely progress. 'We, who grew up in the West, who have always taken our liberty for granted, can go where we like, do what we like, say what we like.'

'You're right,' agreed Zak. 'But fortunately for Albanians, the days when we lacked all those things are in the past. There's a lot of work still to be done – but at the very least, we have those basic freedoms we lacked for so long. And it was only when all vestiges of the old regime had been well and truly eradicated that I myself found out something momentous about my country's history.'

Ruth's forehead creased in puzzlement. 'Which is?' she questioned, eagerly.

'The story of how Albania sheltered Jews during World War II,' responded Zak, his eyes narrowing with the memory. 'How ordinary people, my father, grandfather and great-uncle included, risked their lives over many years to protect the Jewish refugees who, from 1938 onwards, began arriving from Germany and Austria, Yugoslavia and Macedonia. They had been too scared to talk of it, whilst Hoxha ruled, for fear of repercussions.'

'That's incredible!' exclaimed Ruth. 'I had no idea. But...' she faltered, 'why did they do it? When it could have cost them their very existence?'

Zak poured them both some more wine before answering. 'It was partly due to what is called the Albanian Kanun, the ancient lore that governs our deeds and actions. It instructs us that the guest is next only to God in terms of importance and must be protected at all costs. The second part was the notion of *besa*, which literally means "to keep the promise".'

A man at an adjacent table lit a cigarette, the familiar fizz and flare of the match followed by a waft of smoke that tickled Ruth's nostrils. She was so absorbed in Zak's story that, for once, it didn't make her want to light up herself.

'Go on,' she urged, 'tell me about *besa*. I love a tradition, a piece of folklore.'

Zak smiled and nodded. 'It is barely known about outside Albania. But for my ancestors, my fellow countryman, during the war years, it specifically applied to making a pledge, individually and collectively, to save these people who came to our country in so much fear and distress. It was nothing to do with their religion, or ours. *Besa* transcends all such things.'

The bulb in the streetlamp beside the restaurant flickered on and off for a few seconds and then went out, revealing the night-black sea beyond, dotted by a few distant lights of ships in deep water.

'It was a matter of honour,' Zak concluded, 'of a promise bestowed that must be fulfilled.'

Chapter Four

'Psst!'

The girl playing with the hoop in the street carries on, rolling it over the bumpy ground of bare, flattened earth, oblivious.

'PSST!'

I try again, louder this time. I haven't seen her properly, not her face, because she's had her back to me and has been staring down intent on her game. But she looks about the same age as me and I'm bored and want to attract her attention. Plus, I'm sure she is one of the foreigners, like the ones I saw disembarking in the port, who have been arriving for several months now, but recently more and more often, in groups of three, four or a dozen, and I'm curious. I hear the adults' conversations, the discussions after the evening's paltry dinner has been cleared away and they think the children aren't listening, about what is happening in far off lands that is causing these strange folk to arrive on our shores, sad and bewildered, as if washed up on a strong and obdurate tide.

I want to know more: I want to find out her name and how old she is and whether she has brothers and sisters and can she ride a bicycle? Because I can't and I wish I could and if she knows, she could teach me. But even more than

35

that, I want to take the hoop from her and show her how to roll it properly, spinning it so fast that it will go all the way to Leka's hardware shop without falling and we will have to run to catch it up.

'PSST!'

This time, it works. The girl catches hold of the hoop with her hand as she halts and looks around her, first one way and then the other, unsure of where the noise has come from. She turns in a circle, but still she doesn't see me, has not picked me out where I'm concealed behind the log pile that leans against the wall of the nearest house. She pushes her hat back from her forehead, revealing more of her face, of her searching eyes.

I gaze straight at her, into those dark brown eyes, at her rounded face framed by soft, tumbling locks of dark chestnut hair and in that instant I fall in love. I have never seen anyone more beautiful. I know then that she and I will be together forever, that we'll get married and have children and live happily ever after... Obviously that will have to wait awhile, until we're a little older, but until then she is exactly the person who will love to come hunting rabbits with me and pinching cherries from the Akuls' orchard and building dams in the riv—

'What are you doing staring at me?'

I jump as her words interrupt my wandering thoughts. She has spotted me behind the logs, grinning happily at the dream I have concocted of our future, and now comes marching up to me, her sweet face locked into a grimace of hostility and anger, her lovely eyes narrowed. 'Why are you spying on me?' she demands.

And with that, she reaches out her hand and slaps me, hard, across my cheek.

I'm too stunned to move. A girl hitting me? And not just any girl, but the one I adore, who I've already decided will be my future wife. I can hardly believe it.

A chorus of laughter breaks out from somewhere to my left. My gaze darts to the source of the noise and I see my two younger brothers and a group of their friends bent double with mirth at the sight of my humiliation.

Pulling myself up to my tallest and throwing back my shoulders, I step into the centre of the street, feigning dignity. I go up to the girl and my fingers close around the warm, wooden ring of the hoop. I take it from her and she yields it up without resistance.

'You must apologise for hitting me or I won't give you back your hoop.'

The girl looks into my eyes, her gaze steady and unwavering. She's brave, fearless even, I can tell. And even prettier close up than from a distance. I strive to steady my legs, and my resolve, to stop them from weakening.

'I'm sorry,' she says, not sounding it in the slightest, 'but you shouldn't hide and watch people. It's… it's not polite.'

Her Albanian is slow and faltering, but she still manages to sound imperious.

'OK,' I reply, inadequately. I don't know how to respond. I'm sure that I should wait at least a few weeks before I tell her I love her, that convention dictates at least this period of acquaintance and anyway, I don't want to play all my cards at once. It's all so unexpected, so outside my ten (though nearly eleven)-year-old sphere of experience.

I adjust the wide fabric belt around my waist and, with a swagger, roll the hoop a few metres down the street before catching it and handing it back to her.

'What's your name?' I ask casually, trying to sense, without rewarding them with the victory of my attention for the second time, whether my brothers and their stupid friends still have me under surveillance.

'Hannelore,' she answers. On her lips, the name sounds beautiful, exotic and alluring.

'What's yours?'

'Bekim.' I put my hands in my pocket and shrug in a manner I hope is intriguing and enigmatic. 'It means blessing.'

'Oh.'

She doesn't seem as impressed as I want her to be. She should congratulate me on having such an auspicious name but maybe she doesn't get the point.

'How old are you?' I ask, when it becomes obvious that the topic of names is done with.

'I'm nine. How about you?'

I smirk proudly. 'Ten, going on eleven.' Reaching double figures was good but getting to the teens will be even better. There are so many more things I'll be able to do when I'm older, taller, more respected. I can't think precisely what these are right now; I just know they're all to come. But I don't have time to dwell on the rewards of age; there's more I want to know about Hannelore.

'Where are you from and how long have you been here?'

'I'm from Vienna. We came… a few months ago, I think. I lose track, sometimes.' She looks suddenly unsure, vulnerable.

'You have learnt Albanian,' I say encouragingly.

She shakes her head. 'Not much.'

'What language did you speak before? In your country?'

My knowledge of geography is limited. Italy is across the sea, Montenegro and Kosovo to the north, and Macedonia and Greece to the south. That's about all I know – and, I've always reckoned, all I need to know. Though ships come into the port from all manner of countries, I've no idea where they all actually are and I've never really thought about asking. But now here is Hannelore, who hails from a foreign, faraway land, and suddenly I want to know more, want to know everything about her.

'It's a city, actually,' she explains 'A really big city, with wide streets and huge buildings. Not like here. It's in Austria and we speak German. But—'

Suddenly she stops.

A cacophonous noise of banging and crashing, shouting and bellowing, accompanied by a few gunshots, has filled the air. Her face blanches pure white and she looks as if she might be sick. I can see tears forming in the corners of her eyes, widened now in terror. All her bravery, all the pluckiness of that slap disappears in an instant. I can't bear to see her like this; I don't know what's happened, if it's something I've said or done. I have an overwhelming urge to hug her, hold her tight, but of course I can't. Firstly, she's a girl and secondly – well, secondly I just can't. It wouldn't be right, or manly, or anything.

'What's the matter?' I ask instead, urgently, raising my voice above the sounds that are ricocheting off the tightly packed buildings.

But she's gone, running faster than a night fox, and in seconds has disappeared into the jumble of shops and houses that jostle along narrow streets.

'Wait!' I call. 'Come back! I won't hurt you. I'll walk you home.'

I start to follow her, but it's useless. She's so fast and fleet of foot that I'll never catch her with the head start she's got, even if I desired to chase after her, which I don't. She's scared – whether of me or of something else, something I can't see, I don't know – but I will not terrify her further by pursuing her. It seemed to be the noise that frightened her so greatly, but I can't imagine why. It was just a noisy wedding procession, a cart surrounded by stamping, celebrating guests, a few rifles let off in exuberance and congratulation.

I stand and look in the direction in which she has departed and my heart sinks gradually into my old, worn, too-small boots. I don't know if I will ever see her again.

It starts to rain, Albanian winter rain that slicks the skin and turns the dirt roads to rivers of thick mud that sticks to everything. I'm used to it but something tells me that Hannelore probably isn't. That, in Vienna, the streets are paved with stone if not with gold, and everyone is rich.

I turn to leave, to trudge back to my house where perhaps there'll be some food for lunch, and it's only then that I see her hoop, lying flat on the rapidly rain-blackening earth, abandoned. Slowly, as if I were an old, crooked man who finds it hard to bend, I pick it up. I vow then that I'll make sure I give it back to her – and that I won't let her get away again.

But I have to find her first.

Chapter Five

In the end, it doesn't take me too long to seek Hannelore out. A bit of asking around, a few casual questions addressed to my mum and dad, my uncle Altin and various visitors, and I soon track her down to a ramshackle hotel by the port. I don't want to sneak up on her or surprise her this time; I just want to talk to her, to find out what she does all day. Does she go to school? Lucky her if not. I have to go but I sometimes play truant, running off to the river or down to the beach with my friends, Edip and Ilir.

I loiter outside the hotel, and eventually she comes out. But annoyingly she's not on her own. She's surrounded by several other people. Two, a man and a woman, look as if they might be her parents, but there are other adults as well, plus several smaller children, two boys and a girl. They walk straight across the street, though I spot the grown-ups casting anxious, surreptitious glances around them – just like the group I saw last year at the port had done, as if worried about who might have seen them or anticipating being robbed.

I open my mouth to shout to Hannelore but somehow I can't make the sound come out. There's something purposeful about the group that makes me feel that I shouldn't intrude on them, though I couldn't explain exactly why.

I pretend to be absorbed in kicking a loose stone out of the mud whilst observing where they go out of the corner of my eye. All they do is enter an apartment building opposite. It's four o'clock and the darkness is descending fast; it will be a while before the longer days of spring bring the light, hopeful evenings that I love so much. The door closes behind the group and I wait for a moment, checking that they are staying inside. Then I walk up to the building, affecting my best casual and nonchalant gait, ready to shrug my shoulders if anyone should ask me what I am doing or accuse me of trespassing.

It's very quiet, and the noiselessness rings in my ears louder than bells. If they see me skulking around I might get a clip on the ear but my curiosity is greater than my fear – Bekim Shehu is no scaredy cat! Having reassured myself of this fact, I slink up to the nearest window and peer through the grimy pane. It looks only into a hallway, with a staircase leading upwards along one wall. I prowl onwards, to the next window. Here, curtains have been drawn but there's a gap and through it, I can see quite a sizeable group gathered around a table on which stand two candleholders and a tray of something covered with a cloth.

A woman leans forward and lights the candles, then waves her hands and covers her eyes. I can't hear anything but I think she's murmuring, maybe uttering a prayer or incantation. Moving as quietly as I can, I shift my position so that I can see more of the room. With the candlelight, it's possible to make out figures further from the window and I spy Hannelore, in between the two adults I had earlier picked out as her parents. Beside her is one of the small boys. Her brother, perhaps.

I watch as they pass a cup around and drink, wash their hands, then remove the cloth from the tray in the centre of the table, revealing two loaves of plaited bread, different from the round ones we have at home. They tear pieces off the loaves and eat them and my mouth waters; I'm hungry and once again there might not be much for supper tonight. My dad's casual work at the dock is intermittent and unreliable at best and times are strange just now. Recently, days have been going by without any ships coming in, which is unusual. People seem unsettled in some indefinable way and everything is out of kilter.

It looks as if Hannelore and her family and all these disparate friends who are gathered in this room on a Friday night are settled in for an hour or two and I decide, reluctantly, that there's no point in waiting. Likely as not, when she does emerge, she won't be alone and will go straight back to the hotel. Giving one last glance through the window, where I now see dishes of food being passed around, I peel away from the sheltering wall and creep back across the narrow strip of overgrown, untended garden to the road.

When I get home, I ask my father some of the many questions that are burning inside me.

'Who are the people coming to our town, the ones living in the hotel by the port?'

'They are Jews.'

'What are Jews?'

'God's people, just like us.'

I stop to consider this. It seems reasonable.

'Why have they come here though?' I remember Hannelore's description of a great city with wide, paved streets and big houses. What could she and her folk want with the muddy roads and humble, single-storey dwellings in my town?

'They had to leave their countries.' My father opens his mouth as if to expand on what he has said, then shuts it again and thinks for a moment before continuing. 'They have been given permission to come and so they do and, as you well know, our ancient Kanun instructs us to welcome them and to keep them safe.' I don't think it was what he had been about to say but I nod sagely anyway.

He looks me in the eye. 'And so we will.'

I stare back at him, surprised. It hadn't occurred to me to do anything else. But I decide not to ask any more questions. I would take my father's responses as permission to befriend Hannelore and to spend as much time as possible with her. I'd seek her out and take her to the beach and the river and then up to the dry, hot patch of woodland and grass where the tortoises live; they'd be emerging from hibernation, soon. I check my thoughts before they run on again. Perhaps she doesn't like tortoises? Perhaps she has lots of them at home, in her country, and she won't be interested at all. But then I reason with myself that tortoises don't live in towns or on city streets, and I feel excited and optimistic once more, and I know with the utmost certainty that my life will never be the same again now that Hannelore is in it.

Tomorrow, the future will begin. I just have to wait until tomorrow.

Chapter Six

Italy, 2019

Ruth tapped her fingers on the table as she read the email on her screen. It was the day after her fascinating evening with Zak and she had to confess to herself that she was hoping she might see him again soon. When she had climbed aboard that aeroplane at Stansted airport, en route to Italy, the last thing she had expected was to befriend anyone. Least of all an attractive, interesting male. Far from it. She had anticipated weeks spent exclusively in her own company. Now not only did she have a small child to liven up her life, but an equally beguiling adult in the form of Zak.

Ruth thought that Albanian men, unlike French or Italian, weren't generally considered the 'romantic, exotic' sort; rather, they were more likely to be categorised as slightly dodgy. But that only proved how unreliable and dangerous stereotypes were, because Zak didn't seem to be either of those things. In any case, he'd lived nearly all his adult life in Italy so could surely be regarded as an honorary Italian.

Ruth thought of him for a moment more, about his tales of life under an oppressive regime with hints that there was more that he was not saying about his revelation about the sheltering of the Jews, a story she had never heard before. Obviously him asking her out to dinner had just been politeness to make her feel welcome, exactly as he had said. But still. If she had the opportunity to return the favour and treat him, she would take it. There was no reason not to.

Or was there? A sudden dread assailed her. Perhaps he was married or had a long-term partner who was away at the moment. But if that was the case, wouldn't he have said something, mentioned such person? Not necessarily, Ruth reasoned, and definitely not if he were another Simon – in other words, a lying bastard.

Groaning inwardly, she let her head fall into her hands. She was overthinking this whole situation, as she had an unhelpful propensity to do. It should just be taken at face value: a meeting of like minds over a casual coffee or glass of wine. Or Aperol. At the memory of the drink, Ruth reached for the shopping list she was intermittently adding to, and wrote it down. She would buy her own bottle to enjoy on her balcony.

Once this was done, she turned her attention back to her laptop screen where a distraction had arrived in the shape of an offer of some freelance work. An ex-colleague who'd moved from Norwich to London some time ago wanted to know if she'd be interested in researching and writing an article on hidden homelessness amongst young British women.

Research was Ruth's thing. It was how she'd started out in television, working on a consumer programme tracking down the dodgy criminals of East Anglia and the South of England, the hearing aid and driveway salesmen – because in Ruth's experience it nearly always was men – who made a living out of exploiting older people and ripping them off.

Ruth reread the details of the potential commission. The offer of gainful employment was never something to be sniffed at and it was always nice to be thought of. Since she'd lost her job, she'd often lapsed into thinking of herself as lacking any useful purpose, thrown on the trash heap far too soon. It was the kind of experience that left you feeling winded, struck in the diaphragm by an iron blow. The real tragedy was that there was nothing much she could do about it. She couldn't magic herself twenty years younger again, and yet it was her age, she was sure, that meant she was now deemed unsuitable to appear on screen. Of course, no one had actually said any of this to her.

On the contrary, her 'valuable contribution' to the company over many years had been lauded, her 'continual input' into the station's strong brand praised. But neither her value nor her input were enough to save her job. Ruth, sullen and hurting, was secretly sure it was because the senior execs believed that the sensitivities of viewers might be offended by seeing the face of a woman who was past her young and fertile years sullying their television sets.

Ruth scrolled to the part of the email where the fee was mentioned. Of course the cash would be useful, but what was on offer was minimal. She was extremely fortunate that she had received a generous redundancy pay out, and she had savings. So she didn't actually need the money right now and, she reminded herself, she had promised herself that this time in Italy was going to be a complete break from work, that a complete break was necessary in order to come to some sort of conclusion about what to do with the rest of her working life.

Which, despite what the TV executives might think, was most emphatically not over.

Pushing the laptop away, she walked to the front door of her apartment and flung it open. This side of the building looked out over the sea, which was its usual cerulean perfection. Ruth stood for a moment gazing down the road towards the little town perched above the harbour and the steps that led down to the beach. Would she go for a swim? Or a bitter black espresso, perhaps? Choices of how to fill a morning that she wasn't used to and hadn't had for so long.

Deciding on the coffee option, she fetched her bag and sunhat and, locking the door behind her, set off towards the cafe that Zak had introduced her to. It crossed her mind that maybe he would be there. As well as not finding out his marital status, she'd also not got round to asking what he did for a living. In fact, she didn't know anything about his current life – they had only talked about the past.

Pondering this, and wondering if he was a businessman of some sort, or perhaps a creative type, an architect or designer – because he had that air about him, of quiet inventiveness – Ruth was barely aware of what was going on around her until suddenly a pair of hot little arms were clamped around her legs. Daniel. Woken from her reverie, Ruth smiled down at him and then glanced up to see Caroline, weighed down with shopping bags, advancing very slowly up the steep hill from the town.

'*Ciao* Ruth,' shouted Daniel, enthusiastically.

'Hi there,' responded Ruth, as Caroline halted and let the bags rest on the ground for a moment. The poor woman was perspiring heavily and clearly in some discomfort, the heavy load not ideal to be lugging around in this heat. Ruth felt guilty; she had that huge hire car she hadn't even got into for a week. She had baulked at the idea of trying to park it outside the apartment, which would have meant squeezing it into a space barely two inches longer than the car itself, and alongside a fearsomely jagged stone wall to boot, so Caroline had advised her to leave it in the car park at the marina. It was a ten-minute walk away but worth it, in Ruth's opinion, to save herself from the ignominy of certain failure if she'd even so much as tried closer to home. She could have gone to get it, though, and given Caroline a lift to the supermarket.

Saying as much to her landlady, Caroline smiled gratefully. 'You're so kind. I might take you up on the offer next week – I honestly think this is the last time I'm going to be able to do a big shop like this without wheels. Our car conveniently broke down at the beginning of the summer and we won't have the money or the time to get it fixed until the end. Typical!'

Ruth shook her head ruefully. Like a lot of people in the area, Caroline and her husband walked a precarious financial tightrope between the good times, namely the summer, when the cash rolled in, and the quiet times the rest of the year when it didn't.

'Sure,' she said. 'Just tell me the day before and we're on. And Daniel and I need a get-together too, don't we, my friend?'

Daniel grinned broadly and performed a couple of little skips of happiness. Ruth's heart melted. He really was so enchanting. A sudden idea took hold of her.

'Perhaps the water park?' she suggested to Caroline. 'I love a water park!'

Caroline rolled her eyes heavenward as if the angels had descended. 'If you do that, then I'll nominate you for a sainthood,' she replied. 'I hear Pope Francis is open to suggestions!'

'OK, sorted,' said Ruth, laughing. 'I'll help you back up the road with those bags now and we'll set a date for next week. It might be an idea for me to check the weather forecast and choose a less tortuously hot day – if such a thing exists.'

'Good luck with that,' laughed Caroline. 'We rarely get a break before September.'

The bags safely deposited in Caroline's kitchen, Ruth set off once more. Daniel stood at the door waving until she was out of sight. Her heart lurched momentarily at the realisation that came upon her every now and again that she would never have children of her own, that it was too late now. And as for marriage or a life partner, that seemed equally unlikely. The longest relationship she'd ever had was with the dreaded Simon. It had ended extremely badly five years ago, and she'd been so burnt by the experience that she'd barely gone on so much as a date since then. She still had all the apps, occasionally engaged in a conversation with someone, but usually found herself backing out before it got as far as a face-to-face meeting. There was just too much to lose if she got it wrong again.

Like the redundancy that followed, the break-up had left Ruth feeling not only emotionally bruised but also somehow diminished, as if her failure to hold on to a man – even a lying, duplicitous one – reflected negatively on her character at the deepest level. For a moment, amidst the glory of a scorching Italian summer's day, sadness engulfed her and she blinked back tears. She had spent so long grafting and striving, and she'd been so damn *loyal*: loyal to her partner, even when he was cheating on her with at least two other women, making each one believe that they were his one and only, and constantly borrowing money from Ruth to spend it on the other women; loyal to her employers, even when they had passed her over for promotion and given the plum jobs to younger, prettier, perkier women.

And what had loyalty brought her, other than making her look doubly stupid when it was repeatedly thrown back in her face?

Unbidden, the memory of that last, fateful meeting at the news station sprang into Ruth's mind. She'd gone along to it honestly believing that she would be offered the prime-time evening news programme at last, as a well-deserved reward for years of excellent and unstinting service. She truly had had no idea she was going to be handed her P45. At that moment, she had felt that she'd lost everything that had ever been important to her. Even the relationship disaster faded into the background compared to losing her job. She'd put everything into her work. And now it was all gone, evaporated into nothing with a click of the fingers and the opening of a letter which began with the words: 'Thank you for your long-standing service...'

Standing in the hot street, surrounded by beauty, shocking pink bougainvillea pouring over the ancient wall beside her, she angrily shook out her shoulders and forced the memory away. As her mother had told her, trying to help, trying to be reassuring, 'When one door closes, another one opens.'

Though such doors seemed remarkably thin on the ground right now, this was what Ruth had to believe.

At the cafe, restored to some equanimity by the sheer glory of the scene laid out before her, the blue sea, golden sand, azure beach umbrellas, Ruth's eyes flitted around the tables in search of Zak's head of dense, dark hair, but he was not there. Sitting down, she pulled her notebook out of her bag along with her 'Teach Yourself Italian' study guide and a pristine bundle of paper, newly printed and held together with treasury tags, that Zak had given her at the end of their evening together. He'd walked her home then gone to his house to fetch it and bring it back to her. Knowing how precious it was, she handled it very carefully.

The manuscript was Zak's father's memoir, collected, written down and collated over many months by Zak, the telling of the story of the Jewish refugees sheltered by ordinary Albanians. Once she'd ordered her espresso, Ruth ran her hands over the white paper, fingering its smoothness, letting the pages ripple through her eager hands. The Italian course, the notebook hungry for original ideas, the email from her friend, they could all wait.

Reading this book was a far more appealing proposition.

Chapter Seven

Albania, 1939

It's April and the sun is bright, slanting across the wide expanse of beach and glinting on the gently lapping water. It's much too cold to swim but for the first time this year it's warm enough to paddle. I kick off my boots and place them on a mound of dry sand where I'll be able to find them again. They're falling apart and too small anyway, so it's a relief to be rid of them and to feel the soft, shifting sand between my toes.

'Come on!' I shout to Hannelore.

I found her again, after that Friday night when I watched her and her family and compatriots eat their meal. Bekim Shehu knows how to solve a problem. It was just a case of hanging around, making myself available, right time, right place.

Hannelore looks at me doubtfully, her brown eyes both defiant and beseeching.

'I'm not sure,' she mutters, glancing down at her own black patent shoes that are in much better condition than mine. City shoes, that she brought with her from Vienna. Everything she wears seems nicer and cleaner and more expensive than what I have – and it was just the same with the people I saw getting off the boat at the port. And not just the clothes. I can't forget the men's briefcases, the accoutrements of business, indicating a status and income that none of the people I know have ever achieved – or ever will. These Jewish people must have had money once, even if they don't now. That in itself makes them different from us; we've never had a bean. It doesn't mean they're better, nor worse. Just different.

'I can't…' Hannelore stops abruptly, turns away from me and makes as if she is about to walk off, then changes her mind. 'What I mean is, I don't want to. Mother will be cross if I get my clothes wet. They are almost all I have; we were able to bring so little with us.'

She suddenly looks unbearably sad, a wistful, pained expression on her beautiful face. I can't bear to see her so troubled.

'So, what did you leave behind?' I ask. I assume she must mean a few things like cooking pots and that kind of stuff, things that are really essential but also too heavy and unwieldy to carry far.

'Everything,' she replies.

I scuff at the sand with my toes and consider her answer.

'But what is everything?'

'Tush,' she tuts. She sounds impatient now, tossing her chestnut hair over her shoulders and scowling at me. Though I want so much to take care of her, it's at moments like these that I realise that it's not necessarily going to be that easy. She sometimes doesn't seem the type who wants to be protected, who would acquiesce to being looked after.

I watch her gather her words. She's learnt so much Albanian already and it's not as if she's even trying. She says the words just get inside her head and she remembers them. Quite a lot of people in our town can speak German

54

because they've worked or studied there, or Italian like me, because Italy is so close and if you hang out at the docks you meet the sailors and learn from them. But I think Hannelore must be very clever to pick our language up so quickly. It makes me love her even more.

'Everything,' she repeats and then gazes out at the huge, grey-blue expanse of water ahead of us as if she can see all her possessions there, somewhere far out at sea. 'We sold all the furniture and father burnt his personal papers. Our jewellery and watches and silverware were stolen by the Nazis. We weren't allowed to take anything with us except a suitcase each, ten marks per person and what we were wearing. Mother dressed me and David in two outfits each for our journey here. Everything else, all our clothes and toys and books, we packed up to be sent on.'

She looks around her, perhaps imagining that the ship or boat that's carrying her family's belongings is waiting somewhere nearby. 'The container we put it all in was this big.' She stretches her arms out wide and then extends them above her head, standing on her tiptoes to make herself taller. 'Even bigger than that, actually.'

'So it'll arrive here soon and then you'll have it all again.' As I say this, I'm trying to imagine owning enough to fill something of the size she's indicated; I'm sure she must be exaggerating. A quick mental calculation of absolutely everything in my house tells me that it would fit in a couple of wine barrels. I only have one other change of clothes, and a couple of old, worn-out toys – which is all right, because toys are for babies, anyway. Books? There are no books in our house except the Koran, which nobody reads; it's just there because it always has been.

I'm thinking all of this when suddenly Hannelore drops her bombshell.

'It's not coming here, stupid. It's being sent to America, because that's where we're going as soon as we get permission.'

My heart flips over before plummeting down to the soles of my feet and on into the depths of the ruffled golden sand beneath my toes. Despondency settles upon me like the rain clouds that are gathering above.

'When… when are you leaving?' I ask, not really wanting to hear her answer because I can't bear to know that it is soon, perhaps tomorrow or next week, but at the same time not able to resist.

She shrugs again, setting her face bravely against the wind. 'I don't know. Mutti and Vati have been trying to get visas for us for ages – they've been to the consulate in Tirana twice already – but they're not giving them out at the moment. They say the quota is full.'

I have absolutely no idea what this means. The quota of what? What even is a quota? I don't want to look stupid though, so I merely nod, sympathetically and thoughtfully.

'So what will happen to all your stuff?'

Hannelore slumps to the ground, her knees pulled up, and sinks her face into her skirts. 'Who can say?' comes her muffled reply. 'I guess it doesn't really matter anymore anyway.'

An overwhelming urge to comfort her suffuses me. Maybe I was wrong about her not being the protection-needing type. Though her distress twists into my very being, a tiny part of me is pleased. Perhaps I can help her after all, make her need me and love me like I love her.

I kneel down beside her. 'It'll be OK,' I say, trying to sound as if I mean it. I put my hand into my pocket and pull out the package my mum gave me as I left the house.

'Share this with your friend,' she had said. 'Altin brought the nuts, and the honey is what's left of what we gathered last year in the mountains.'

I unwrap the paper and nudge Hannelore with my free hand. 'Look,' I say, displaying it before her as if it is an offering to a god. '*Shendetlie!* My mum made it and it's really good.'

Slowly, she lifts her head and looks at the precious slices of honey and nut cake nestling in my palm. A smile creeps across her face and relief floods my body. I've saved the day for now, taken her mind off her family's troubles and perhaps – just perhaps – made her realise that I am someone who can be relied upon in any situation. It's always wise, I reckon, to establish something as important as that early on.

We take a piece of cake each and munch in silence. It tastes even better than I thought it would, eating it here on the beach with a fresh breeze blowing and Hannelore beside me. I've taken her being here for granted, understanding her only from the moment I first saw her with her hoop, not even thinking about the journey she had to undertake to get here, the life she must have left behind. Not imagining that her future might be somewhere else, that her presence here in Albania might not be permanent.

'Tell me all about it,' I say to her now. 'I want to know everything.'

And so she tells me about catching the train from Vienna across somewhere called the Brenner Pass into Italy, the searches by the border guards, the army, the police, the constant fear that they would be apprehended and sent back, that the temporary visas granted them by King Zog through the Albanian embassy would be dismissed and disallowed. The hunger, due to only being allowed those ten marks per person, soon spent. Things got a little better once they reached Rome, where a Jewish organisation helped them with money and accommodation and even sightseeing, and got them to the port of Bari so that they could travel by night across the Adriatic to my city, Durrësi in Albania.

By the time she finishes her story, the *shendetlie* is long gone, the last traces of sweet honey and crunchy nuts nothing but a lingering memory on my taste buds.

'But what I still don't understand,' I say, picking up handfuls of sand and letting it drift downwards between my fingers, thousands of grains per second rejoining the infinite number upon the beach, 'is why you and your family were so unhappy in Vienna that you left.'

Hannelore lies back and gazes up at the sky, so wide and blue-black above us, scudding clouds racing inland towards the Accursed Mountains.

'We weren't unhappy – not until recently. But then everything changed. At first it was small things – we weren't allowed to go to cinemas or museums or to the park. Next they raided our cultural institute. They did everything they could to humiliate us – even forcing my mother and other Jewish women to crawl on their hands and knees to clean the pavements. Finally, last year, in November...' she falters and stumbles, seeming to be finding it difficult to carry on, '... last November – there was Kristallnacht.'

Chapter Eight

I've no idea what the word 'Kristallnacht' means but it sounds pretty, like the tinkling of a thousand bells.

'What is that?' I ask Hannelore, curious to find out why this word seems to frighten her so much.

'It was at night.' She takes a deep breath and juts her chin forward, forcing her hands into the sand on either side of her until they are submerged, invisible. 'It started with the noise – so much noise, sounds I'd never heard before. Shouting and breaking glass and hundreds of feet running and the pounding on the door, oh God, the worst thing was the thumping on the door. Vati didn't open it and eventually they went away but the noise continued. People – soldiers, the Hitler Youth, anyone – rampaged through the streets, burning our synagogues, looting our shops, breaking windows, kicking down doors and dragging people outside to be beaten and killed.'

She stops and looks me straight in the eye. I'm speechless. I've got nothing to say, but I think I must have been wrong about the bells. I can't imagine such horror. Deep inside me wells up a feeling that I want to go and find the people who did this and smash their faces in, break their necks, trample them into the ground. I swear if I knew where they were, I would do that. And if anyone ever tries to hurt her, my Hannelore, again, I'll be there.

'After that, everything was different, worse than it had ever been. We were not welcome in our own country. That's when Mutti and Vati knew we had to go. There was nothing left for us in Vienna. So we came here.'

I nod, as if I understand, which I don't. It is all incomprehensible.

'Have you got any more of that cake?' she asks, while I'm still contemplating the helplessness I feel at what she's had to go through. Her question breaks through my anguish and makes me laugh.

'No. But when I do, I'll save it all for you.' I stand up and pull her to her feet. 'And now – let's paddle.'

She opens her mouth as if to speak, just as she had before, and then shuts it.

'What's the matter?' I ask. 'Not afraid of the sea are you, after all you've told me about?'

She digs her elbow into my side in response. 'Shut up,' she says. 'Of course I'm not afraid. It's just that – well, I don't know how to swim.'

I stop dead in my tracks and can't stop myself grinning, though I don't want her to think I'm making fun of her. 'We're not going to swim, you idiot. We'd die of cold. We'll just dip our toes in and then – when summer comes – I'll teach you.'

Inside me, a little voice is whispering, 'If you're still here…' but I quell it by jumping into the first tiny wave and sending seawater spraying all over us. I taste the salt tang on my tongue and will myself to believe that I'll have Hannelore in my life forever, that the mysterious 'quota' will never materialise, that she'll still be here the day I'm old enough to tell her that I love her.

Later, as we're walking back to the hotel, hurrying because the clouds are spitting rain at us, a few things occur to me.

'So if you weren't allowed to take any of your money,' I ask, 'how do you buy bread?' I indicate up to the hotel that's now in front of us. 'And how do you pay to live here?'

Hannelore bites her lip. 'We get a bit of money from a charity in America, and a bit from your government. It's not enough – but now Mutti is working, teaching German to a rich family, and Vati – well, Vati mends bicycles at a shop in the centre of town.' She sticks her chin out in that way that I've now learnt is what she does when she's feeling proud, that indicates she refuses to be cowed. 'He's an engineer so he's good at that kind of thing. But neither of them gets paid very much.'

I'm trying to think of something to say that won't sound dismissive when a cart rattles cacophonously past us. As it recedes, one of its massive wheels throws a stone against the hotel window and it cracks with an explosive shattering. Just like when the wedding rifle had sounded, I see the fear whiten Hannelore's beautiful face and sense how it freezes her blood in her veins. In the second in which her terror renders her incapable of movement, I grab her arm to prevent her from fleeing like she had before.

'It's OK,' I say. 'It's nothing. Just a broken window pane. Nothing to worry about.'

Tears are spilling out of the corners of her eyes and I see her trying to squeeze them back. I say again, 'It's OK, don't worry. There'll never be a Kristallnacht here, I promise.'

I feel the tension dissipate and her terrified limbs relax.

I reach into my pocket and pull out another package. I give it to her. 'I did have some more *shendetlie*, but my mother told me, on pain of a beating, not to scoff it myself because it is a gift for your mother. An Albanian treat to welcome you to our country.'

Her brown eyes nearly dissolve into tears again but she holds them back. I watch as she goes into the hotel, turning to wave at me before the door opens and the dark hallway swallows her up.

Walking home, I strive to suppress the heavy fear that drags at my heart. Though I had tried to reassure Hannelore, an air of unease hangs about the quiet streets. There have been whispers, rumours, adults talking in corners in hushed conversations that I have strained my ears to hear, but managed to catch only wafts of odd words here and there that make little sense. Words like 'war' and 'Italian' and 'army'. I don't know what it all means and I'm sure it doesn't have much to do with me, but making my way along roads rutted with wheel tracks as the rain gathers pace, all I can think of is that I hope Hannelore doesn't hear the gossip and the tall tales that are flying around.

I want so much for her never to be scared again, to put her bad memories, so tremulously described, behind her. To forget all about it and never experience such fear again.

But even I, usually able to see the positive side of things, find it hard to convince myself of this.

'Where on earth have you been?' My mother, usually so patient, snaps viciously at me as I walk over the threshold of our house, her voice taut as a violin string.

'At the beach,' I protest, rage at this unjustified attack growing rapidly inside me. 'You knew I was there; you said I could go. You gave me cake.' My feelings of reproach cause my voice to crack in a very unmanly way and I try to pull myself together.

Mother sighs and wipes her hand across her brow. 'Yes, you are right.' She glances outside. Dusk is gathering but it's not late, only around six o'clock. 'But now we have been ordered— advised,' she quickly corrects herself, 'to stay inside.'

'Why? Who by?'

'Never mind why or who,' interjects my father, coming into the room. 'Just do as you're told.'

That night, a wind howls around our small house, wailing down the chimney, finding the cracks in doors and window frames, and the sky is pitch black, prescient of an ominous future. In the early hours of the morning I'm woken by the sound of gunshots, shattering glass, shouting and screaming.

Kristallnacht!

I leap out of bed and throw on my coat, racing to the door. It's still barely light and I don't even see my father standing there, have no idea where he is until I feel his iron grip on my forearm.

'What do you think you're doing?' He gestures furiously towards the window. 'Stay low. And for the love of God, stay here.'

A booming sound like I've never heard before rents the air, causing the walls to shake and the roof tiles to rumble.

'What is it?' asks my little brother, Lefter, whimpering in fear.

'Guns,' replies my father. 'Big ones.'

Guns? But I have to get to Hannelore to comfort her. I promised her it would be all right, that Kristallnacht could never happen here, and now she will never believe another thing I say.

'What's happening, Dad?' I ask. My voice is trembling and I don't even care. All I can think about is Hannelore and how scared she will be. At the same time, I'm trying to make sense of it. Bombs? In Durrësi, our sleepy little town where the most that ever happens is that two ships come in at once and one has to wait at anchor until the other has been unloaded as we only have docking for a single ship at a time? It is scarcely believable.

'It's the Italians.' Dad's voice is short and curt. 'They've invaded. We are resisting but' his words trail away like vapour from a boiling pot. It's clear from the 'but' that our cause is hopeless.

The Italians will win.

It seems like hours before there is a break in the fighting. Dad goes out, despite mother's admonishments and pleas for him to stay put. He says he has to find out what has happened, and when he returns half an hour later, he brings the worst news. The gendarmes, joined by ordinary townspeople to make a force numbering three hundred and sixty, bravely resisted with three machine guns for a few hours but were powerless against the tanks, guns and heavy weaponry of the invaders.

We sit in silence, everyone deep in thought, immersed in the nightmare. Even Lefter and Fatos, my irritating brothers, stop their senseless prattling for once. The heavy dread of what is to come fills every corner of our small house and, I imagine, every house in town.

When the knock on the door comes, we all jump out of our skins. I remember Hannelore's words, how the

Nazis hammered at the doors and, if let in, dragged out Jews to attack them on the roadside. Will the Italians do that to us?

We all sit, motionless, nobody daring to speak.

And then I hear it. A voice, calling.

'Bekim? Bekim! Are you there?'

A beautiful soft voice. A desperate voice.

'It's Hannelore,' I say, and leap up to open the door before anyone can stop me. Over the threshold stumble Hannelore and her brother, David, her parents and another man, elderly, with twisted glasses and little hair.

'We had to leave the hotel. They came by sea – the fighting – it was all around us. There were dead men – bodies – in the street. We didn't know where to go. And then I thought of you.' As she says this, all five pairs of eyes are upon me, plus the four of my own family, boring into me. 'You said you'd always help us. Can you do that? Can you help?'

I don't know what to say. Though so big in my promises, what could I, ten years old, nearly eleven, really offer her?

And then my father is in front of me, ushering them in and gently closing the door behind them.

'Come in,' he says. 'Welcome. You are our honoured guests and you will always be safe here. Sit down. Eat.'

And so the day ends with us sharing a meagre meal of bread and lamb stew while the boots of Italian soldiers echo through the streets around us.

Not Kristallnacht.

Something worse than that or not as terrible, we simply don't know. But one thing is clear: with the port blockaded and a foreign force in power, Hannelore and her family won't be leaving Albania any time soon.

And I can't avoid thinking that perhaps the Italian
occupation is not such a bad thing, after all.

Chapter Nine

Italy, 2019

For the next three nights, Ruth went every evening to the little osteria that Zak had introduced her to for a glass of wine and a light meal. Every evening she wondered if she would see Zak there, but there was no sign of him. The tinge of disappointment she felt about this she put down to unassuaged curiosity. She wanted to talk to him about the book, about these characters who were coming to life the more she got to know them – Bekim, Hannelore and their families. It seemed so extraordinary that there was this whole untold story – about a country, not far away or on the other side of the world, but a European country – that Ruth had never heard before and was sure most people hadn't, either. Whenever Albania came into the news, it was always about drugs or child refugees or gangs, rarely something good, something noble like this.

Ruth had so many questions to ask Zak but she was obviously going to have to wait.

When she wasn't reading, she channelled her need to take action towards her healthy eating and fitness campaign, going for long runs in the cool of the morning, striking out through fields of parched brown grass studded with olive trees and down lanes hemmed in by hedges of honeysuckle and oleander. Ever mindful of her commitment to take part in the half-marathon, she tried to regularly cover twelve to fourteen kilometres, which she could just about do. That was no mean feat, she knew, but nowhere near the twenty-one kilometres she'd need to pull out of the bag for this dratted race. Why hadn't it been a 10K she'd signed up for? Ruth could only hope and pray that the adrenaline, the roar of the crowd and the impetus provided by the other runners would help her along.

Later, she would go to the beach and swim, crisscrossing the bay over and over again, getting the laps in. Once she had tired herself with front crawl, she would stop and simply float, enjoying the sun on her face or turning onto her front and examining the extensive underwater life that proliferated there, all sizes of fish darting hither and thither, rippling banks of seaweed, rocks dotted with globe-like sea urchins.

Gradually, despite her initial difficulties and misgivings, she relearnt the art of pottering, of doing nothing very much at all and, crucially, enjoying it rather than beating herself up about her lack of achievement or her idleness.

One day she fulfilled her promise of taking Daniel to the Splash water park a little way up the coast. The picturesque drive there made her determined to do a bit more exploring, though the exhaustion engendered by six hours spent flying down water flumes under a sun that beat relentlessly down ensured it wouldn't be for another week or so.

'I'm going to need a bit of time to recover from that,' Ruth joked with Caroline, as she carried a sleeping Daniel inside and deposited him on the sofa. 'He conked out the second the engine started and he hasn't stirred since. As for me – I feel like my hard drive's been erased!'

Caroline laughed. 'You are honestly so unbelievably kind,' she repeated, over and over. 'And in return, Enzo wants to offer you a free trip on one of the boat excursions. I recommend the evening outing to the grottoes – they're really spectacular. Plus,' she added, 'I spoke to Zak yesterday. He wanted to get in touch with you but he doesn't have your number or email. I couldn't give him your details without your permission; I know we've become friends but I still have to be mindful of data protection and all that.'

'Oh!' Ruth suppressed a tiny, incriminating blush at the mention of Zak's name. 'Well, you have my permission now; it's fine to pass them on.'

'I will,' replied Caroline, 'and in the meantime, he wanted me to give you his.' She scrabbled around amongst a pile of paperwork, located a business card and handed it over.

Back in her apartment, Ruth read it carefully. On one side was his name and business position, and on the other his contact details.

Zak Shehu
Managing Director, Exert Components Ltd

Deciding that there was no time like the present, she picked up her phone and dialled the number, wondering as she did so what Exert Components dealt in. She felt ridiculously nervous, as if she were fifteen years old and ringing up a boy who she wasn't sure fancied her but who'd left a message so she had to call back, even if it turned out that all he wanted was to find out what the maths homework was.

Well, that wasn't going to happen today, Ruth assured herself as her heart beat loudly in her chest. Thank God the horrors of teenage crushes were well and truly over. But it was amazing the power they still had to rise unbidden into the mind and strike terror into the soul, their potency undiminished by a thirty-five-year distance.

The phone rang just once before being answered briskly in Italian with what was obviously Zak's business voice.

'Z-Zak,' Ruth began, falteringly. 'It's Ruth, you know...'

'Ruth!' Before she'd said much more than her name, Zak had intervened. 'Thanks so much for calling. Did Caroline pass on my number?'

They chatted for a bit and then Ruth plucked up the courage to ask Zak if he'd be interested in coming on the trip to the grottoes; Caroline had said it was a 'plus one' invitation. When he said yes, she felt a frisson of anticipation unlike anything she'd experienced in a long time.

That evening she strolled down to the marina to find Enzo, the boat *The Efemera* and Zak, hiding her excitement underneath a studiedly casual pace. The evening was perfect, the sun slowly descending in the sky, the sea calm and waveless, striated clouds dotting the arching blue heavens above.

Enzo helped her and Zak aboard, and then the other four or five people booked onto the trip. The speedboat was luxurious, with cushioned seats and a well-polished deck. Caroline had told Ruth that it was an investment Enzo had felt he had to make, to be sure of attracting business, but that paying off the loan was a constant burden. It reminded Ruth once more that, though the lifestyle here in this gorgeous part of the world seemed idyllic, it was actually pretty tough going. Perhaps she should send the fantasy of relocating to Italy to run a guesthouse to the same place that the Norfolk smallholding had been dispatched to – namely, the trash can. As countless TV documentaries constantly portrayed, starting a new life in a new country was a lot easier said than done, especially on your own and not speaking the language as it would be for her.

Zak gestured her to a seat at the front of the boat and came to sit beside her as Enzo navigated out of the crowded marina into the open sea. Once there, he opened the throttle and the boat leapt forward. The last rays of the dying sun made fiery diamonds of the flying spray, each one flaring brightly before fading back into the blue velvet deep. They sped past the end of Santa Maria del Mare, the last few stone houses and concrete villas petering out until it was just the barren, rocky cliffs shooting by. Rounding the headland, Enzo reduced speed and headed towards the shoreline, eventually stopping and letting down the anchor. The boat bobbed on the gentle undulations of a benign sea and Ruth waited, expectantly. She hadn't been sure what to expect of these grottoes, but right now she couldn't see anything at all, just stubby grey rocks climbing from the water.

'Are you up for this?' asked Zak.

Ruth laughed. 'I don't know whether the answer to that is yes or no, because I've no idea what we're doing!'

Zak smiled. 'You'll see. As long as you're OK to swim underwater and hold your breath for a moment or two.'

Ruth grimaced and rolled her eyes comedically. 'Oh my goodness, you're worrying me now. But I'll give it a go.'

And with that, Zak had taken off his T-shirt and shorts and dived over the side of the boat. Somewhat stunned, Ruth stood motionless for a moment, mouth open in astonishment. For some reason, she hadn't expected Zak to be quite so athletic. Within seconds he had resurfaced and was treading water beside the boat's bow.

'Come on!' he called, with a broad grin. 'What are you waiting for?'

Enzo moved towards Ruth. 'It's all right,' he said to her, encouragingly. 'You don't have to go in like that. Use the steps.' He pointed towards the stern where metal stairs led down into the water. Gratefully, Ruth accepted, descending gracefully and swimming towards Zak. The other tourists were still aboard, fussing over cameras and towels and talking excitedly in Milan accents. At least, Zak had told Ruth they were from Milan, whispering the information in her ear; she wouldn't have had a clue otherwise, still having barely mastered a few words of Italian so far.

'We'll get a few minutes to ourselves if we're lucky,' said Zak as Ruth approached. She followed him as he swam closer to the cliffs. Right beside a rocky outcrop, he stopped.

'Come beside me now,' he instructed, gently. 'We're going to take a deep breath and dive down. Hold onto my arm and I'll lead you. It's ten seconds underwater, no more.'

A quiver of apprehension rippled through Ruth's belly. She wasn't entirely sure that she wanted to do this. But then on the other hand, bottling it would make her look like a prize chicken. And if Zak was so sure it was safe, then it must be. Gulping a huge mouthful of air, she followed him beneath the surface.

The underwater world was mottled green, blue, and aquamarine, dotted with plump white fish the shape a child would draw, and purplish-black anemones. Ruth tried to concentrate on the beauty of it all, rather than her incipient fear. Just as she was starting to panic, Zak was pulling her upwards. Their heads broke the water and they emerged into a wonder world of vaulting light and dark, glowing stalactites and intricately patterned rock formations. The sea inside the cavern was limpid, crystal clear and dead calm. Treading water, Ruth swirled herself round and round, head tilted back to take in the full expanse of the cave.

'This is amazing!' she whispered, awed into near silence by the magic of nature.

'I thought you'd like it.'

Zak began to swim lazily onwards, further into the cavern, which seemed to stretch right back into the bowels of the earth. 'Look,' he said, pointing at the roof. An enormous stalactite hung, Damoclean-style, over a jutting piece of rock, into which millennia of drips had formed a hole at least twenty centimetres deep.

They explored the cave for an hour or more, diving down to gaze upon fish and seaweed and rock creatures, counting the stalactites, getting to three hundred and giving up, and wondering how far the water penetrated when the cave became too narrow to follow further.

'Not that I'd want to go in there,' said Ruth, suppressing a shudder. 'I've never liked the idea of caving or potholing. And since those Thai boys all got trapped by a flood in that cave complex – urgh. That's put me off for life.'

Zak grinned. 'I know what you mean. But this is caving-lite isn't it? And so beautiful.'

Ruth nodded. 'Absolutely stunning.'

They swam back towards the entrance and a few minutes later were back on board the boat, where Enzo was distributing water and cold beer to the guests.

'Now we visit a small beach accessible only by sea, and we have Prosecco and canapés prepared by my wife,' he announced, once everyone was settled back in their seats.

The tiny cove was snuggled up beneath high, unscalable cliffs, protected from all but southerly winds. The beach shelved steeply just a few metres from the shore, enabling the boat to get close enough for the passengers to walk ashore. Zak helped Enzo to carry the wicker baskets of provisions and the group was soon lolling on rugs, drinking sparkling wine and eating snacks; tomato and olive bruschetta, Grana Padano and prosciutto pastry cups, mini pizzettes and countless other scrumptious treats.

It was ten p.m. before they got back to the marina. Ruth felt pleasantly exhausted from the sea air and the adventure. Zak pointed his house out to her as they passed, a beautiful white-rendered single-storey building with a wide veranda at the front. Instead of leaving her to walk on to her apartment alone, he insisted on seeing Ruth safely to her door.

It had been such a perfect evening, Ruth did not want it to end. Outside her apartment, she paused for a moment and then decided to go for it and invite Zak in for a nightcap. She hoped he wouldn't think she was being suggestive, or that it was some sort of come-on. But she had so much still to ask him about himself, and the book. Apart from anything else, she desperately wanted to smoke and having someone with her whilst the craving was at its height might prevent her from giving in to it. Obviously, she had no cigarettes in the house but there was a very convenient mini-mart just down the road which seemed to stay open all hours so temptation was sadly always within reach.

Settled at the table on the balcony, she poured them both a glass of Negroamaro, the local wine which she was developing quite a taste for, though she'd never been much of a red drinker before.

'So these people,' she ventured, as they sipped their drinks, 'Hannelore and her family – did they survive?'

Zak laughed. 'I'm not telling you that yet. You have to read the book and find out.'

'Killjoy!' retaliated Ruth. 'I'm one of those people who reads the last page first. I don't like surprises.'

Zak shrugged, his dark eyes twinkling. 'Well, you can do that if you like. But you should know that the very last chapter has still to be written.'

'Oh, very cryptic!' Ruth grimaced dramatically, forehead furrowed. 'I guess I'll have to just wait and see then. But you know it's stopping me from doing anything else, don't you?' she teased, thinking of the article which she'd finally turned down today. 'Like work.'

Zak clinked his glass against hers. 'You haven't told me anything about your job. What is it you do?'

Ruth sighed and shrugged. It had always been inevitable that the moment would come when she had to reveal the truth about her employment – or lack of it. 'I used to be a TV newsreader and journalist,' she explained, her voice heavy with regret. 'But not anymore. My employers decided they could do without me and so here I am, taking a break whilst I sort it all out in my head. The work I just referred to was a piece of freelance writing that a mate offered me. Not a proper job or anything.'

'I'm sorry to hear that,' sympathised Zak. 'Such a blow is hard to bear. But I'm sure it's not as bad as it seems. You'll find something else, won't you? If that's what you want.'

Ruth sniffed, aware of incipient tears behind her eyes. 'I suppose so.'

There was silence for a moment.

'For now though, you're on holiday,' Zak reminded her. 'You shouldn't be working, or even thinking of it. Cut yourself some slack, as I believe the young people say. Sit on the beach and look out across the sea to Albania and imagine all the things that were going on there nearly eighty years ago.'

Ruth smiled. 'I will,' she said, grateful for his empathy, though wishing it wasn't making her want to cry. The kindness of strangers. It always got to her. 'I most definitely will. And by the way, if we're on the subject of occupations, what's yours? I saw your company name on your card but it doesn't give much away.'

Zak took a sip of his wine. 'It's pretty boring, I have to confess. I run a factory manufacturing electronic components.'

'OK,' responded Ruth. 'I suppose that must keep you busy?' Electronic components were a closed book to her so she wasn't sure what else to ask.

Laughing, Zak nodded. 'It certainly does. Though I have some measure of flexibility, being the boss.'

At that moment, a dull buzzing sound began to emanate from Zak's person. It took Ruth a moment to realise it was his phone. She didn't know what the time was, but it must be getting close to midnight. Who would be calling at this hour? A partner checking up on his whereabouts? No sooner had Ruth thought this than she dismissed it. Bloody Simon and the suspicious mind he had bequeathed to her. For sure Zak would have mentioned a significant other by now if there were one. Wouldn't he?

Pulling the phone from his pocket, Zak stood up as he answered. Leaning over the balcony rail, he conducted a short, brisk conversation in Italian. Ending the call, he turned back to Ruth.

'Well, that was bang on cue,' he muttered, frowning. 'Having said I can be flexible, there are times when I can't be. And now is one of them. Trouble with the night shift at the factory I'm afraid, and I'm going to have to go.'

Jumping out of her chair, Ruth went to the door to see him out. Strange that he should be the one who was on late-night call out. Or perhaps, as he had intimated, it was the penalty for being the boss, the rough that went with the smooth.

By the door, Zak paused and turned to her.

'Ruth,' he said, his voice low in consideration of the neighbours, his idiosyncratic pronunciation of her name making her smile. She became acutely conscious of the rapid beating of her heart, of the sultry night heat invading the cool of the air-conditioned interior, of Zak's eyes upon her.

'It's been a lovely evening,' he continued. 'I've enjoyed myself greatly.'

And with that he was off, out of the front door and down the steps to the street in seconds. Though nothing disturbed the calm equanimity of his demeanour, his body had the look of a carefully coiled spring that might unfurl at any moment. A tension that was almost tangible hung in the air, gradually dissipating once Zak had gone.

Ruth stood for a moment, listening to the cicadas, her nostrils catching the scent of the sea upon the air. Then she returned to the balcony overlooking the orchard and finished her wine, disappointment vying with happiness within her. It had indeed been a lovely evening... and she was an idiot to think there was any more to it. What was wrong with her? She should be glad to have found a friend, not be sitting here on her lonesome pathetically hoping Zak liked her. Because, despite all her internal protestations to the contrary, she realised that she liked him, perhaps a little bit more than was wise.

You silly fool, she told herself. She looked at the moon, almost full, hanging in the navy sky. Pull yourself together. Even if he is single, you're far too old for a holiday romance. Surely you should know that by now.

Chapter Ten

Albania, 1939

After the upheaval and shock of the Italian invasion and occupation, it's almost strange how quickly things settle down and go back to something that is not much different from normal. I thought – hoped – it might mean that there was no more school but no such luck. I still have to attend every weekday morning and waste my time learning stuff that's of no interest to me at all. Hannelore and the other children she came with from Austria are taught by their parents in an apartment in the town centre. So whilst the sun is shining outside, both of us are bored to pieces sitting in schoolrooms. Although maybe it's only me who is bored because Hannelore tells me that she likes studying.

Whatever.

One thing that's out of the ordinary is that Hannelore and her family are still staying in our house, so at least I get to spend time with her every day. Bliss! I don't see any problem with them remaining here forever; I never think of my house as small. Two rooms are all anyone I know has, maybe three or even four if their father has a permanent job, not just casual work on the docks when it's available, like my dad. But, with five extra people in it, I think my mother does find the cramped conditions difficult. And Hannelore's folks definitely do. They sleep in the main room where the kitchen is and we sleep in our bedroom as always, and sometimes, in the night, I can hear the sound of crying through the wall between us.

'What's wrong with your mum?' I ask Hannelore one evening. We're sitting on a couple of barrels outside the greengrocer's store on our road, eating olives that the shopkeeper's wife has given us.

'She misses home,' Hannelore replies.

She watches as I spit my stone right across the road and into a bucket outside my uncle Altin's house. Altin is my favourite person ever; he's tall and strong and brave and he was one of those who attempted to hold back the Italian invasion. When I grow up, I'm going to be just like him. In fact, I've already started. He's the one who taught me to fire a rifle and who gave me the knife I carry with me at all times.

I watch Hannelore as she delicately removes her olive stone from her mouth, holding it in her cupped hand and then dropping it to the ground for the dirt to swallow up.

She looks around her. 'Obviously,' she adds, disparagingly.

I spit another stone even harder and further. It pings against the house wall and falls neatly into the bucket.

'Bullseye!' I cry, triumphant. '*Obviously*' what? I'm thinking.

'Everything is so different here,' Hannelore continues, answering my unasked question. She puts another olive into her mouth and rolls it round and round with her tongue. She told me that she had never eaten olives before she came to Albania and at first she hated them, but now she loves them. I think about that now. Doesn't it logically indicate that one can get used to anything? Mrs Frankl will love being in our house if she just sticks it out, in the same way her daughter's learnt to love olives.

'In Vienna, we had an apartment with eight rooms just for us. We had a toilet you could sit down on, not like the ones here, that you have to,' Hannelore's lips curl, revealing her disgust, 'squat on, and there were no rats and cockroaches and ants, no horrible insects and vermin and creepy-crawlies at all. But...' she sighs, helplessly, uncharacteristically at a loss for words, 'I don't think it's even any of that. I think it's not having any privacy she hates the most.'

I am silent. I'm not sure what to make of what she's said. Privacy isn't something I've ever given much thought to. What's in my head is private and that's all I worry about. As for toilets – what can that matter to anyone? It's not as if you spend much time there. But Hannelore's words have cast doubt on my certainty.

'It's different for you and your family,' says Hannelore, as if she could read my mind. 'You're used to living all close together and on top of each other. But we're not. My father was a rich man in Vienna; we had everything we could ever want – food, clothes, books, toys, not just a bathroom but one that was inside...'

Somehow Hannelore can say things like this, can list in such detail all the unimaginable things she used to have, and it doesn't even sound like boasting.

'And we went to proper school,' she adds, 'and when school was out, we had holidays in the mountains and by the lakes.'

I had been feeling somewhat disheartened – there was so much of Hannelore's past that Albania could not possibly offer her – but now I cheer up. 'We live by the sea and we have holidays in the mountains!' I cry. 'So we're not so very different from you.'

Hannelore looks at me. Her eyes seem to take in my threadbare, outgrown clothing and my scruffy, worn-out boots. I even seem to read in those eyes that she knows that when we go to the mountains, it's to work, not to sit in deck chairs and rest or fly down snow-covered slopes on skis like I've seen pictures of Europeans doing.

OK, so I'm completely different from her. But that's all right, I tell myself defiantly. It's us who are helping Hannelore's family now, sharing our home and our food, even though we have scarcely enough for ourselves.

'It's OK, Bekim,' she says, her voice soft with understanding. 'Please, don't think we are ungrateful. You took us in when we had nowhere to go and we'll never forget that. We could never have imagined that complete strangers could be so kind.'

She pauses, as if searching for the words to carry on. 'I think one of the reasons that Mutti is so sad and Vati so tense, is that we can't practise our religion and do the things God told us to do, like eat special food on Friday nights. Even in the hotel by the port, we could do that. But now – we had to let Passover go by with no ceremonies at all, thanks to the Italians choosing this holy time for their invasion. It's hard for my parents. For all of us. We're not the same, are we? You are Muslim and we are Jewish and nothing will change that.'

I feel sick. I don't want any more olives now, even if they are just about the only thing about Albania that's better than Austria. I don't know if what Hannelore has just said means that we can't ever get married but I've got a horrible feeling it might do. It's not something I'd even considered before.

I have the overwhelming urge to do something crazy like climb the tower at the mosque, which I've tried before though I didn't get very high, or jump off the bridge and into the river below. That's the most terrifying thing I've ever done but, after I did it, I felt like a king. I want to feel like that again – and I will. When it's warmer and school is over for the summer, I'll do it. And Hannelore will see how brave I am – braver than any Austrian or any Jew, and that will make up for all I and my country lack, I'm sure, and, and…

Lefter comes to call us back to the house and I get up, slowly and reluctantly. We walk back in silence, me in front, Hannelore behind. Though only a few inches separate us, it's as if a chasm has opened up between us.

That evening, things get even worse.

'Please, take this,' I overhear my mother saying to Hannelore's mother. She hands her a fire-blackened pan; she has two that are similar but I know this is the one she likes the best. 'I have another one and you'll need it for your cooking.' She laughs and adds, 'If the house was burning down, my big old pot is what I'd rescue. How else could I feed my family?'

Hannelore's mother has only learnt a few words of Albanian so I know she won't understand anything of what my mum has said. But I've understood, and what I've heard has alarmed me.

'What's going on?' I ask.

'Mr and Mrs Frankl are moving out,' my mother replies. 'They've managed to find a small apartment not too far from here, so I'm giving Mrs Frankl a few things to help her set up house.'

I look at the tiny pile of items my mother has gathered together – the pot, a bowl, a knife and fork, a couple of plates. It looks pathetic, even to my inexperienced eyes. I think of Hannelore's home in Vienna, imagining the riches it possessed, the chandelier lamps and the silver cutlery on a dining table polished so highly you could see your face in it.

We don't even have a table – and unless there's one in the apartment they're renting, neither will they.

–

I don't see Hannelore for a few weeks after she and her family move out. She barely says goodbye to me when they go, too busy bustling around after her mother, closing suitcase lids and admonishing David for messing around and not helping.

I tell myself I don't miss her – honestly, it's better not to hang around with a girl. I have plenty to occupy my time, anyway. Now spring is here, my friends and I have been building a dam in the river and using it as a defensive position from behind which we can fire catapults at our arch-enemies, some boys from the neighbouring district. We go there as soon as school is over; it's a battle every day to shake off my brothers but they can't run as fast as me so I always manage to escape them in the end. I come home soaking wet and barefoot; my boots have finally copped it and I won't get another pair until winter comes again. There's no need for them in the hot weather.

I can't deny it, though: I get a bit bored of the game after a while. So when Hannelore starts to come round again, I'm much more pleased to see her than I let on. Once I've established that she's never seen a tortoise and only ever read about one in some weird story where a tortoise and a hare race each other, which is plainly nonsense, I take her to the place where they live. Watching her pick them up and cradle them, or feed them berries and leaves, or tickle their wizened necks makes me burst with pride.

'I love them, Bekim,' she says, over and over again, every time we visit. 'Can I take one home as a pet?'

I shake my head. 'You wouldn't be able to look after it properly,' I say. I know this because I've tried. 'It would escape and get away and maybe get run over. In the winter it has to hibernate and it probably wouldn't survive, and apart from all of that, they can live for fifty years so you'd have to look after it until you are an old lady.'

Hannelore looks at me as if she's about to argue but then she doesn't. 'You're right,' she concurs, reluctantly. 'It's better just to be able to come here and see them in the wild, where they're free.'

She sits down, placing the tortoise she's been holding on the ground next to her and stroking its intricately patterned yellow-brown shell. 'We all want to be free, don't we?'

I know there's something more to her words than musings on the life of a tortoise, but I can't quite work out what it is. Tears are gathering in the corners of her eyes and it makes me sad in a way I cannot begin to define.

On the way home, we see the Italian soldiers who have come in increasing numbers to the town. They are everywhere. But in all honesty, they take little notice of us and we of them. They just *are*, as if they've always been.

For the rest of the summer of 1939, Hannelore has to go to see the tortoises alone. As the weather gets ever warmer, my family and I decamp to the mountains, taking the old, familiar route, on buses, carts and on foot. The work there is as hard as ever and, now that my birthday has passed and I'm eleven, and bigger and stronger with it, I'm expected to do more and more of the labouring chores, whilst Lefter, Fatos and the little kids watch the flocks. As I lift and carry and chop and load I lighten the burden with thoughts of Hannelore, her chestnut hair and melting brown eyes.

A long way away, in countries I know nothing of, the war is raging. Every now and then we hear snippets of news that tell us so. But to me all it means is that I get to keep Hannelore a little while longer.

Chapter Eleven

Albania, 1940

A whole year passes before the events of the war intrude into our lives again. It's not until May 1940, a month before my twelfth birthday, that things change again. Word goes around that Hitler has forbidden Mussolini to allow any Jews to enter Italy. And whether what happens next has anything to do with this or not, we'll never know, but soon after this declaration, one terrible night brings fear and desperation to our threshold once more.

I rattle through the door with all my usual clamour, to find Uncle Altin and my father in the kitchen. Dad's face is drawn in concentration and both men are tight-lipped, arms folded. My father is a gentle person, quietly religious, never making a show of anything. But now he starts to pray, words from the Koran. We are not regular mosque goers, but even so the murmurings are familiar from numerous holy days and family gatherings. He's asking for protection, for God's guiding hand. But not for himself, nor for me or my brothers, his children, nor for my mother, his wife.

It is for Hannelore and her family that he's uttering his incantations.

'What's going on?' I shout. I look from one to the other, my head swiping back and forth like a crazed pendulum, my heart pounding.

'They've arrested Mr and Mrs Frankl,' says Altin, shortly. 'Your mother's gone to fetch the children here. It's all under control.'

Altin is always like this. Calm, reasoned, thoughtful. Calculating. But underneath the composure, even he seems nervous and unsettled, his black eyes glowering beneath knitted brows.

The door opens and my mother enters, Hannelore and David held in either hand. They are pale and silent, wearing their terror on their white faces.

Hannelore sees me and stumbles on the rough floor, falling to her knees, her tears splashing to the ground and staining the brown stones black. David, too, is sobbing.

'Mutti,' he whispers, over and over again, 'Mutti, Vati…'

I go to them, kneel down beside them. I want to help but I don't know what to do.

'Bekim,' wails Hannelore, holding my arm and tugging on it, almost pulling me off balance. 'Oh, Bekim, what shall we do? They've had Mutti and Vati for two days already. We have lost so much, if they are gone, we have no one.'

You have me, I want to say. *I'll never leave you*.

But of course, I don't utter the words. Because I know that they are not what she wants or needs to hear; they are meaningless. Her parents are taken and, right now, she doesn't know if she will ever get them back.

On and on and on, the adults talk. My father, my uncle and even my mother. Usually she would come to bed and leave the men to deal with men's business. But not tonight. It was only because she went to call on Mrs Frankl, to bring her some eggs she had been given by Altin's wife, Sarah, that Hannelore and David were found, alone in the house, petrified. Mr and Mrs Frankl had gone out one evening for a stroll in the fresh air and not come back. The two children had waited and waited, not knowing what to do.

My heart breaks when I hear the story. Why had Hannelore not come to me? To think that she had been too terrified to go anywhere is terrible. I know from my conversations with her, from all her descriptions of Vienna, that Albania is a wretched place in comparison. But in all my days, all my nearly twelve years, I have never, ever looked despair in the face like she is now. And in a sudden flash, I understand what Hannelore had been getting at that day with the tortoises. She would not take away an animal's freedom, put at risk an animal's life, because she knows from personal experience what those things feel like.

I square my shoulders and stand up straight. If anyone can help the Frankls now, it is us – the humble Shehu family from Durrësi, with not a gold coin nor a precious jewel to our names – nor even a dining table, polished or otherwise. And help them we will.

All night, the adults confer. I try to stay awake to listen, but the voices are faint and hard to hear, rising and falling like the rhythm of breathing. Every now and again, I hear a word spoken louder than the rest: 'bribe', 'permit', 'police'. But then the cockerel is crowing outside and the light is streaming through the window and it's morning again and I realise I must have fallen asleep. I judge from the position of the sun that it's eight o'clock already; I have slept longer than usual, worn out by the emotional scene of the night before. Hannelore and David are still lost in dreams, curled around each other like Hansel and Gretel in the forest. At least they won't get caught by the wicked witch in our house. Here, they are safe.

I creep into the kitchen to find mother making soup, stirring her big pot – the one she didn't give to Hannelore's mother – over the stove. She's so intent on her labour that she doesn't hear me enter and jumps when I speak to her.

'Where's papa?' I demand, sensing danger in the fact that he isn't there, though this is ridiculous because he always leaves the house at 5 a.m. to go to the docks to see if there is any work for the day. 'And Altin?'

Altin and his movements are more of an enigma. He flits like a firefly, illuminating the darkness wherever he goes but alighting nowhere for long.

Mama purses her lips and continues her robust stirring. She seems to be considering what to say, how much she should reveal to me.

'They've gone to the police station.'

My belly flip-flops.

'To get Mr and Mrs Frankl out?' I ask, stupidly. Why else would they pay the police a visit? The only time anyone in our family has willingly spent time in the presence of the forces of law and order was when Altin fought the Italian invasion. And look how that turned out, I can't help thinking.

Mother shrugs. 'To talk,' she replies, hefting the pan onto the hearthstone and giving it a final stir before replacing the lid.

My heart sinks. 'Talking', in my experience and when adults are involved, can go on for a long time and still end up resolving nothing.

'I should be there,' I state, determinedly. Even if talking is a waste of time, if that's what the men of the family are doing, then so should I. I'm a man, or near enough – and at times like these, everyone should be working together, gaining strength from numbers. I'm the one who found Hannelore in the first place, after all, and it's because of me that they came to our house for succour when they needed it.

'You should be at school,' mother says to me, as if suddenly remembering that such a thing as school exists.

I curse inwardly. I'd hoped she'd forget but no such luck.

'What about Hannelore and David?' I ask. 'They should get up, shouldn't they? What about their school?'

Mother sighs heavily and shrugs again. 'I think not today.' She reaches out and lands a light slap on my cheek. 'But you – off! And take Lefter and Fatos with you.'

I set off, shouting to my brothers to join me. At the school building, I wave them on ahead, pretending to stop to pull a thorn out of my foot. As soon as they've disappeared inside, I turn around and leg it out of the gates. I've got absolutely no intention of going to school and wasting a day in a classroom when there's an emergency to deal with.

It is several hours before Altin and my father emerge from the police station. They are silent until they've cleared the perimeter but as soon as they are out of earshot of the gendarme on sentry duty, they lower their heads and fall into a deep and furtive conversation.

I tail them, staying as close behind as I can whilst still keeping out of sight. They disappear into a side alley and I cautiously creep to its entrance, flattening myself against the wall and peering around the corner. Fleetingly, I see them vanish through a doorway, melting away into the bowels of the building, where I cannot follow.

I head back to the house where Hannelore and David sit silently on the floor in the kitchen. Untouched bowls of soup stand beside them.

'They'll eat nothing,' mother says to me, raising her hands in despair.

I don't blame them. I'm not hungry either; in fact, my stomach is knotted into balls and the thought of food makes me nauseous. But people not eating is the thing that my mother hates the most because it screams abnormality and wrongness. People like us, people we know, are always hungry, unless they are ill.

'They won't go out; they're too scared,' she continues. 'They say people taken by the police were not seen again, in Vienna, before they left.'

She pronounces 'Vienna' oddly; a weird, strangulated sound that accentuates the city's foreignness, and perhaps also the terrible things that Hannelore and David have witnessed happening there.

Mother doesn't have any news about Mr and Mrs Frankl, and even if she did, I don't think she would tell me for fear of being overheard and causing more distress to the children cowering in the corner of our kitchen.

I go over to them and sit beside them. In my pocket, I have a small rubber ball and half a dozen small stones. I pull them out, lay them on the floor and ask them if they know how to play jacks. They don't. At first, they aren't that interested in learning, but after I've demonstrated a few times, David cautiously holds his hand out for the ball and has a go, and once he has relaxed and started to play, some of the tension seems to lift from Hannelore's hunched shoulders and clenched jaw, and she joins in, too.

We pass some time this way, and when my brothers turn up and begin playing with us, I manage to slip quietly away and go in search of my father and Altin. I don't have to look far. They are in the coffee house just down the road, sitting amongst a group of men, all smoking, a game of chess spread out before them.

Rage fills my heart and I feel my blood boiling. I want to go to them and overturn the chess board, ask them what on earth they are doing wasting their time like this when the Frankls are in a police cell. But I don't. I'm wary of Altin, a wariness born out of equal parts respect and fear. He is uncompromising and can be brutal; I've been on the receiving end of one of his beatings before when I vexed him and it's not something I want to experience again. Instead, I ease my way into the midst of the men, sidling past Altin, trying to keep a low profile. I needn't have bothered to be so surreptitious; no one takes the blindest bit of notice of me.

I soon pick up on what is going on. They have ascertained that the Frankls are still in the police cells, that they are being kept in isolation and that the problem is that their papers are invalid. They were granted a visa to come to Albania, but not to stay indefinitely. It's a petty detail that would normally be overlooked, but the police chief in Durrësi is hoping for promotion. He wants to be noticed by the Italian occupiers for his conscientious attention to detail and duty, and is thus behaving unnecessarily officiously.

It may be possible, however, to rectify the situation.

Altin, incredibly, has a contact in the Ministry of the Interior. The beach in Durrësi is lined with beautiful houses belonging to rich people from Tirana. They come in the summer and stay for a few weeks, then lock the houses up and go away again until the following year. One of the houses is owned by the Minister himself and once, many years ago, Altin saved his son from drowning in the sea; he had gone out too far and got into trouble and Altin swam out to rescue him.

This is one of the reasons people look up to Altin. Why he has an almost God-like influence in our town. He seems to know everyone and everything. Today, he has been to Tirana and back already to ask for the Minister's help in securing the Frankls' release and now all the men can do is wait. Hence the game of chess, the coffee and the smoking.

It is another twenty-four hours before the Frankls are let out. When they are finally freed, my father is waiting for them outside the police station. Altin has had to go somewhere on unspecified business.

I watch Hannelore and David as they fall into their parents' arms and feel tears prick behind my eyes. But I also sense something terrible in the air that night. Some kind of intuition tells me what they are thinking, the secret fear that none of them will ever voice. That perhaps Albania isn't the refuge, the sanctuary that they had first imagined.

From that night on, I keep my knife sharpened at all times. I never know when I might need it.

Chapter Twelve

Albania, 1940

Against all the odds, the summer of 1940 is a glorious, carefree time. After the horror of the Frankls' arrest and the relief of their release, we are all a little high, joyful in a desperate kind of way, as if every second must be savoured. The war continues in all its savagery across Europe and in North Africa, but there is no fighting in Albania. Or at least, none that impacts on us down by the sea. In the highlands, there are said to be partisan training camps and military bases, but no one talks openly of such things and so, if you want to, it is perfectly possible to ignore it.

For some reason that I never quite get to the bottom of, we don't go to the mountains this summer. Once set free from the tyranny of school, we spend most of our time on the beach, Hannelore and I, David and my brothers, when we are put in charge of them, and several of my friends. We have a base camp near the tamarisk trees where we can seek shade at the hottest part of the day, or just lie in the sand and look up at a blue sky through dark green leaves. Hannelore's parents are glad to see her and David occupied as, with the onset of the holidays, her mother is no longer tutoring the rich family's children. Without this income, they cannot pay their rent or buy enough food so Mrs Frankl is taking in sewing.

I see her nearly every day because I always walk Hannelore and David home. I tell them that I have to pass their house to get to mine anyway, so it makes no difference to me, but they both know this isn't true. There are all manner of shortcuts I could take if I wanted to. But I don't want to; since the arrest, even though I know it was one over-zealous official who won't try the same trick twice, I need to make sure they get back safely. If there is any kind of trouble and my fists are not enough, my knife is ready and waiting.

Mrs Frankl, though grateful for the children's daily absences, seems to think it's quite unusual to be outside all day, every day, which makes me wonder about life in Vienna and what people do there when the sun is shining.

I ask Hannelore.

'Do?' she repeats, as if it's the strangest question she's ever heard. 'Well, in Vienna we do – did – what all…' she hesitates and I wonder if she's forgotten already. If she has, that would be good, because it might mean she's settling in here and that, when the war is over and travelling is possible again, her family won't want to leave after all.

'We did normal things, I suppose,' she says, dashing that particular hope of mine. 'We went to the park and the boating lake and the museum and to visit relatives.' She looks around her, her eyes seeing not the beach upon which we are sitting but another place in another time. There's an implicit suggestion that I greatly resent that the Vienna way of spending school holidays is superior to the Durrësi one.

'And if we weren't doing any of those things, we would stay inside and read.'

'Read?' I repeat. It seems extraordinary to me that anyone would waste a summer doing something so pointless and boring.

'Why don't you read here, then?' I ask, petulantly. 'If you like it so much.'

She looks at me sharply. 'Why do you think?' she asks, and before I have a chance to reply, she continues, 'Because I haven't got any books, of course.'

We both sit in silent contemplation of this indisputable fact for a while. And then she grabs my hand and we run to the sea. I have made good on my promise to teach her to swim. At first, she was reluctant, scared of the water, of going to the depth that's needed if one is to become buoyant. You can't swim properly where it's only knee deep. But gradually, she learnt to trust me and I cajoled and encouraged and praised her until she managed her first few flailing, untidy strokes – and then, after three weeks of my expert tuition, she could swim.

Though we don't talk about it again, the subject of books remains at the back of my mind over the next few days. It's August, baking hot, the sun relentless in its ferocity. The beach houses are full, everyone who can do so having bailed out of Tirana and come to the seaside. But rather than relish the cool sea and the freedom of being waterborne, Hannelore's words niggle at me endlessly. I think about how, where and when I could procure such an item as a book for Hannelore. There are German-speaking people in Albania – before the war, many men went there to study or work and came back with a German wife. So it stands to reason that there must be German books. Somewhere. I just don't know where.

I need to find a way to get my hands on one. I wander around for a week or so, waiting for Providence to help me out, but I soon realise that's not going to happen. I'm going to have to be much more proactive than that. I need to find someone German and somehow gain access to their library.

It takes a few more days of loitering up and down the beach, creeping along the side passages between the houses, listening intently to all the conversations I can hear, before I strike lucky.

A young woman is sitting on her veranda, nursing a baby. A man dressed in a bathing suit – her husband I presume – comes out and starts talking to her. They don't look Albanian and my suspicions are confirmed when I recognise that they are speaking German. I've picked up quite a lot from Hannelore and I understand what they're saying; something about him not being too long and her going inside for a rest quite soon. They're not taking any notice of me but anyway I pretend to be engrossed in poking a stick at the sandy trickle of water that runs beside the house and down onto the beach. In the winter, it's probably a proper stream but now, after weeks without rain, it's all but dried up.

The man bends over and kisses the woman on the cheek and then throws a towel over his shoulder and leaves, taking the steps down onto the beach two at a time before running athletically towards the water.

The woman lays the baby in a cradle, pats it and sings a lullaby. On the table beside her is not just one book but a whole pile of them. One is lying open and face down, as if she was in the middle of reading it when the baby awoke and she had to stop. I eye it covetously. I know nothing about books, but it looks appealing and desirable, with its coloured cover and the bold print on the spine. I'm sure that Hannelore would love it.

The woman withdraws her hand from the cradle and sits up. She stretches and yawns and then turns and she's looking straight at me. I freeze. She's going to ask me what I'm doing there, why I'm hanging around. She'll tell me to make myself scarce or she'll send her husband after me. I stand stock still, my stick in my hand, a scowl fixed upon my face. But all she does is smile at me, the sweetest smile – apart from Hannelore's, of course – and I relax and smile back. Then she looks away again, gets up and goes inside the house. There's no sound from the cradle; the baby must be sleeping soundly.

I've no idea how long she's going to be gone for but if I don't do it now, I don't know when or if I'll get another chance. Hastily, I discard the stick and take a running jump onto the raised frame of the veranda. Hauling myself up, I'm just taller than the wooden railings that run around the sides and across the front. I glance towards the house. There's no sign of her, but then again the light is so bright outside that it's impossible to see into the darkness. The pile of books is just out of my reach. I dart towards the table and I'm about to pause and try to extricate a book when I hear a shout from inside, accompanied by the sound of hurrying footsteps.

She's seen me and she's coming back. There's nothing for it but to seize the open book right at the top and leg it – so this is what I do. I don't bother with the steps at all; just take a flying leap from the veranda onto the soft, yielding sand. It's so thick and dry that I skid on landing and roll over and over, but I'm up in a flash and off down the beach, the book clasped firmly in my hand. There's no way she could catch me and anyway, I know she won't come after me. She wouldn't leave the baby alone in its cradle; mothers never do.

Once I'm so far down the beach that I can't even see the house anymore, I slow to a walk, bending forward and panting for breath, my heart pounding and my lungs ready to explode. I'm sorry I took the book she was reading; she might have been enjoying it and will be annoyed at not finding out how it ends. But she has lots more so I'm sure she'll be OK. I stand still and hold the book up in front of my eyes, scrutinising it. It has a picture of a cow with a bell on her collar, and a blonde-haired girl. It looks just the kind of book that Hannelore will love.

When I give it to her the next day, her face lights up with joy.

'Heidi!' she says. 'But I love Heidi so much; how did you know?'

I shrug modestly.

But then she puts the book down and stares at me, her eyes narrowed in suspicion. 'Where did you get it from?' she demands. 'Did you buy it? But you can't have done, you never have any money.' She waits for my answer, her lips pursed into a tight line.

'I didn't steal it,' I proclaim, nonchalantly. 'I... borrowed it.' Well, that was true, really. Sort of true. 'When you've finished it, I'll take it back. It's fine.' Once you've started a lie, it's easy to carry on.

'All right,' concedes Hannelore, her desire for the book clearly overcoming her doubts. She picks the book back up again and hugs it to her chest. 'If you're sure.'

I think she knows that I'm not sure but she wants to believe me because she really, really wants the book. That's the difference between us: Hannelore would never do anything even just a tiny bit bad, however much she desired something, whereas me... well, I think it's fine to bend the rules a little if you have a good reason to. Maybe that's what it means to be either Austrian or Albanian, I don't know. But I spend the rest of the day bathed in the warm glow of Hannelore's delight in her new treasure.

–

Two days later, my feel-good glow is eradicated in an instant.

I call for Hannelore as usual but she tells me she's not well and she doesn't want to come out. I spend the whole day in a bad mood, convinced that she isn't ill at all but just wants to stay in and read the book. Dratted thing! A summer here rather than in the mountains was time with Hannelore I hadn't bargained on. If I'd known some pieces of paper bound in cardboard were going to take Hannelore away from me, I'd never have got it for her.

But the next day, it's Mrs Frankl who comes to the door. She has dark circles round her eyes as if she's been up all night and her forehead is creased with worry. She tells me Hannelore is really sick.

Over the next week, Hannelore gets worse, not better. I'm not allowed in to see her but eventually, though money is tight, the Frankls have to call the doctor. He diagnoses malaria and advises complete bed rest while she fights the infection. But Hannelore's fever climbs as does the temperature outside, and on a further visit, the doctor confirms that she also has typhoid. She's really sick and she needs to be transferred to the hospital in Tirana, the only one that can treat such a serious disease.

Altin arranges Hannelore's transport. As I watch her being loaded into the ambulance, I realise I've never seen such desolation on anyone's face as Mrs Frankl's. Mr Frankl goes with Hannelore to the hospital, and when he returns the next day he tells us that she's been put in an isolation ward and that no one can see her for at least a fortnight.

For days, weeks, Hannelore's illness continues. No one says it but everyone's eyes reveal it: she might die.

Her birthday comes and goes; she's turned eleven whilst being cooped up in that place, steeped in pain and fear at death's door. I say every prayer I've ever known and a few I make up for her, willing her to get well. They don't work, though, and I wonder why God is not looking out for her. Surely she deserves to get better?

August turns to September and it's the date of the annual swimming contest that is held in the harbour. This is an event that Altin excels at, always winning at least one prize, either for swimming or diving or both. Usually it's one of my favourite events of the year, but not this year. This year, all I can think about is Hannelore and I end up slinking away, pushing through a forest of spectators' legs, unable to bear the joviality and high spirits when my heart is heavy as lead. Once I'm through the crowd, I look back and see Altin above all the heads, executing the most perfect high dive. He glides through the air, his body in perfect alignment, as if he has mastered the art of human flight.

If anyone could do it, it would be him.

A huge cheer goes up and I suppose he's completed his dive and entered the water cleanly and with barely a splash. But even this triumph cannot induce me to stay. I skulk in the shadows all the way home and, once there, I lie face down on my blankets, hoping, willing Hannelore to make it.

Just when I think that things can't get any worse, they do. There are problems between Italy and Greece and the prospect of fighting on our borders gets even closer. The government decrees that all Jews must leave Durrësi. Apparently, they say, the port is too important and non-Albanian residents might put it in jeopardy. I don't see how or why they would, but nobody I know ever understands the reasoning behind anything that comes out of government.

The Jews are ordered to go to Berati. Nobody says what they should do when they get there. Where would they live? How would they get money to survive? If a small town like that is suddenly full of newcomers, there will not be enough work to go around, and probably not enough houses, either. Life would be even harder for the Frankls and the others like them, than it is already.

And most important of all, if they go, I might never see Hannelore again.

Through all of this I carry the truth in my heart, where it is heavy as lead and as poisonous, too. I know why these things have happened, why Hannelore is sick, hovering between life and death, and why my prayers aren't working and the refugees are being sent away: it is because I stole the book. Hannelore's illness is punishment for my sin. If she doesn't get better, it will be my fault.

Chapter Thirteen

Italy, 2019

After Zak's hasty departure due to the late-night call from the factory, Ruth didn't hear from him for a few days. She toyed with the idea of calling him but didn't. Instead, she busied herself with her fitness regime, her 'teach yourself Italian' campaign and, of course, with Zak's manuscript. She wanted to know everything about Bekim, Hannelore and all the Frankls and the Shehus. But she resisted the urge to gobble the story up too quickly, forcing herself to take her time, to relish every word. That meant rationing herself to a few pages a day so as not to finish it too soon.

Three evenings after her and Zak's wonderful trip on the boat, she was reading the BBC news online when she took a violent swipe at a particularly persistent and annoying mosquito. In so doing, she knocked over the bottle of wine she'd been enjoying and, as she reached out to rescue it, the whole table went flying. Her phone skittered off the upturned surface, fell on to the tiled balcony floor and then further down to the garden beneath. It landed with a resounding smash on Caroline's small flagstone terrace.

Shit!

It was eleven o'clock, too late to disturb Caroline to retrieve it. It would have to wait until the morning.

First thing when she woke up, she went downstairs. Caroline hadn't been outside yet but she immediately took Ruth out to investigate the scene of the accident. There lay the phone, the screen of which was, as Ruth had expected and despite its protective casing, completely shattered.

'Oh dear,' breathed Caroline, bending down to pick it up before Ruth could get there. 'That doesn't look good.'

Ruth sighed. 'No, it doesn't.'

Caroline groaned as she straightened up. 'Oh, my back, it's absolutely killing me.' She handed the phone over to Ruth. 'There's a place Enzo knows in Leuca that's really good at mending mobiles, laptops, everything. I'll find out the name of it and let you know.'

'Thanks, Caroline,' replied Ruth. 'It's only a phone – but it's a bloody nuisance. So careless of me.'

Caroline grimaced in sympathy. 'I know. Phones… can't live with them, can't live without them. Bit like husbands, really.' She was joking but there was an edge to her voice that made Ruth look sharply at her.

'Is everything OK?'

'What, apart from the aching back, swollen ankles, enormous belly and boobs the size of melons? And Enzo always at work…?'

Ruth wanted to give Caroline a hug but she looked too hot for that to be either welcome or comfortable.

'I'm sorry, you poor thing,' she sympathised. 'Where's Daniel, anyway?' she asked, suddenly aware that she hadn't heard the little boy since she'd come down.

Caroline mustered a weak smile. 'Don't worry, I haven't locked him in his bedroom – not yet, anyway! He's gone with Enzo for the day. I know Enzo doesn't like taking him – he can get in the way – but I think he realised I needed a break.'

'I'll take him out again soon,' Ruth promised. 'In the meantime, don't do anything else today. Just rest. And don't worry about the phone place – I'll look it up online and if I don't find it, I'll come down and ask Enzo when he's back this evening. You are not to even think about it!'

Taking her wreck of a phone with her, Ruth went back upstairs to her flat. When she heard a knock on the door a short while later, she sighed resignedly, assuming it was Caroline disobeying her instructions and coming up with the information anyway. Ruth hadn't actually got round to googling the shop, but she would do at some point.

Opening the door, she was taken aback to find standing there not Caroline, but Zak.

'H-hi,' she spluttered, before quickly recovering herself. 'How nice to see you. What are you up to? Would you like to come in for a coffee?'

Zak stepped inside. 'I'm conscious of my rather abrupt departure the other night,' he began cautiously, raising his arms in a gesture of remorse. 'It is the necessary inconvenience of my position, but I wanted to say sorry.'

Ruth nodded. It was just as she had thought. The buck stopped with Zak and so he had no choice but to do whatever was required.

'Please,' she remonstrated, 'it's no problem. But would you like that coffee?'

'Thank you,' Zak replied. 'That would be lovely.' He followed her into the kitchen. 'I'm here to ask you something. I tried to call but there was no reply. So I took the liberty of coming over.' He deposited a bag from the best pasticceria in town onto the counter beside the coffee machine. 'And of bringing breakfast.'

'Thank you so much! How did you know that I've got nothing to eat here apart from some salami and half a stale baguette?'

Zak chuckled, his eyes twinkling attractively. 'Call it intuition,' he said.

Ruth took a couple of plates from a cupboard, arranged the pastries and took them to the table.

'Sit down,' she urged Zak, as she handed him a plate. 'And this is why you didn't get any response from my phone.'

She lifted up the handset to reveal to Zak the fractured screen.

'Ah,' smiled Zak, 'I see the problem! What happened?'

'Dropped it, quite spectacularly,' Ruth said, making the coffee.

'I can get it fixed for you,' Zak suggested. 'I know an expert. And I've got a spare handset you can borrow in the meantime.'

'Really?' Ruth was so rubbish with her phone, having very little idea how it actually worked. 'Can I do that?'

'Well, it's not an iPhone so it won't take your sim card – but it would mean you had something in case of emergencies.'

Ruth laughed. 'I can't think of what kind of emergency I could possibly find myself in here,' she joked, 'but thanks for the offer.'

She handed him his cup of coffee. 'So – what did you want to ask me?'

'Well,' Zak said, 'I wondered if you'd like to do a spot of sightseeing.' He paused and took a sip of the coffee. 'If you can spare the time, of course. Everything is running smoothly at the factory again now so I can take a few hours off. And there's somewhere I'd like to show you.'

Ruth stifled a yawn. She'd not slept that well, not because of the phone disaster but due to the amount of noise overnight. Helicopters had hovered overhead until the small hours, their whirring appearing first in her dream and later actually waking her. It was an unfamiliar sound in Norfolk where she lived, and certainly not one she expected to hear on the coast of Puglia. But she wasn't feeling too groggy to turn down a day out.

'I'd love to come,' she answered as brightly as she could. 'I'll just get my bag.'

Sitting in the car as Zak drove, lulled by the motion, Ruth could not stop herself from yawning again. 'So sorry,' she apologised. 'I assure you I'm not bored. Just a little sleepy.' She explained about the helicopters.

'Drugs,' responded Zak, briefly. 'We have a problem here. And I hate to say it, but it stems from my homeland. Cannabis is grown in the mountains there, where the conditions are ideal – plenty of sun, plenty of rain. The farms are very isolated, but nevertheless their existence is often common knowledge, and they frequently operate with the collusion of the local police.

'When the crops are harvested, they fly the goods over here in Piper aircrafts and drop them into designated pick-up points in the fields, or bring them by sea in high speed powerboats. Other routes include by mule over the mountains into Montenegro and on to central and western Europe that way. The ingenuity of the Albanian gangs is legendary; they're pretty good at coming up with ways to get around the forces of law and order. They know there just isn't the manpower to apprehend them.'

'Gosh.' Ruth looked out of the window, as if there might be an illicit package of contraband lying there amongst the parched grass and silver-leaved olive trees.

Zak shrugged. 'Yes, gosh indeed. But there are not many jobs or opportunities for young Albanians, particularly men, and when they see the spoils that can be made by farming cannabis... well, what's not to like? It's easy money, compared with other, lawful, means.'

'Oh dear,' sighed Ruth. 'I was beginning to think of Albania as that unspoilt, undiscovered Mediterranean paradise we all dream about – only to find out that there's a dark underbelly lurking in the background.'

'Yup,' agreed Zak. 'The police do what they can but there is always a sense that they are fighting a losing battle.'

They had arrived in Santa Maria di Leuca and Zak negotiated some narrow back streets before stopping in front of a small shop with an array of mobile handsets and other devices in the window.

'I'll put the phone in for you, shall I?' he said. 'I know the guy and he gives me a good price.'

He was back out again in minutes. 'All sorted,' he pronounced. 'Mo will have it done by today or tomorrow and his colleague will drop it right back at the apartment; he lives in Santa Maria del Mare so it's no problem.'

'What about paying for it?' asked Ruth.

'On me.' They were on their way again. 'It's the least I can do after abandoning you the other night.'

Ruth wasn't sure what to say. She was used to looking after herself, to managing all her affairs on her own. It was strange to have someone else stepping in and taking over. Not unpleasant – but definitely weird by dint of being so unfamiliar.

'Th-thank you,' she said, falteringly. 'That's very kind of you... and him for returning it. I appreciate it.' They bowled along for another forty-five minutes or so, chatting about this and that, discovering that they both had fennel and celeriac, as well as celery, on their disliked foods list. Although when Ruth mentioned Brussels sprouts, Zak had no idea what they were and her description of them as foul-tasting – and smelling – mini-cabbages failed to enlighten him, though it did make him laugh. Eventually, as they were still chuckling amicably, they entered the village of Santa Maria al Bagno. The car slowed down and Zak pulled up outside a nondescript-looking building.

'Here we are,' he announced.

Ruth still did not know where Zak had taken her; he'd remained tight-lipped despite all her questioning. The sign above the entrance stated that it was the Museum of Memory and Hospitality, which frankly left her none the wiser.

Entering, she sighed with pleasure as the air conditioning hit her. Just the few short steps from the car to the door had left her roasting; the weather, though it hardly seemed possible, was getting hotter and hotter. Searching for enlightenment as to what this place was exactly, she found a board just inside that informed her about the museum's purpose; it was a commemoration of the displaced persons of Europe who had been housed in villages in the Salento region at the end of World War II. Many were Holocaust survivors, liberated from the concentration camps and desperately searching for a new, safe home. But there were also refugees from all over the continent – including those who had lived out the war years in the relative sanctuary of Albania.

In the main exhibition hall, a wedding dress and an accordion took centre stage, items lent to the Jewish refugees by the local Italian people and returned to their owners years later, to end up on display here as a symbol of a friendship across nationalities and cultures. Photographs studded the walls and Ruth studied them, scrutinising the faces of those depicted. The majority were young, and there was hope in their eyes, but behind that lay the strain of horrors witnessed and experienced. *Everyone here will have lost people they love*, she thought, gazing at a group of teenagers perched on the side of a boat lying on Santa Maria al Bagno beach. Maybe their whole family, because many, she read, arrived as orphans. *How do you survive that*, she thought. *How do you carry on?*

She remembered a school trip of many years ago to a Holocaust exhibition at the Imperial War Museum in London. The image that had struck her the most deeply had been of a pile of children's shoes heaped up outside a gas chamber, on the very top a pair of pristine, patent leather buckle-ups with dainty heels. A treasured pair of shoes, party shoes, dancing shoes, shoes to be proud of. *Exactly the sort of impractical shoes I would have worn on such a special journey*, Ruth, who had a bit of shoe obsession, could remember thinking. Perhaps those children had thought they were on the trip of a lifetime when they got on the trains and rattled across borders blown away by war. What they didn't know was that, for the vast majority, their journey to the concentration camp would be their last. Ruth could hardly comprehend the tragedy of it all.

In another photo, a young mother posed proudly beside her pram. The caption informed her that over two hundred Jewish babies were born during the time of the camps' existence between 1945 and 1947. So people kept on trying, Ruth thought, tears filling her eyes; despite everything they'd been through they carried on, doing what humans do, falling in love, getting married, having babies. Though every effort had been made to break their spirit, evil had not succeeded.

Zak appeared by her side and they both stopped in front of an arresting picture of a young girl, about sixteen, staring straight at the camera with an unabashed gaze. Although the photograph was black and white, Ruth could tell that the girl's eyes were brown, the kind of eyes that seemed as if they held the secrets of the future and of the past in them. The caption announced her as Hildebrand, newly arrived from Albania. Ruth imagined Hannelore looking just like this girl.

She smiled. 'Albanians,' she said. 'They're like buses. You don't meet one for your whole life and then a whole crowd arrive at once.'

Zak chuckled in agreement.

They'd reached the end of the exhibits and went outside to the vine-draped terrace of a small cafe, against the walls of which a hot pink bougainvillea clung and scrambled. A tabby cat lay on a chair lazily sunning itself while a host of untroubled little birds chirped and sang by a water fountain.

'I love the fact that the Allied authorities housed them all – refugees, concentration camp survivors, displaced persons – in holiday homes requisitioned from the wealthy. Imagine trying to do that now!' exclaimed Ruth, as she and Zak drank freshly squeezed orange juice that smelt of sunshine.

Zak nodded. 'Different times, I suppose. You can see some of the villas they used in Leuca – I'll point them out to you on the way back. They're pretty grand, a lot of them!'

When they'd finished their drinks they ambled back to the car, Ruth's footsteps dragging in the heavy midday heat. Zak zapped the central locking off as they approached.

'Maybe wait to get in until I've turned the air con on,' Zak suggested.

'Good idea,' Ruth laughed. 'You get to the point where you can't even imagine ever being cold again, can you? But I'm making the most of it because once I get back to Norfolk, the picture will be reversed pretty quickly.'

Zak grimaced sympathetically and opened his mouth to say something, but before the words were articulated, his phone rang. Glancing at the screen, he shot Ruth an apologetic look.

'I'm going to have to take this,' he said, striding hurriedly away to stand under the shade of a large parasol pine.

Ruth idled by the car, opening the passenger door and flapping it to and fro in an attempt to let some air in, though doubting it would do any good. Outside was no cooler than inside. As she waited, she felt a familiar tickling in her nose. Damn! She was prone to spontaneous nosebleeds that came out of the blue. Putting one hand up to her nose to stem the flow, she searched frantically in her bag for a tissue. There were none, and her sundress lacked pockets that might be harbouring one. Diving into the front of the car, she frantically looked around to see if Zak had any, but no luck. With only a moment's hesitation and a flash of discomfort, she unlatched the glove compartment. She wouldn't normally search around in someone else's vehicle, but desperate times called for desperate measures and all that.

With a surge of relief, she found not only one tissue but a whole packet right there at the top of the glovebox.

Ruth grabbed the packet, and had already snatched a couple of tissues and pressed them to her nostrils when the sight of what lay behind the tissues hit her like a blow to the solar plexus. With a gasp of shock, Ruth's legs almost gave way beneath her. Stumbling, she backed out of the car, fear and shock coursing through her body. Because there, in Zak's car, was something Ruth had never seen in real life before.

A gun.

Ruth regarded all firearms with a typically British horror and revulsion. So alien was such an object that she almost imagined that it could operate autonomously, that just by dint of being discovered, the pistol could come to life and begin shooting.

Pinching the bridge of her nose to try to staunch the flow of blood, she spoke sternly to herself. Stop being so hysterical, her inner voice instructed her. It's just a gun. This isn't Britain; the laws are different here – what were Italian gun laws? Ruth had no idea. But it was probably perfectly normal for someone to own a gun. Nothing to write home about; nothing to see here.

She was deep in this chain of muddled and incoherent thought when she became aware of a presence behind her.

'Ruth.' Zak's voice was calm and measured as always. But when Ruth turned to meet his gaze, his face blanched white and in an instant his expression morphed to one of horrified alarm.

Despite the befuddlement plaguing her mind, it immediately occurred to Ruth what he might be thinking: that she'd found the gun, injured herself?

'Nosebleed,' she muttered, her voice muffled by the layers of tissue. 'They happen sometimes, come out of nowhere. I looked for some tissues – so sorry – found that.' She gestured towards the gun, nestled in the glove box.

Zak's face relaxed, his shoulders visibly dropping. 'No need to apologise,' he insisted, his habitual composure restored. 'And I'm sorry you made such a… startling discovery.'

He leant into the car and snapped the glove compartment emphatically closed. He gestured to Ruth to get into the passenger seat as he climbed in the other side and settled himself behind the wheel.

'You're probably wondering why I possess a firearm,' he stated, as he fired up the ignition.

Um, just slightly, thought Ruth. What with the nosebleed, the gun and the heat, she was feeling a bit faint. She reached out her hand and cranked up the air conditioning to full pelt.

Before she had said anything in reply, Zak was continuing. 'I'm sure you are well aware of the Mafia. We have a problem with it here. I've had threats, attempts to extort money from the factory, harassment of my security guards. The police have warned me to be alert, to take care, especially when I'm on night duty. Hence the weapon, which is for protection only. I really wish I didn't have to have it, and I'm so sorry if it frightened you.'

Ruth shook her head. 'No, no, not at all,' she asserted, with a conviction she didn't truly feel. 'I'm the one who should be apologising. It's none of my business whether you have a gun or not. I shouldn't have been poking and prying. And I wouldn't have been, if it hadn't been for this.' She indicated towards the bloody pile of tissues she was holding, waiting for the opportunity to dispose of them.

A sudden rush of empathy for Zak flooded through her, that he needed to own a lethal weapon even though he hated having to do so, that he might have felt his very life to be in danger. To a holidaymaker such as her, everything seemed so idyllic in Santa Maria del Mare and its environs. But clearly this wasn't quite the full picture.

'I'm sorry that you've had trouble with the Mafia. The stories I read about them – it – terrify me. It must be awful. Scary.'

Zak made a dismissive gesture with his head. 'You get used to it. Par for the course, part of the job.'

Ruth saw the opportunity to ask the question she hadn't so far posed. 'But what about... I mean, do you have family who might be targeted? Threatened? That would be terrible, if so...'

Zak smiled, slowly and sadly. 'No, no family. Never been married. Married to the job, I suppose. No children either, though I would have liked them. Maybe one day.'

He glanced towards Ruth. 'Bit pathetic, isn't it? Sometimes I wish...' His voice trailed off.

Ruth felt a rush of compassion. Secret firearms notwithstanding, Zak was a lovely man, attractive, interesting, thoughtful. She couldn't believe that there wasn't a phalanx of women lined up to marry him. If he went on one of those dreaded dating apps, he'd be inundated, more matches than Bryant and May.

'That makes two of us,' she said, blankly. 'I put work before everything and look where it got me. Put out to grass long before I'm ready. And as for relationships... I'm a walking one-woman disaster zone.'

'We're made for each other then, aren't we?' laughed Zak. 'So much in common.'

Ruth joined in, chuckling at his joke. But at the back of her mind his suggestion flared and smouldered: that they were, indeed, very well suited. I mean, when else had she met someone with the exact same taste in vegetables as hers?

Seriously, though, she could not deny that she was developing feelings for Zak that perhaps were unwise. Maybe it wasn't just her who felt this way, as she'd thought after the trip to the grottoes.

She fiddled with the air con again; it was too cold now, blasting her with an Arctic chill. She'd be gone soon, back to the similarly frigid wild winds of Norfolk. It was stupid to think of things that could never be.

'So the big question is,' she said, pushing the image of the gun firmly from her mind, along with any thoughts of romance, 'did Hannelore come here, to Italy, to one of the displaced persons camps?'

Zak smiled his enigmatic smile. 'As I said, you'll have to wait and see. You'll find out all in due course. Be patient.'

Ruth sighed. Patience was not one of her virtues. But she was clearly going to have to develop some.

Chapter Fourteen

Albania, 1940

At last, some good news. Hannelore is back from Tirana.

Somehow she has managed to fight off the infections and survive. She's on the mend, though still too sick to get up or to see me. This obviously means that she can't possibly travel to Berati. But anyway, no one is happy with that proposal and plans are afoot to come up with an alternative. Just as when Mr and Mrs Frankl were arrested, the men stay up late into the night discussing the problem. The word I keep hearing, that crops up time and again, is 'papers'. The issue is papers, or rather, the Frankls' lack of them.

Forgeries could be made, false Albanian names and addresses given. But they will only stand up to scrutiny or inspection if they have the correct stamp – and no one has the solution for this.

I ponder the problem endlessly, turning it over and over in my head. And one night, in the darkness before the dawn, I hatch my plan. It is dangerous. The penalty if I'm found out would be severe – imprisonment, at the very least. Probably for a very long time.

But I'll take the risk because it is my chance to make good on the damage I have done, on the misfortune I have brought down on Hannelore. It's my chance to prove that I'd lay down my life for her.

The local authority headquarters is an austere, imposing building. Three storeys high, it has small windows with external bars and internal shutters. At night, all possible access points – doors and windows – are barred and locked. It is a mini-fortress.

Breaking in is impossible. The only way to carry out my plan is to do it in broad daylight, in full view. To be so audacious that no one will suspect me of any crime but instead will assume I'm meant to be there.

I set out early. I need time to calm my nerves, to steady myself, to force my heart to a normal rhythm. If I look unsettled, uneasy, I'll invite suspicion. In my hand, I carry the photo I've spent all the lekë I have to purchase. Arriving at the double wooden doors that lead into the wide, echoing hallway, I pull myself up to my full height, which is all of five foot, and readjust my hat. It gives me at least another couple of inches. Even so, the sentry on duty regards me as if I'm a tiny and insignificant insect. It doesn't fill me with confidence. When he demands that I surrender my knife, I feel even more insubstantial. Nevertheless, I march inside, my face set firm whilst my legs are nearly giving way beneath me.

'Identity cards?' I demand of the officer stationed at the reception desk.

Wordlessly, he points to the wide stone staircase that stretches monumentally upwards and then curves away to each side. I take a deep breath. The further I go, the harder it will be to get back out. But I mustn't let my guard down, mustn't let slip the façade that I'm here legitimately.

The weather is still good and my parents won't buy me new boots to replace the outgrown, fallen-apart ones until autumn comes and it's absolutely necessary. As my mother says, a young boy's feet can grow two sizes over the summer. So I've borrowed a pair of shoes from Altin, telling him I cut my toe and I need to protect it until it's healed. They're much too big for me, and they slap down onto the stone treads of the staircase with a comic flopping noise that I'm convinced must be giving me away. But the two people who pass me on their way down as I am ascending take no notice of me.

Taking strength from this, I fix my eyes rigidly ahead and set off down the long corridor towards the sign that reads 'Identity cards'. The secretary working there studiously ignores me. She turns her face away as I approach, pretending to search for something in an overloaded filing cabinet, and then engrosses herself in a form that is clearly already filled in and cannot possibly demand any more of her time.

I feel my self-appointed stature and status slipping away and have to give myself a stern talking to; I am an important member of the public who deserves attention.

'Excuse me,' I say sharply, trying to give the impression that I will take no nonsense.

The secretary glances towards me with a look of ineffable boredom.

'My identity card has incomprehensibly got lost and I'm here to get another one.'

She looks barely older than me but glares as if I am nothing but an irritation.

But then our eyes lock and in hers I see a glimmer of understanding. Working for the authorities she might be, but she is not one of them. She, like me, is one of the little people, and because this is Albania, this unites us in a way that needs no words.

I lean towards her. I pause whilst I look all around me, checking that we are still alone. 'I need blank identity cards,' I whisper. I hold her gaze with the force of some invisible magnetism.

She nods rapidly, and then stands up.

The knots in my stomach unfurl like released elastic. Thank heavens for the Albanian way; ask no questions and you'll hear no lies.

I point to the pile of forms by her side. 'Is this what I have to fill in to report the loss?' I ask, speaking at normal volume now.

Detaching a form from the stack, she passes it over to me and watches as I painstakingly input my details, making up a name and address. Once completed, she takes it, gives it a cursory look and pulls out a pile of blank ID cards from a locked drawer beside her. She transcribes my name and details onto the top one and attaches the photo. Then she retrieves a stamp and ink pad from another drawer and stamps it, once, with a precision born of long practice. Meeting my eyes with hers, she places my validated ID card on top of the pile and slides the whole lot over to me.

'There you are, sir,' she says, in a loud, clear voice. 'All done for you now.' And then, in a much quieter voice, she mutters, 'Now scarper, before I get into trouble.'

I pick up the cards and put them in my capacious pocket. But I can't leave yet. Because there's another problem. Without the correct stamp, the cards won't be valid. That's the whole point of me being here, the reason why I have taken such a risk to come. I withdraw my card and stare at it intently, as if examining it for accuracy. As I do so, I point wordlessly at the stamp, which is still sitting on the desk, just out of reach.

The secretary's expression veers from puzzled to astounded to furious all in a few seconds.

'Oh no,' she whispers. 'No, you can't have that. That's more than my job's worth.'

I think fast, trying to decide what to do. Leave with the cards and hope for the best? Threaten the girl until she hands the stamp over? Perhaps we could make a similar one from a piece of rubber or a potato – anything. I look at the mark on my card and see that that is a stupid idea. It's much too complex, too detailed, to replicate.

At that moment, a paunchy man in a European-style suit emerges from a room behind the filing cabinets, looks impatiently around and then, spotting the secretary at the counter, calls to her loudly to come to his office. She jumps at the sound of his voice and, nervously smoothing down her skirt and her hair, she shoves the stamp and ink pad back into the drawer, turns the key and rushes off in his direction without a backwards glance.

I linger, considering. The thing that I so desperately need is right there, inches from where I'm standing. Unreachable. If only I had my knife with me, I could jimmy the drawer open. I curse the policeman who took it away from me.

Casting my eyes around, helplessly hoping for inspiration, I spot on the counter a metal paper knife. The whole room is deathly quiet. It's now or never.

My heart pounding, I leapfrog over the counter, grab the knife, force it into the gap between the drawer and its frame and slide it, gently but forcefully, from left to right. Unbelievably, it works. I feel the lock give way.

Pulling open the drawer, I grab the stamp and the ink pad. I'm hot with fear and my hands are slippery with sweat, but I manage to get them out. Just as I'm clambering back over the counter, a shout echoes around the stone walls.

'Stop, thief!'

I freeze. My heart is in my mouth and I feel sick. The sound of running footsteps increases in volume as the police officer who's seen me comes tearing down the corridor. The door behind which the secretary and her boss had retreated is thrown open and I hear both of their sharp intakes of breath before the man yells, 'Catch him! Get him!'

I fling my legs towards the floor but as I'm doing so, one of them is grabbed by a pair of strong hands. I kick frantically, powerful in my terror and desperation. My foot slips easily out of Altin's oversized shoe, releasing me from my captor's grasp. I get both feet to the floor and I run, an uneven, energy-sapping gait with one foot uncomfortably shod and the other bare. As I race along the walkway to the staircase, which seems twice as long as it had on the way here, the ink pad slides out of my sweaty grip. For a split second, I think about stopping to pick it up. But then, out of the corner of my eye, I see a flurry of boots approaching from the opposite direction. Simultaneously, a rush of air brushes my cheek and an arm swipes out at me. My wrist is clenched in an iron grip.

I've failed.

The hand tightens its grasp. The fingers are long and tensile, seeming to wrap around my flesh and bones with the intention of squeezing the life out of me. For a moment, I give up, resigning myself to my fate. I imagine myself behind bars for years, wasting away, missing my family. Missing Hannelore. A picture of her lying on a hospital bed, face white as the sheets, frail and suffering, flits through my mind. It renews my energy and determination.

With all the strength I can muster, I struggle to break free, twisting and turning, kicking and biting, squirming and writhing. My captor's grip loosens; I can sense him weakening. With a final violent thrust, I push him away from me and I'm down the stairs and out of the door in moments. I run and run, cursing the one shoe I still have but not daring to stop and take it off. I keep going until I'm streets away from the headquarters before I finally give in, slumping against the wall of the nearest building and sinking to a squat, my head in my hands, my lungs bursting even more than they had when I took the book, my heart pounding against my chest.

When I've recovered enough to move again, I put my hand tentatively into my pocket. I have the cards, and the stamp. But I've lost so much. The ink pad, Altin's shoe, and above all my traditional knife, razor sharp, that Altin gave to me to keep for always. The officials in the building have all seen clearly what I look like; even though I gave a false name and address, I'm sure they could easily find me. They could come and get me anytime they like. And what good will I be to Hannelore then, when I'm in prison or doing hard labour?

The tears begin to form behind my closed eyelids and then to fall, fast and furious, dropping onto the dusty pavement like salty raindrops.

Stupid, stupid, stupid.

Why did I think a boy like me could do a man's job?

When I get home, the fact that no one has even noticed that I've been gone only serves to compound my disappointment. I wait all day, and it's only when, after our dinner of lamb broth and bread, the conversation turns once more to the evacuation that I confess all. Placing the cards and the stamp in the middle of the floor, I turn to confront the puzzled faces of my family.

'I got these,' I say, deliberately not going in to details, 'but I dropped the ink pad. Sorry.'

Everyone stares in disbelief. I'm not sure they understand.

'These are the blank ID cards you said you needed,' I reiterate, concentrating on my dad as the person most likely to cotton on, 'and here's the stamp that they must have. It's just ink that's missing.'

I affect a nonchalant tone. I'm not sure if anyone will care what method I used to come by them – surely anything's legitimate when the stakes are so high? – but I don't want to take any chances. You just never know with adults.

My dad goes to fetch Altin and it's he who breaks the silence. He picks up one of the cards and turns it over and over in his hands.

'This is a miracle,' he says, finally, definitively. 'You are a miracle,' he adds, turning to me with an enormous grin, and then reaching across and grabbing me, pulling me into a bear hug of such vigour that it winds me.

Once the mood has been directed by the all-powerful Altin, everyone joins with their congratulations and expressions of surprise and delight. Even Lefter and Fatos bury their normal competitiveness and antipathy to anyone else's success – particularly mine – for long enough to say 'well done'.

I deem it safe to own up to what went wrong. I confess that I lost Altin's shoe and he just laughs like a drain and says they didn't fit him, either. But I can't bring myself to talk about the loss of my knife, my most precious possession, or the fact that, if they chose to track me down, they could easily do so. The secretary especially, who saw me so closely, could incriminate me in seconds. I don't want to dull the party atmosphere or lessen the adulation that is being directed towards me. I'm starting to feel like a man again, and there's no way I'm going to let my mistakes turn me back into a boy.

Over the next few days, the arrangements are made. Altin makes ink from a plant he gathers from the forest outside the city and it looks pretty good. You would have to be an expert to tell the difference from the real thing. Each member of the Frankl family is given an identity card in a false name; if questioned, they will say they are German cousins of ours. This is perfectly plausible due to the number of people in the town who have German relatives and no one would be able to tell the difference between a German accent and an Austrian one.

Altin and my father go to tell the family the plan. I beg to accompany them. I have to know how Hannelore is, if the curse I put on her by purloining the book has been lifted by the provision of the identity cards. I know the Koran says that two wrongs don't make a right but in this case I choose to ignore such teachings. Whoever wrote the holy book probably hadn't even considered the kind of situation we are in now, and if they had, they would have known that desperate times call for desperate measures. That's what I tell myself, anyway – plus of course the fact that, even if stealing from an individual is a sin, stealing from the state, for the purposes of saving lives, can't possibly be. That wouldn't make any sense.

And it works.

As soon as the cards are delivered, Hannelore starts to recover. By the end of the week, she is out of bed for the first time in weeks. By the end of September, she is up and about and much more like her former self.

'Thank you, Bekim,' she says to me, one day when we are sitting inside her tiny apartment whilst the autumn rain pours down outside. She's thinner and paler but still as beautiful as ever.

'My mother and father actually sleep soundly at night now they have the cards. You do so much for us – you and all your family. We can never repay you.'

She has said those words many times since the family first arrived in Albania. In the past, I had no answer to give. Now I know for sure that it's not repayment I want. All I want is to keep the family safe, to help them get through this war. To keep Hannelore safe.

I shrug.

'You are our guests,' I remind her. 'As such, we must protect you with our own lives, if necessary.'

This is the law, the Kanun, by which all Albanians live, but all my life until now, they have just been words. Now they are more than words, more than deeds. They are everything.

Hannelore leans over and kisses me on the cheek. Her lips are soft as down, her breath sweet as fresh-baked cinnamon bread.

I walk home on air that evening.

But in the way this war has of constantly throwing up new horrors, that night a noise awakens me and all the family. We go outside, gazing up at the dense clouds, no idea what is making such a racket, what force is causing the windows to rattle like an earthquake.

And then, in the heavens right above us, the planes appear, half a dozen of them, with British RAF markings.

They rumble past. What seems like minutes but is probably only seconds later, the bombs begin to fall, on the docks and the warehouses. We smell the cordite and the fire, and soon the distant glow of flames is visible, lighting up the sky long before the dawn.

It's hard to know what to think. Except that the idea of normality has been shattered into tiny pieces once again.

Chapter Fifteen

Albania, 1940-42

We are moving to Shkodra.

It's all happening really quickly. Altin's wife's father died a few months ago and the person who's been running his coffee shop, drinks stall and tobacconist business in the northern city can no longer do so. It's profitable and can provide a living for all of us – Altin and Sarah, plus the entire Shehu family – and it will be better than father's casual work on the docks. Which anyway is drying up with every advance in the war and every bombing raid; they're coming almost every night now and we will all be glad to get away.

With papers that are good enough to satisfy the Italians, should they ask for them, the Frankls are coming with us. The old gentleman has long since disappeared, gone to friends in Vlore, so I'm told. But we will be accompanied by another refugee family who evacuated to Berati but suffered such starvation and deprivation there that they crept back to Durrësi under cover of darkness and took shelter with the Frankls. They are Mr and Mrs Albrecht, their four-year-old son, Albert, and a maiden aunt called Brunhild.

The houses the Albrechts and the other refugees were assigned in Berati had no electricity or running water;

both families seem to find this unbelievable and unbearable. Listening to their stories, I think about the mountain village where my family comes from. I often plan a trip there in my mind and imagine showing Hannelore the beautiful lakes, trees and wild flower meadows, the free-flowing streams that quiver and glint in the sunshine like green snakes. But the dreams recede as I listen to her gasps of horror about the primitive conditions in Berati. I realise miserably that she would never want to visit the mountains, where things are even more basic, and that if she did, she would hate it. But I cheer up when I think about Shkodra, a city with all modern conveniences. Even the Frankls are sure to feel at home there.

We load our possessions — the few that we have — onto the back of a donkey cart and set off with hope in our hearts. A new start, away from the bombing, will be good for all of us. I'm sad to leave my friends behind, but Hannelore is coming and that's all that really matters. In the cart, bumping up and down over potholes and stones, she holds my hand every inch of the way; I have proven that I am a man by procuring the identity cards. I feel unassailable, as if nothing can touch me.

Once we reach the main road that runs from Tirana to Shkodra, we unload everything and wait for the bus that will take us the rest of the way. We are waved through every checkpoint and Italian military installation without so much as a question asked. I should be glad that the cards have not been necessary; instead, I feel slightly aggrieved at being denied further opportunities to bask in the glow of Hannelore's approval.

Eventually, we arrive in Shkodra; I've never been to another town or city similar in size to Durrësi. My eyes are out on stalks and my neck aches from peering all around me at the sights and sounds that greet us. There are so many shops selling so many things – brooms and brushes, pots and pans, knives and guns, clothing, footwear, garden implements. My head aches with taking it all in. And the people! Crowds and crowds of them, all walking or cycling with purpose, looking like they have somewhere urgent to go.

It's late in the evening by the time we pull up in the main square and unload our possessions once more, distributing the load so that everyone is carrying as much as they can. We walk the short distance to our new home, still struggling to take in the vibrancy and chaos of our surroundings. We are to live in the flat above the shop, Altin and Sarah with her mother, and the Jewish families in a small house that Sarah's mother has found for them. When I finally fall into bed at around midnight, I'm dog-tired and sleep the sleep of the dead.

Over the next few days we are so busy learning the ropes of the business, that I don't have time to see Hannelore at all. Now I'm nearly thirteen, I'm to work alongside my father whilst Lefter and Fatos complete their elementary education. Meanwhile Hannelore and her brother, I find out later, have been enrolled in an Italian school which they'll have to attend for six hours a day. I'm relieved to be released from such purgatory.

For some time, nothing much disturbs our new life in Shkodra. In the spring of 1941, Germany occupies Yugoslavia, and our nights are once again regularly disturbed by the rumble of bombers overhead. But running the business takes up all of our time, and I, for one, more or less forget about the war. When summer comes, my mother, brothers and I travel to the mountains to help with the harvest; father stays behind as he can't take the time away from work in the city. It's a glorious time, the weather superb, the air fresh and vibrant, every day taken up by the satisfying tasks of gathering the crops that will see the community through the winter – but I miss Hannelore and don't enjoy it as I normally would.

We return to Shkodra in the autumn, and in December of that year, Hannelore invites me to join the Jewish families in their celebration of Hanukkah. It's the first time I observe the ritual, which seems strange and beautiful to me. One of the few precious things the Frankls managed to take with them from Vienna is an ornate solid silver candlestick that's sacred to this festival. I lift it and marvel at its weight and the fact that they've managed to carry it everywhere with them, that they've kept it safe and never been tempted to sell it to supplement their tiny income and often meagre food supplies. When I question Hannelore about this, she is appalled, as if I'm asking whether the family would sell their grandma for something to eat. From this I understand how important the candlestick is.

The winter of 1942 is remarkable, in fact, due to the lack of hunger. For the first time ever, the cold months pass without mother ever having to say that there's nothing for dinner, or father going out day after day, only to return without having worked and with no money. I feel that things cannot get any better. Not only do I have shoes that fit and a warm jacket, I also have the thought of Hannelore to warm me when wool is not enough.

By the time the weather starts to heat up again in the spring of 1942, it's nearly time for Sarah and Altin's baby to arrive. Poor Sarah gets fatter and fatter and looks more and more tired each day. She barely works with us anymore – she's too fatigued – and her swollen legs mean she can't be on her feet all day. I haven't given it much thought until now, but as Sarah's belly grows, I start to be aware of how rarely Altin is around these days, and how fleeting his visits are when he does put in an appearance.

One afternoon, my mother sends me to Sarah's house across the road with a tray of food and a glass of cold, sweetened mint tea for her lunch. She and Altin have always had a bed, rather than a mat on the floor, and they brought it with them when we moved. I find her lying on it on her side, trying to catch a breeze from the open window. Her skin is clammy with sweat and she seizes the drink from the tray and gulps it down greedily before sinking back into her pillows.

'Are you all right?' I ask, tentatively. I'm worried about her, but I don't know what I'll do if she says she's not OK. What if the baby is on its way? At least her mother and my mother are not far off; I can call them for help if necessary.

'I'm fine,' she replies, 'just bored. All this waiting is getting to me.' She holds out her hand and takes mine. 'Come and sit down. Keep me company for a moment. I know you're busy,' she hastily adds, as she sees me about to protest that I need to get back to work, 'but they can do without you for a few minutes. After all, you're only a boy.'

I feel my cheeks flush with indignation. What an insult! I'm thirteen now, not far off fourteen. But she looks so hot and weary that my anger evaporates in a flood of pity. I sit down on the floor beside the bed. She's still holding my hand and she places it onto her stomach, vast and protruding.

'Feel the baby kicking,' she says, sounding dreamy now, staring at a spot above my head.

A tiny bump vibrates across her skin stretched taut beneath her dress. I flinch and pull my hand away in disgust. But then curiosity makes me put it back and I leave it there until the baby settles down and the kicks subside.

'That's... weird,' I say, finally. 'To think that there's a *person* inside you... it's... well, it's weird.' My vocabulary lets me down as I try to express my fascinated revulsion.

Sarah seems to come back to life. She laughs. 'It's going to be a big strong boy, just like you. And he'll make me so proud, just as you do your parents.'

Now my cheeks are red with embarrassment.

'I just hope Altin is back soon,' she continues, gazing wistfully towards the window as if her longing might conjure up his presence there. 'I'm sure he should be here any day.'

I'm not sure if she's referring to the baby or to her husband.

'Wh-where is he?' I ask, tentatively. I've just assumed he's back in Durrësi, looking after his property and business interests there. But, I see now, if that were the case then Sarah would know when he would return, would be able to contact him by phone or post or send a message. It's odd that she doesn't seem to have any more information about his movements than the rest of us.

'He's... busy.' She doesn't elaborate but I can't leave it there.

'Busy doing what?' I demand.

Sarah takes my hand off her stomach and rolls over onto her other side. There's a short silence and then a strange snuffling noise. I kneel up and peer over her. She's crying, great fat tears rolling down her cheeks.

'What's the matter? Aunt Sarah, what's wrong? Shall I get someone?' I'm panicking and I force myself to calm down. A real man is always strong in a crisis.

'He's in the mountains, Bekim. Far away.'

I don't know why he would be there at this time of year. There will still be snow on the high ground, and it's not until later in the year that the real farming work begins.

'Why? What is he doing?'

Sarah wipes her eyes and hauls herself into a sitting position. She looks so uncomfortable with her huge belly. I think that it would be so much better if babies were born in shells and hatched like baby chicks. While I'm imagining an infant popping its bald head out of an over-sized egg, Sarah speaks again.

'He's with the partisans. Training, planning, fighting. There are thousands of them, hiding out in the hills, learning about war. And I know it's right and I know he's brave and I know he'll be fine because he's Altin and he always is... but at the same time... I'm so scared. And I don't understand it, Bekim. This is not our war. What has it got to do with us? Why are we involved? No one in Europe cares about us; we're just caught in the crossfire and some of our men will be killed, for certain. And for what?'

I'm flabbergasted and enthralled by this speech in equal measure, by the revelations about Altin, by Sarah's passionate tirade against the war. But most of all, by the glory of the struggle, by the idea of the partisans, of men rising up and fighting against the evil oppressors. Sarah swears me to secrecy. For any of the men – or women, because there are female members too – to be found out would be certain death. Then and there, I determine to be part of it. If not now, then soon. I don't care whose war it is; I'll do my bit for my country and my people.

I'll do it for Hannelore.

Chapter Sixteen

Albania, 1942-43

That night, Sarah has the baby. No one goes into details, but from the bits and pieces I pick up I understand that things didn't go easily for her. Her mother, my mother and Mrs Frankl were all in attendance, as well as a midwife who Altin had left money to pay for.

At eleven o'clock in the morning, Sarah's mother comes downstairs with a minute, mop-haired baby girl and introduces us to the newest member of the family. Sarah has named her Majlinda, which means 'born in the month of May', and we all fall instantly in love with her. As she wraps her tiny fist around my finger, I whisper in her ear, swearing to her that I'll join the partisans and defend her and all our women and children to the death.

The unexpected consequence of Majlinda's arrival is that I see ten times more of Hannelore than I have been doing. She's completely transfixed by the baby and turns up in every spare moment to look after her. Sarah is delighted to have the help and I'm delighted to have Hannelore close by once more, as the apartment the Jewish families have rented is a thirty-minute walk away. Hannelore gets around by bike; her father has set up shop for himself now, building and repairing cycles, and as there are far more people in Shkodra than in Durrësi, all of whom seem to adore cycling, he's doing well.

One hot summer afternoon, I watch her arrive, lean her bike against a lamppost and turn, not to Sarah's home, but towards the drinks stall on the pavement where I am leaning idly against the wall, waiting for customers. It's the quiet time in the early afternoon; it'll get busy again in a couple of hours, as the heat recedes and people come out to enjoy the relative cool of the evening.

'Hi, Bekim,' she calls as she approaches.

'Hi,' I reply.

She looks utterly beautiful. Her hair has been cut and it hangs in loose chestnut curls around her heart-shaped face. Now we all have enough food she's filled out a bit and, aged thirteen, she's nearly as tall as me.

'What are you staring at?' she asks, impatiently. 'Look, since you're not doing anything,' she continues, without waiting for an answer, 'come with me.' She grins as she beckons me towards her. 'There's something I want you to do.'

I look over my shoulder to where my mother is serving a customer in the tobacconist.

'Mama,' I call, 'can I go for half an hour? I need to see Hannelore.'

My mother nods her assent. 'Be back by five,' she says, 'for the rush.'

I leg it before she can give me any more instructions or remember anything she needs me to do. Hannelore grabs the bicycle and sets off at a run, the wheels throwing up a small cloud of dust and tiny stones. I chase after her, no idea what she is up to but not caring. Life in Shkodra is wonderful and I love being able to contribute to the family income, but sometimes I hanker for the carefree days of my childhood, of hours spent on the beach or in the woods, by the river or at the port, when the only clock was the sun and the only thing directing my time was the emptiness of my stomach. These days, my belly is full but sometimes my soul feels empty of fun.

We arrive at the square which has a mosque at one end and a church at the other. In the middle is a dusty garden dotted with pine and tamarisk trees, and ribboned with wide, winding paths. Here Hannelore stops and I lurch to a halt behind her. She turns to me with a look of triumph and holds out the bicycle's handlebars.

'It's time for you to learn to ride a bike,' she says, her eyes shining with eager brightness. 'Then, when we have free days, we can borrow another cycle from father's shop and go so much further. We could visit the bridge of Mes or go up to the citadel.' She shakes the handlebars to encourage me to hurry up and take them. 'But you have to learn first!'

Tentatively, I reach out and grab the hot metal handles. I'm torn between wanting to do it and not wanting to look stupid by falling off. But her smile is so encouraging, her enthusiasm so infectious, that I cannot possibly say no, and anyway, I think, there's nothing that Bekim Shehu can't do, nothing he can't achieve if he puts his mind to it.

Bolstered by these thoughts, I swing my leg over and take up my position on the saddle. It's a little low but secretly I'm quite glad. I haven't taken my feet off the ground or tried to actually move yet and I'm already feeling insecure.

'So,' says Hannelore, in the kind of voice I think she must have learnt from her teachers, 'you put your right foot on the pedal. Make sure it's in the most upright position, push off with your left, put that foot on the other pedal and… well, just keep going.'

She's brimming over with glee at the surprise she's sprung on me and the pleasure of being able to teach me something. Other than the bits and pieces of German she's impressed on me, most of the time she's spent in Albania has been me showing her and teaching her things. I think back to the first day I saw her, playing with her hoop in the street. I had wondered then if she could ride a bike; for years I have wanted someone – her – to teach me. I had never said so – yet somehow, she must have known.

'OK.' I take a deep breath and clench my hands tighter around the handlebars. My palms are slippery with sweat and so too is my forehead. I put my right foot on the pedal, then raise my eyes to look straight ahead of me. Suddenly the idea of being able to balance on two thin wheels seems utterly preposterous.

'Go on, then!' urges Hannelore. 'What are you waiting for?'

I can't put it off any longer. I give a mighty push and I'm off. But my left foot can't find the pedal and my right loses contact and in less than five seconds I'm falling to one side and landing in a sprawling heap in the dust with the bike on top of me.

Hannelore collapses in helpless laughter.

Leaping to my feet, I haul the bike upright and get straight back on again. Damn her for laughing! The second time I go a bit further and stay upright for all of ten seconds before I'm once more on my backside on the ground.

I keep trying and Hannelore keeps laughing, as does every passer-by who happens to see my humiliation, but that only makes me more determined. Eventually, as my time draws to an end and I'm aware I need to get back to work soon, I do it. I manage a complete circuit of the square with only a couple of wobbles (because of stones on the path, nothing to do with my lack of control) and Hannelore runs up to me and flings her arms around me. I'm so surprised – by her hug and my own achievement – that I take my hands off the handlebars and immediately we collapse to the ground, me, Hannelore and the bike.

And now I start laughing, and I laugh and laugh so hard that my body is too weak to get back up and Hannelore is laughing too and I think that this is the best moment of my life, lying in the hot dust with Hannelore beside me and a heap of metal on top of me, the last of the sun shining through the tree branches and not a worry in the whole wide world.

We wander back to the shop, recounting the adventure, the thrills and spills of my very first bicycling encounter, joined in the easy, happy camaraderie I enjoy with no one else but Hannelore.

The joy does not last long.

A bad atmosphere has descended on the shop and cafe. Everyone seems agitated, on edge. Father shouts at me for spilling tea on a customer and when Fatos drops a bottle of beer, the glass shattering into a thousand pieces and the liquid splashing out over walls, floor and furniture, he's sent to bed with no supper.

Eventually, I find out the cause of the unease. Altin has been injured. Badly.

No one ever talks about what he is doing, and I only know that it must be because of his partisan activities because of what Sarah told me. When he appears, two days later, limping down from the Accursed Mountains under cover of darkness with his arm in a bandage and his face furrowed with pain, he must stay hidden or risk imprisonment or worse if his identity is revealed. He looks five years older than when I last saw him, lines around his eyes and across his brow that he never had before, his hair noticeably tinged with grey.

Though he dotes on baby Majlinda, because of his wounds he cannot hold her. Instead, he kisses her curly head and whispers lullabies in a voice so tender it belies the brave resistance fighter I know him to be.

That summer passes slowly as we all wait for Altin's body to heal. Reports of the war's progress are terrible, and everyone is forced to confront the possibility that the Germans may win. Despite the bright days of endless sunshine, we seem to be living through the darkest of times.

The Communists are calling for young people to join their ranks and I start to prepare; I'd go straightaway but I'm told I'm still too young. I curse the loss of my knife at the police station in Durrësi, and wonder if it was worth it. After all that effort, no one has ever asked for the ID cards.

When autumn comes, more shocking news reaches us. Hannelore and her family have travelled to a town further south where many Jews who fled Yugoslavia after the Germans invaded now live. They go for the holy days of Rosh Hashanah and Yom Kippur but the stories they bring back from those driven out of Belgrade are not of celebration. They are of mass executions, forest shootings and prison camps from which no one is ever released. We are forced to confront the evil that has swept across Europe, and to wonder what will happen to us here in Albania.

In that bleak period, only watching baby Majlinda grow and flourish brings a relief from the strain we're all living under. She smiles and pumps her little fists in the air and kicks her tiny legs. When I see Altin whispering in her ear, tickling her toes and kissing her palms, I know that it is his love of her that, far from keeping him by her side, will send him back to the mountains to plot and plan and train and fight. He will never, ever give up.

On the day that Altin leaves again, he says goodbye to us with eyes that glint with steely purpose. We all know he is not completely fixed yet, that his arm still throbs with pain. He sets the example for any man's life; one in which personal suffering is considered insignificant in the face of the greater good. I have always modelled myself on him, wanted not just to be like him, but to actually be him. So I watch and listen and learn and determine to always follow his example.

Over the following weeks and months, we hear of ever more audacious partisan attacks on Axis forces, sabotage of military installations and raids on army bases. In my mind, I have Altin at the centre of all of these actions and the hero-worship I've always felt towards my gallant, handsome uncle increases tenfold. I long to join him; my fingers itch to take up a weapon in the name of freedom; my soul craves the glory of the fight. But apparently, even though I'm now thirteen, I am still too young and I must wait.

It is the same story, whoever I ask.

Another year rolls around and 1942 turns to 1943. We spend the summer in the mountains but by September are back in the city. Hannelore and I are out walking in the streets one day when she suddenly pulls me roughly by the arm and forces me to flatten myself against the wall of the house beside us. She's strong these days, from helping her father in the bike shop and almost as tall as her mother. We're both getting older, growing up, taking on ever greater responsibility, but still, all too often, treated as children.

'Bekim,' she hisses, agitatedly.

'What's wrong?' I ask.

Wordlessly, she points around the corner and I lean forward and peer in the direction her finger indicates. I see nothing but a couple of soldiers standing in the street, tall and upright, surveying the passers-by with stiff-necked glances.

No big deal, I'm thinking, there have been foreign soldiers on our streets for years now. But as I'm about to turn to Hannelore and ask her what's up, I stop abruptly, suddenly aware of something. I creep right up to the front of the building and crane my neck to see the soldiers more clearly. Their grey-green uniforms are smart and close-fitting, their rifles polished and shiny. Immediately, I know what is wrong, and why Hannelore's beautiful face has gone so deathly pale. Italy has capitulated and the Italian troops have gone. These soldiers are German.

The Nazis are here.

Chapter Seventeen

Italy, 2019

Reading the next few chapters of the story left Ruth breathless, heart thumping in her chest. She could hardly imagine the fear that must have run through these youngsters' veins when they caught that first glimpse of the German forces. Over seventy years later, the word 'Nazi' still had the power to terrify.

Ruth would have loved to discuss it with Zak. But she woke up to a text message on the borrowed phone informing her that he would be at the factory all day and until late into the night, and that the next morning he was catching a very early flight to Tirana. His father had taken a turn for the worse, and at the age of ninety, there was no telling what would happen. Zak would be gone for a week or so.

Ruth could not prevent a sinking feeling of disappointment from coursing through her at the prospect of dining alone every night, with no possibility of Zak's company to alleviate the solitude. She shouldn't let herself indulge such feelings, she knew. Zak was a friend, nothing more, and she had no right to expect his company or to think she had any ownership of his time. And of course his first obligation would always be to his father, exactly as it should be.

Eating breakfast on the balcony one day when she'd woken early, she set herself to studying the Italian primer, repeating phrases out loud to herself. Surely it was not beyond her to master such simple feats as asking someone their name, ordering a meal or buying a book of stamps. But somehow nothing stuck and eventually she became too irritated by her incompetence to continue.

Not feeling in the mood for running, she decided to go out for a walk in the relative cool of the morning. At the bottom of the stairs she bumped into Enzo, checking the mail boxes.

'There's something here for you,' he told Ruth, after they'd exchanged greetings and Ruth had enquired as to how business was going.

'Thank you,' responded Ruth, surprised, as she took the jiffy bag he handed to her. She hadn't expected to get mail. Enzo called a hasty goodbye and rushed out of the building, clearly in a hurry to get to work, leaving Ruth opening the package. Inside was Ruth's phone, returned exactly as promised and looking pristine once more.

In fact, it was better than it had been before because there had been a few scratches and cracks on the old screen. She checked it over and it seemed to be in perfect working order.

The arrival of the package gave rise to a sudden change of plan. Forget the walk. Instead, she had a sudden urge to return to Zak the spare handset he had lent to her. She could take it to the factory and drop it off – and that would also give her a chance to say goodbye. Running back up the stairs, she retrieved the phone, then grabbed her handbag and car keys. Zak's business card was in her purse and she pulled it out and scrutinised it. The physical address, clearly of far less importance than the website, was printed in tiny font in the bottom left-hand corner and she had to screw her eyes up to read it. The location was Santa Maria di Leuca, but given that Ruth had only ever driven through the town on the way to the museum with Zak, she had no idea where it was. She was about to look it up on Google maps when she caught sight of Caroline dragging the washing basket into the garden down below, Daniel trailing behind her.

'Hi there,' she called down.

'*Ciao*, Ruth,' the little boy called back to her.

Ruth blew him a kiss and then went down the stairs to help Caroline hang the washing out.

'I thought I'd drop by Zak's factory to return a phone he lent me to use while mine was broken,' she told Caroline, as casually as she could. 'He's off to Albania for a short visit.'

'Yes, he does go back and forth fairly often,' Caroline agreed. 'It makes me anxious for the future, when my parents get older. I'll have to do the same between here and the UK.'

'I suppose so,' mused Ruth. 'But you don't have to worry about that quite yet, do you? Your parents are still fairly young, aren't they?'

Caroline nodded. 'Fortunately, yes. And so helpful – they'll be here soon to give me a hand with the new baby.'

The two women fell silent for a moment as they steadily pegged up towels and sheets.

'So Zak,' ventured Ruth, screwing up her eyes as she moved into the full glare of the sun, 'does he, um, well, I guess he's probably got some close friends back home in Albania? As well as his parents and family, of course.' She paused as she bent down to pull the last pillowcase from the washing basket. 'Perhaps a special friend?'

She would have struggled to explain it, even to herself, but the doubt that Zak wasn't as unencumbered as he had said kept niggling at her. After all, that is what Simon had averred. Only for Ruth to find out he was keeping wives (in all but name) in three separate cities and even had a child with one of them. Who was to say that Zak was any different? People – women – always think they would know if something fishy was going on – but Simon had successfully hoodwinked Ruth for over two years, and internet chat forums were full of similar stories.

Caroline pressed the pegs more firmly down on a towel that was slipping loose and then slotted the prop post into position. With a huge heave, she raised the line high up to expose it to the sun. Ruth, who hadn't managed to get there in time to do this for her, winced. She was sure doing all this heavy work wasn't good for a lady in Caroline's condition.

Wiping her hand over her brow, Caroline frowned in consideration of Ruth's question. 'I don't think so,' she replied, slowly. 'He's never mentioned anyone. But on other hand, I suppose I've never asked so...'

She let the conclusion to this remark fade away and Ruth knew she had to let it go.

'I'm not sure exactly where his factory is. Do you know?' she asked, picking up the empty basket. 'I'll carry this in for you,' she added, as they turned back towards the house.

'It's really easy to find,' Caroline assured her. 'It's in the industrial estate just off the main road on the way into town. Just look for the "*zona industriale*" sign – it's a right-hand turn – and follow the one-way system. You'll soon spot it.'

'Great. Sounds simple enough even for me,' replied Ruth. She didn't remember seeing the place Caroline was talking about when she and Zak had driven through Leuca, but then she hadn't been looking. Following Caroline into her apartment, she put the washing basket down by the utility room door. 'I'll be off then. I'm going to go on into town and do some rubbernecking.'

Santa Maria di Leuca boasted a number of attractions, including a basilica, a lighthouse and a waterfall that all seemed to merit a visit, and she ought to tick a few things off the bucket list. She'd been here long enough without going anywhere very much at all.

Retrieving her car from the marina car park, she set off. It was much easier driving down here than around the airport in Brindisi, the roads quiet with little traffic. The sea drifted in and out of view, impossibly blue under an azure sky. The tarmac was edged with a rustic stone wall, behind which olive trees dripped with ruby-red fruit. Every now and then a restored *trullo* nestled in a roadside dell.

As she approached the town, there was the sign for the industrial park, just as Caroline had said. Ruth flicked the indicator and made the turn. The estate resembled such places the world over; large, single-storey buildings ranged over a wide area, all similarly bland and unappealing. What a difference from the charm of the *trulli* and all the other traditional houses Puglia boasted. Feeling like an imposter, her hire car out of place amidst the vans and lorries parked up alongside the bunker-like properties, Ruth cruised along the smoothly paved road, keeping her eyes peeled for Exert Components. She had passed only a few other enterprises before she found it, a factory larger and bigger than those that surrounded it.

Pulling into a parking space, she fumbled in her bag to make sure the borrowed phone was in there, and got out. The heat hit her like a furnace; bouncing off the huge expanses of white walls and soaking into the hot tarmac. It seemed ten degrees hotter here than where she'd come from. Wafting her T-shirt up and down to try to aerate herself, Ruth then smoothed down her hair and headed for the front door.

Inside, an immaculate receptionist sat at the front desk, engaged in an extremely loud and avid conversation with two men in overalls. Ruth nearly turned straight back out to leave; she hadn't really thought about the language barrier. But they had already seen her and immediately fallen silent, eyes fixed upon her. They continued to stare as she approached, a mixture of puzzlement and curiosity upon their faces.

'Uh um.' Ruth coughed to clear her throat. '*Scusi*,' she began in Italian, before switching back to English. There was no way she could explain what she was there for in any tongue but her own. 'I'm… er… wondering if Zak is here. Mr Shehu.'

The receptionist steepled her fingertips, revealing her flawlessly polished nails. How did Italians do it? So effortlessly well put together, so stylish and chic. Ruth could quite simply never measure up. And then it occurred to her that these were the sort of women Zak was surrounded by and she almost laughed out loud at having any idea that he might ever in a million years take a romantic interest in her.

'Do you have an appointment?' asked the receptionist, whose badge declared her to be Aurora.

Even her name's alluring, thought Ruth, beautiful and elaborate, just like her.

'Er... no,' admitted Ruth, feeling about six years old under Aurora's supercilious gaze.

'And the purpose of your visit is...?' Aurora flicked her eyes towards the two men, a barely suppressed frown on her mouth. Were random female callers really that unwelcome?

'I... it's... I just have something of his I need to return to him,' spluttered Ruth, pulling the phone halfway out of her handbag as she spoke. One of the men raised his eyebrows to the other in a look that said, 'we've heard that one before'. Or maybe it didn't and Ruth was being paranoid. She had a sudden terrible sense of déjà vu. A moment just like this had occurred when she had gone to Simon's workplace. He had left his house keys on the table and she was about to embark on a work trip for a few days so would not be able to let him in.

Though his office was over an hour's drive away in Bury St Edmunds, Ruth had set off, happy to do something helpful for her partner. But when she had got there, the receptionist had looked at her in surprise before informing her that Mr Elliott had transferred to the Cambridge office some months previously. Simon, of course, had brushed it off, saying that the move was only temporary and he hadn't thought it worth bothering her with. She was always so busy on her own projects, he had said pointedly. If she were more available to him and interested in him rather than obsessed with her work, he might have felt more inclined to talk to her about it. And about a lot of stuff.

Suitably chastised, Ruth had said no more. Simon's explanation was eminently reasonable and his affronted attitude had warned her off delving deeper. More fool me, she could not avoid thinking now, as she looked back up at the pristine Aurora.

'I'm afraid Signor Shehu is not here at the moment,' said Aurora, smoothly. Her unfriendliness was like a force field around her. Did Zak know that she treated people like this? Or was it a deliberate strategy to ward off bothersome visitors? Perhaps her animosity was due to the fact that she herself had designs on the eligible Signor Shehu. Surely not, she was years younger than him. Ruth's imagination was running away from her and she had to force herself to keep calm and to think and behave rationally. 'You are welcome to leave the – item – with me,' Aurora was saying, 'and I will make sure he gets it. But he is not expected back for some days.'

'Oh, right.' Involuntarily, Ruth gripped the cool metal reception counter. So Zak had left for Albania already, ahead of the schedule he'd shared with her. Or gone somewhere, anyway. 'In that case, don't worry about it,' she added hastily. 'I'll… it can wait.'

Shoving the phone hurriedly back into her bag, she turned on her heels and left, aware of three pairs of eyes following her through the door. Outside, she ran her hand over her forehead where beads of sweat had gathered. That had been an uncomfortable and thoroughly discombobulating experience. She felt stupid that she'd even come to the factory, and that what Zak had told her of his plans was not correct. She was sure it was nothing, just an oversight on his part, or a last-minute change of plan. Definitely not that he was spending his last few hours before leaving, with another woman. *Stop being so distrustful*, she hissed at herself.

And then another thought struck, accompanied by a tight feeling in her chest. Perhaps Zak's father's condition had suddenly worsened and he'd had to bring forward his departure because of that.

Ruth sincerely hoped not. Getting into the oven-like car, she focused on navigating the road into the town centre, thinking that sightseeing would take her mind off worries about Bekim's health. And Zak's receptionist. Thankfully, she found a car park with spaces almost immediately.

Leuca was as beautiful as promised and its sites certainly worth seeing, but loneliness descended upon Ruth as she joined the tours that were packed with families, couples and groups of friends. The presence of all these happy people, along with the visit to the factory which had seemed to exacerbate her solitude, lodged a sense of despondency like a dead weight in her heart. At the lighthouse, situated at the point where the Adriatic and Ionian seas meet, instead of appreciating the beauty of the scene Ruth simply felt miserable. The view was stupendous, but were views enough? More and more she felt the emptiness of her life. The success she had once thought she had achieved had evaporated. Her single status seemed unlikely to change any time soon. She desperately needed a new direction. But as she surveyed the endless blue of the water stretching to an infinite horizon, she could not fathom where such a direction might lie.

Next day, Ruth was still down in the dumps. Daniel would cheer her up but she felt too lacking in energy to even contemplate spending time with him. That was one advantage to being childless, she tried to convince herself. No obligations, complete and utter liberty to do exactly what she liked. Partners, too, could be restrictive, wanting you to go along with their choice of activity, to go to the holiday spots they picked out of the brochure. It was far better to be a free agent.

All the internal tough talking Ruth could muster, though, failed to lift her from the doldrums. Moping around the apartment, she recalled being dumped by a boyfriend in her twenties and a friend, with whom she'd long since lost touch, making her listen to the soundtrack of Les Mis on repeat for a whole evening. Ruth had sobbed and wailed, the wine had flowed freely, and by the end Ruth was no longer sure if it was her broken heart that she was crying about or the cheesy music.

Contemplating locating the musical soundtrack on YouTube, she was almost at the point of typing it into the search bar when she abruptly slammed her laptop closed. Enough already. Determinedly, she collected her tote bag and paperback novel she'd picked up at the airport and not even opened yet and strode forth towards the beach. Forget the Italian book, forget Zak's manuscript and Hannelore and Bekim's burgeoning love which Ruth really couldn't bear to read about right now, and forget any notion of writing her own book. The broken-hearted only pen self-indulgent nonsense, Ruth was convinced, and there was enough of that floating around without her adding to it.

Stopping at the mini-mart, she stocked up with enough unhealthy snacks and soft drinks to last the day and, with an air of defiance, pointed out the packet of Benson & Hedges Gold and a lighter she also wished to purchase. Back outside, she couldn't wait to reach the line of loungers on the beach but instead ripped off the plastic wrap right there and then. Experiencing a frisson of anticipation, she flipped the cardboard lid open and tapped out a cigarette. Lighting it, she took her first, glorious puff. It was delicious, heavenly. Why had she been depriving herself of such pleasure? Inhaling for a second time, Ruth was suddenly bent double in a fit of coughing and choking. Hastily, she grabbed a can of coke and tore open the ring pull, taking a huge slug of the cold liquid to calm her raging throat. Before she'd even begun the third puff, Ruth faced up to the inevitable.

She no longer enjoyed smoking. It wasn't a treat anymore, but a torture. She ground the butt into the pavement to make sure it was out and then picked it up, wrapped it in tissue and stored it in her bag to put in the bin later.

Bang goes that vice, that method of taking my mind off my worries, she thought to herself as she selected a lounger and sank down onto it. Losing the taste for smoking should be something to be pleased about, an achievement to be proud of. But without anyone to share it with, it felt hollow and worthless.

As she had at the beginning of her holiday, once more Ruth stayed on the beach until the sun went down and the teenage lad who managed the loungers came to gather them all in for the night. Wondering briefly what he'd do if she pretended to be asleep, Ruth soon thought better of trying to find out and meekly packed her bag and left. She placed the almost-full packet of cigarettes on the end of her sunbed; the boy chain-smoked so he might as well have them.

In her apartment, she ate a desultory supper of avocado on toast, not even having the heart to smash the fruit in some trendy cosmopolitan way, but instead opting for good old-fashioned slices. Tonight, her culinary sensibilities had well and truly deserted her.

Chapter Eighteen

Albania, 1943

The day after our first sighting of the German soldiers, their numbers swell innumerably. On the ninth of September, all Albania is occupied by the German 2nd Armoured Division. The Nazis sweep in to take over where the Italians left off, but with extra helpings of brutality, ruthlessness and repression. Life suddenly takes a terrible turn for the worse.

Notices appear all over Shkodra informing residents that housing, harbouring or hiding Jews is prohibited. The penalty for anyone found committing such a crime: death. Not only that, but all residents are instructed that they must report to the authorities with their identity papers. At the same time, word goes around that house-to-house searches for Jews have begun and are intensifying in number and enthusiasm.

Altin is the first to recognise what needs to be done, coming back to Shkodra to make arrangements.

'They must get away.' His voice is hard with exhaustion and gravelly as if he's swallowed half the dust on the roads he's travelled to get here. 'Now.'

He tells us that Jews who obey the regulation and turn themselves into the authorities are going to be rounded up and sent to Kavaja. The Frankls and the Albrechts are immediately terrified. Rumours about camps in Poland and Germany have become stories of hard labour and starvation, disease and death. Though it cannot possibly be as bad as people are making out, nevertheless nobody wants to take the chance of finding out.

'To have gone through so much,' moans Mrs Frankl, her head in her hands, 'and now this.'

I've never seen her so despairing, or heard her sound so tired and downcast. It is as if she is giving up hope.

Hannelore and David cry and cry, and I try to comfort them.

'It'll be all right,' I say, but even I know that I don't sound convincing. Hannelore takes her brother's hand, and then her mother's, too.

'As long as we are all together, Mutti,' whispers Hannelore. 'We can look after each other.'

But Altin has no intention of letting the Jews go to Kavaja. He has another plan.

'We will take them to the mountains.' He looks at my father and mother, at Lefter and Fatos. 'You will stay here – you need to run the business and look after Sarah, Majlinda and the new baby.' For Sarah, who stands stoically beside her husband through thick and thin, never complaining about his prolonged absences, is pregnant again.

He turns to me, reaching out and putting a strong hand on my shoulder. He pretends that the break in his arm is fixed and that he is fighting fit, but I catch an almost imperceptible wince of pain as he stretches the limb out. It still hurts, I can tell. But Altin would never admit to weakness of any kind.

'Bekim will lead the party,' he commands. His tone is unequivocal; I cannot and will not let him down. 'I will accompany them as far as the village, and then he will be in charge. He's fifteen now, ready to take on the responsibilities of manhood. He has shown in the past that he is brave and resourceful. This task will test those attributes to the limit.'

My heart swells with pride even as the blood in my veins runs chill and my guts clench in fear.

Despite the apprehension, I feel immeasurably older than that day when I first saw Hannelore playing with her hoop in the street. We were children then, selfish and silly and, for my part, oblivious to the fact that our world was irrevocably altering. I look at Hannelore now and suddenly see how much she has changed, how, at age fourteen, she is more of a woman than a girl, with breasts that swell beneath her embroidered blouse and long legs that allow her to keep pace with me when we are walking. Her face, slimmer, framed by her chestnut curls, is more beautiful than ever. There has been an increasing self-consciousness between us for months, that I've been aware of and yet reluctant to face up to. But at this moment, strange feelings stir within me that I cannot suppress. I struggle to take my eyes away from her; it's as if Altin conferring the status of a grown man upon me has given me permission to see her in a completely new light.

I'm nearly five foot nine these days, but it's not just my height that has transformed over the years since the Frankls arrived in Albania. My understanding of the world is also completely different and I see clearly that everything is far more complicated than I ever imagined back in my boyhood. And yet it is also very simple: I have been entrusted with the safety of these people who I have grown to love so much, who have become part of my family. And I will protect them to the ends of the earth and back.

–

The walk to the mountains will take over a week with so many people of varying degress of fitness and agility. Because of the ever-increasing presence of the enemy, the Jews are being spirited away from big cities all over the country, not just from Shkodra, but also from Vlore down in the south and from the capital, Tirana. Durrësi has been completely evacuated as the Germans are mining the city, fearing – expecting – an invasion by the Allied troops. They've reached Sicily already; surely, we all whisper amongst ourselves when far from prying ears, it can't be long until they reach us? Or the Russians will come. Surely they will.

But until that time, we must be constantly on our guard.

Our group originally comprised only the Frankls and the Albrechts, but before we set off we are joined by seven more people – a woman travelling alone, a family of two adults and two children aged six and eight, and two young men, friends not brothers, in their early twenties. They are from Hamburg and their names are Moses and Chaim. I never ask them what happened to their parents, or any of their other relatives. And they never mention them. Immediately, I bond with these youths, glad that I'll have their male company on our long march. David, too, has grown up – he's a tall, strapping lad of eleven now and keen to take his place as protector of his parents and sister.

Altin, with his unerring ability to lay his hands on anything that the situation requires, manages to procure three donkeys and two horses to facilitate our journey. The donkeys carry the packs, and the horses the women and children, taking turns to ride. Just before we leave, my father passes me something. I take it into my hands, feel the weight of metal, the hard edge of well-worn leather. Looking down, I already know what I will see. It is my father's watch, handed down to him by his father – our family watch. And now it is mine. I clasp it tightly, hold it to my chest, feel the metal warming in my palm as hot tears gather behind my eyes. I know exactly what it means that he has gifted it to me.

It means that I am worthy of it.

We travel early in the morning and late at night, keeping to back roads and paths across fields and through woods, avoiding the main highways at all cost. These are dotted with German checkpoints and we would have no chance of getting through unchallenged.

As we walk, David, Chaim and Moses chat in German, every now and again spontaneously bursting into song. The music lifts all of our spirits. In the evenings, before we sleep in the shelter of a country barn or a protective thicket, I tell tales around the cooking fire, of grappling with wolves and fighting off bears, of soaring eagles and blundering boars. The stories gently scare the children but even they can see that wild animals are preferable and more predictable foes than the Nazis who are crawling over our country like maggots on a piece of road kill.

We pass through woods of pine and beech, through groves of olives in parched brown fields, alongside gushing rivers and sluggish streams. I know the paths and trails like the back of my hand; we've been coming this way for years. One day we reach a copse made up of ancient oaks, one of which has a hollowed out trunk big enough to hide in. My cousins and I discovered it when we were young and we never miss going to visit it as we wend our way to the mountains.

Eager to share this precious memory of childhood with David, we leave the others resting in the shade as I guide him to the tree. When the Frankls first came to Albania I barely took any notice of David. He was just Hannelore's baby brother, nearly five years younger than me and therefore warranting little of my so-much-more-mature attention. During the time we've all spent living in Shkodra, I've got to know him much better and begun to see that he has many of Hannelore's best traits – loyalty, humour, kindness and strength. Yet though he acts grown-up, the reality is that he's still a child. When I was a boy his age, a hollow tree trunk was one of the most exciting things I could imagine. Perhaps by showing it to him, I can give him a little bit of joy to alleviate the tension that surrounds us.

Gratifyingly, David is as delighted with the tree as I hoped he would be. He examines it carefully, marvelling at every detail, especially the deceptive spaciousness within, the way the opening folds over itself like a pair of lips so that the hollow interior is effectively hidden from all but the most avid searcher. I watch as he climbs in and out, trying the hollow for size, laughing as he peeps out from the entrance and I pretend I cannot see him.

Despite the fun we are having, we cannot stay long and must get on our way. Our final destination is only a few days' walk away, and reaching that haven unscathed is the aim we all hold close to our hearts. The sooner we get there, the better. Nevertheless, we have to eat, and we always take a break at the height of the midday heat. A short distance from the hollow oak copse is a roadside cafe run by a distant cousin called Rezar. Though on a minor road, it sees enough traffic from those taking their goods to and from their farms and the towns nearby to give him a living. Outside of local farming people, however, the route is little known so Altin and I deem it safe for us to have a drink and a meal here; the long days of travelling are taking their toll. We could all do with some rest and a good hot meal.

Altin doesn't stay with us at the cafe. He has business to attend to and will catch us up further along our route. He disappears into the sun-baked landscape, his proud, erect form soon mingling with the hills and trees and fields and melting out of sight. As we ascend higher and higher into the Accursed Mountains, I imagine partisan hideouts all around us, bands of men armed to the hilt and continually engaging in acts of sabotage and the many small insur- rections designed to weary and weaken the enemy. They haven't succeeded yet.

But surely, in time, they will.

I settle down on a bench, taking a long swig of fresh spring water. The Jewish people are inside, sheltering from the sun, resting on the plump blankets and cushions Rezar has provided. All I can hear is the singing of the birds and the rustle of the leaves in the soft breeze; it's a beautiful day.

Until suddenly I become aware of something. There's a rattle, and the rumbling sound of thick tyres on hardened mud followed by the squeal of brakes. My heart flips over and begins to beat like jungle war drums. Slowly, I raise my eyes from my water cup and force myself to look. I see a truck, green and black, and another one behind; their wheels covered in dust but the symbols on their sides unobscured.

Swastikas.

Chapter Nineteen

Albania, 1943

I casually stroll to the door and put my finger to my lips, gesturing to the Jews that they must be silent. The building is built against the side of the hill and the back opens out into a natural cave in which Rezar stores the drinks – beer, lemonade, cordial – to keep them cool. I can hear loud voices demanding, commanding. Rezar speaks only a few words of German but he'll know what they want. We all do.

In a split second, I have shoved two barrels to the side, flicked open the latch of the wooden door that leads to the cave and gestured to our guests to go inside. They wear their fear on their ashen faces but they all obediently creep, one by one, into the room. They have become accustomed to hiding, are old hands at the art of concealment, of melting into the background, of existing outside of normal society.

It's only as I'm shutting the door that I realise who is missing. Hannelore, and David.

My heart thumps and my blood chills in my veins. Where are they?

I force myself to composure. Picking up a tray I saunter outside, affecting a casual nonchalance that is a million miles from the reality of the pounding in my chest, the sweat rising on my palms. I assume that they've gone to the toilet. They often accompany each other; Hannelore is terrified of the huge rats that hang around the bathroom areas and David, who isn't bothered by them, scares them away for her.

The toilet is on the other side of the outdoor seating area. I need to get to them and warn them, before they are noticed. My pulse quickens and my heart is beating at a pace I didn't realise it could reach as I stroll past Rezar and the Nazis, straining to take in as much as I can about them without looking as if I'm looking, using the collecting of empty coffee cups and water glasses as a pretext to be there.

I see taut, clean-shaven faces under perfectly positioned caps and expressions that exude hostility.

Rezar calls me over. He mutters to me rapidly in our dialect, knowing that, even if the Germans speak Albanian, they won't know it the way we speak it.

'They are looking for Jews. They've been told there are unregistered people in the area and it is an order of law to hand them over.'

I shrug and shake my head, the universal signal of knowing nothing.

A noise erupts from the second of the Nazi trucks. I snatch a glance towards it and see that it is full of men, hunched on the benches. An argument has broken out amongst them. One of the German soldiers goes to the truck, takes the butt of his rifle and smashes it against the provocateur's head.

'Prisoners of war, going to hard labour,' he says, as he comes back, although no one had asked for an explanation. I assume it is a warning.

I think of Altin, somewhere out on the mountain roads, plotting and planning with the other partisans. If they find him, they will take him, too. The thought makes me brave.

But the feeling doesn't last long. At that very moment, David comes sauntering round the corner from the direction of the toilets, hands in pockets. He sees the soldiers, and halts, his mouth dropping open, his eyes darting wildly to and fro. Guilt and fear are written on his face; he knows immediately that there's no escape.

'Papers,' snaps the Nazi who seems to be in charge. They have immediately spotted that he is not one of us; they haven't asked Rezar or me for any form of identification.

David doesn't have his ID card. Mr Frankl has the whole family's. A situation had not been envisaged where a child on his or her own might have to produce one. Looking at David now, he doesn't seem like a child. But neither does he seem like an Albanian. The cards are an irrelevance; even if had one, the Germans would see in an instant that it was fake.

'Name?' barks the senior officer.

There is a terrible silence. A wood pigeon coos into the black hole that is David's desperate search for an appropriate answer. I see his hands shaking before he clenches them tightly shut.

'David Frankl,' he mutters finally, his voice faint with terror and hopelessness. In his anguish, he could not even invent a made-up name.

'You will come with us,' says the officer. 'Put him on the list,' he orders one of his men.

165

The soldier clicks his heels together, at the same time as he efficiently produces a clipboard onto which he writes David's name, date of birth and country of origin.

The sun is beating down on our heads and I'm feeling dizzy; there's something bizarre and surreal about being here, surrounded by the enemy, our precious guests holed up in a cave, David about to be carted off to God knows what fate. And Hannelore God knows where.

'All in good time, gentlemen,' says Rezar, in his most jovial tone of voice. 'First, of course, you must accept Albanian hospitality and take a drink; we cannot let guests leave without refreshments.'

I recognise Rezar's actions as delaying tactics and inwardly congratulate him for his lightning-fast thinking.

'Bekim, quick… rakia all round, please, and send to the kitchen for byrek.'

The Germans seem, if not happy, at least willing to take some time out from whatever acts of brutality they're supposed to be engaged in and settle themselves down at a table under a vine-draped pergola. Hastily, I bring plates, trays of byrek filled with spinach, mince and onions, cheese, along with glasses of home-distilled quince rakia that looks like water and tastes like the hottest fire on earth.

As I'm laying it on the table, out of the corner of my eye, I catch sight of a flash of white. Hannelore.

I'm breathing so hard I'm sure the Germans will wonder what is wrong with me. I sense, rather than see, Hannelore observing us, sizing up the situation, choosing between fight or flight.

'Who is this?'

It's too late. The commandant has spotted her.

I stand upright, feeling nauseous, struggling to keep my legs from giving way beneath me.

Hannelore walks over to us. 'Good afternoon, gentlemen,' she says in Albanian. 'Sorry for my brief absence; I'm sure my husband here' – she points at Rezar – 'and our employee' – she points at me – 'are making you comfortable.'

I nearly faint in relief; her fluency in our language, and her presence of mind, might just save her. I have no idea if the Germans have understood what she said – but she was so convincing, I don't think it matters. As she stands there, smiling despite the terror that must be surging within her, I also realise for the first time how compeltely unalike she and David are. They bear no resemblance to each other at all. David has blond hair and small, deep-set eyes and a much fairer complexion than Hannelore. You would not place them as brother and sister if you did not know; the Nazis won't guess she and David are related. But they know there is more than one Jew they need to round up.

The commandant takes a long swig of the rakia I've served him and then saunters casually over to Hannelore. He stands right before her, much too close. Anger heaves in my belly. He reaches out a hand and lifts her chin as if inspecting her, then strokes her cheek with a feather touch of his fingers. Hannelore remains impervious. I've always known she was strong, but never guessed that she had nerves of quite such unbreakable steel. She does not flinch.

'She's a pretty one,' the commandant says, sneeringly.

I'm waiting for him to add, 'for a Jew'. My breath is no longer coming in pants; it's barely coming at all. The tension in the air is palpable, thick as the heat on an August day.

Abruptly, the commandant drops his hand away from Hannelore and swivels around. He goes back to the table and sits down.

Cool as you like, Hannelore makes a small curtsey in his direction and then, picking up the tray I've discarded, disappears in the direction of the kitchen. I'm sure she knows that she should stay out of sight but, because of David, she can't bear to. So, as the Germans are tucking into the byrek, she returns and starts to gather glasses and bottles and place them onto the tray.

As she moves near to David, sitting between two of the soldiers, trembling in fear, the poor boy emits a pathetic whimper.

An enormous crash echoes through the still air, resounding off the walls of the building. Hannelore has dropped the tray; there's glass and bits of crockery everywhere. The Germans laugh and clap and cheer and I can see Hannelore straining with every cell not to cry, not to break down and weep for her brother.

'She's clumsy, your pretty wife,' barks the commandant and they all laugh even louder. 'You should beat her for this – isn't that how you peasants treat your women?'

They must have noticed how young Hannelore is but they've accepted that she's married. They probably think that child brides is only what is to be expected of such primitive people as us Albanians. My heart blazes with fiery rage anew; it banishes all fear.

Rezar is lucky Hannelore isn't Albanian and isn't really his wife. An insult like that would call for a fight to the death. But even if she were, the Germans are in charge and can do what they like. My blood boils anew at the thought and I want to take each one and wring their necks. Instead, I put my hands deferentially behind my back and offer them more rakia, realising for the first time in my life what a foul, bitter taste subjugation has.

By the third round of rakia, things are getting merry. One of the soldiers starts singing and the others join in. It doesn't sound very tuneful to me, more the sort of rhythm you'd beat a carpet to. But they seem to be enjoying themselves. David is still sitting motionless, as if frozen. In all the commotion, I'm not sure that anyone but me notices that he's thrown up, a little pile of vomit at the end of his toes, spatters of it staining his boots.

They can't think he's that much of a threat if they haven't bothered to tie him up, I think. And then I realise that they haven't bothered because they know he has nowhere to run to, that if he did make a break for it, they would simply shoot him.

The soldiers get drunker and drunker. I watch Hannelore plying them with alcohol, not letting the humiliation of earlier get the better of her. One of them pinches her bottom when she leans forward to clear a glass. I remember the slap she gave me on the first day she met. I wish she could do that to this brute. But she giggles and smirks and you'd never guess that inside she's dying of embarrassment and on fire with rage. Just I, who understands her so well, knows this must be the case.

Rezar's whispered idea to me is that soon the soldiers will be so drunk they'll forget about David, but I'm not convinced. He's their prize and they're not going to let go of him that easily. Imagine the praise they'll receive from the Oberführer when they get back to base, bringing a real live Jewish prisoner. I shudder to think about David's fate.

We're trying to keep the soldiers drinking for as long as possible, to buy ourselves time. Rezar keeps sending me to the kitchen for more food and drink and tasty titbits to tempt them to stay – but no coffee. He doesn't want them sobering up. As I'm slicing peaches in half, the brainwave comes to me.

'Back in a minute,' I whisper to Lela, Rezar's actual wife, who has remained in the kitchen throughout, preparing the food, too scared to come out. Which is good, though the Germans think we're so benighted they probably wouldn't question a man having two wives, an older and a younger one.

I rush out to the back of the cafe and grub around in the ground until I find what I need. Returning to the kitchen, I go back to my tray of peaches. There is one that is overripe, especially on one side. I would have put it in the bin but it will be perfect for my purpose. I remove the stone, and replace it with the acorn I fetched from outside. Placing this fruit, squidgy and a darker, more livid orange than the rest, on the tray closest to me I hope and pray that I'm doing the right thing, that my plan isn't going to prove to be a monumental mistake. Fear clutching at my stomach, I venture back outside to the singing soldiers and to Rezar whose rigid stance reveals the tension that his cheerful exhortations to 'drink up' cannot hide.

As I approach the group, the tray trembles in my hands. My blood runs cold in my veins and bile rises in my stomach. I choke back the nausea but I can't stop the flush of guilt that's rising on my cheeks. I tell myself that I have to go through with this – and that David will understand what the acorn means. It might be his only chance.

But if I'm caught…

I'm not going to think about being caught. I just need to keep going, to stay calm, hold my nerve.

Willing my hands to steadiness, I hold out the tray of peaches to the group. Rezar tuts, and points at the gone-over one with the acorn in the middle. I can tell that he's worried that the food won't find favour with the Nazis, that the mood might change and go against us – and make things even worse for David. Though how they could be worse, I'm not too sure. And anyway, his reaction is exactly what I wanted.

'I'm sorry,' I say. I take the peach and thrust it into David's hands. 'He can have the bad one,' I say in German, and chuckle as if I've done something really clever.

All the soldiers roar with laughter, too, like I've made the best joke ever. I use the distraction to give Rezar a surreptitious wink. Then I pass around the rest of the fruit, putting my body between David and the soldiers, willing him to realise what I've done. Rezar pours yet more rakia and I tell them a stupid, long-drawn out German joke about a talking horse that Hannelore taught me and next time I look around David is gone.

Relief makes my grip weaken and I lean forward to put my empty tray down on the table, but miscalculate the distance so that it clangs onto the wooden surface with a loud, metallic crash. Suddenly the soldiers are alert, their drunkenness evaporated as quickly as steam from a boiling kettle.

The commandant leaps to his feet, glaring around him. He strides to the truck where the prisoners are slumped all over each other, sweating in the hazy heat of the afternoon. He marches back to the table, staring at the spot where David had been sitting. He's trying to look imperious, but I see him blinking as if attempting to rub out the alcohol and focus on the empty seat. Swivelling round on one heel, he shouts a command I don't understand to the soldiers.

In seconds, they too are on their feet and they've grabbed hold of Rezar and me and they're dragging us to the wall of the cafe and forcing us up against it and they have their hands to our throats and they're shouting and swearing, furious words from furious mouths.

'Where is the boy?' they scream, over and over again. '*Wo ist der Jude?*'

Rezar clamps his mouth shut and says nothing. I do the same.

Hannelore is there, behind us, watching. At least they won't interrogate her; what would an Albanian woman know?

The commandant is livid, his cool, smooth face bright red with anger, his eyes blazing through narrowed lids.

He strolls towards us, slowly now, maximising the fact that we are locked into position, our arms pinioned against our sides. He stops. Languidly, he draws his gun from its holster. He takes one more step forward and comes to a slow and deliberate halt, his face two inches from Rezar's. He lifts the gun and places the barrel against Rezar's temple.

'Tell me where is the boy? The Jewish boy?'

Rezar's eyes stare straight ahead, fixed at some point far in the distance, avoiding the commandant's piercing gaze.

'I don't know,' he says.

The commandant drops the gun, spins it around his finger and then turns to me.

As the cold metal meets my flesh, my legs shake. I'm going to collapse. My stomach turns and I swallow back the bile that rises in my throat.

'Tell me where he is,' says the commandant. 'This is not a request; it's an order.'

There's a silence as deep as the ocean and this time there's no cooing pigeon to fill it with its gentle, familiar song.

I breathe in, steel my nerves. I look him straight in his nasty, brutish eyes. The only thing in my favour right now is that I'm no use to him dead. I'm not wearing the watch on my wrist but it's in my pocket, burning my skin through the thin fabric, reminding me of my duty.

'I don't know.' I say it in German, loud and clear. '*Ich weiss es nicht.*'

My father's words echo inside my head, drowning out the terror and the temptation to confess.

To save a life is to go to paradise.

I'd sooner my son were killed than break my promise, my besa.

You must lay down your own life for a guest.

The thoughts are confused and all mixed up but I know what they are telling me. They are saying that it is quite literally more than my life is worth to give David away.

The commandant steps back, twirling his gun. He looks down at the ground, at the dusty, stony mud floor beneath us, flat from the trampling of many feet, where only a few scrappy weeds dare to poke their heads.

A chicken appears, its tiny head bobbing back and forth, its beady eyes surveying the scene with blank disinterest. It picks its way over the stones, occasionally pecking at the dust, strutting between the commandant and me with utter insouciance. The commandant raises his gun, takes aim, fires.

The fowl flops to the floor.

A few feet beyond it, the bullet is embedded in the ground. It has passed straight through the poor chicken's head, in one side and out the other.

The commandant laughs and all his men join in.

'This is what will happen to you if you do not tell me the truth.'

And then the gun is back, against my temple, hard and bullying.

I will not give in. I will not.

'Where is the boy?'

'I don't know.'

He turns to Rezar, who denies any knowledge. But Rezar really doesn't know what's happened to David so when he answers, he is telling the truth. It is only me who is lying.

When the gun is raised again, I know this is the final time. I feel a slithering in my guts. I need the toilet, desperately, and I want to cry. I lean back into the cafe wall, feeling its firm surface against my back, needing its support.

In my peripheral vision, I can just make out the shape of Hannelore. She's relying on me to save her brother. Nobody else knows where I have sent him. If he isn't collected, the Nazis will pick him up somewhere along the road at some future point in time when he has to venture out for water, for food. I rub my wrists against the rough-hewn wood of the planks from which the building is constructed, willing the pain of the splinters that pierce my skin to take my mind off what is to come.

Does it hurt, when you are shot through the head? Do you know when you are dead?

'This is your last chance. Tell me where the boy is.'

The gun's smell of hot metal intensifies, mingling with the wood smoke from the cooking fire and the pine resin from the unfinished boards behind my back. The pigeon coos and I know that this is the last time I'll hear that lilting, familiar sound.

'I don't know where he is.'

The trigger clicks.

I wait for the explosion in my head that will tell me that it's over.

Chapter Twenty

Italy, 2019

'Ruth! Ruth, are you there?'

Alarm searing through her, Ruth sat bolt upright in bed, her heart beating at double time. For a moment, she had visions of jackbooted soldiers outside, tracking her down, coming to take her away. Nazis, who would threaten to kill her in cold blood just as they were doing to Bekim.

It took a few seconds for Ruth to realise that the voice calling from outside was Enzo's. He sounded panicked, an impression corroborated by the frantic thumping at the door that accompanied the shouting.

Leaping from her bed, Ruth pulled on a kaftan she'd left lying on the back of a chair and rushed to the door. Her mind was already turning over every eventuality: Daniel was ill; Caroline was ill; the unborn baby... Before she'd had time to formulate the last thought, she had flung the door open to reveal a dishevelled looking Enzo standing on the doorstep, wild-eyed.

'Oh Ruth, thank God you're here,' he exclaimed. 'Caroline has gone into labour. She's three weeks early so her parents aren't due over for another fortnight. Can you look after Daniel while I take her to the hospital? My mother will come in the morning but I don't like to wake her so late and ask her to drive through the night at her age.'

Right on cue, an agonised wail drifted up from Caroline and Enzo's apartment, where the door was standing open after Enzo's hurried exit.

'Of course,' said Ruth. 'Let me just get some clothes and my glasses, otherwise I'm blind as a bat. I'll be right down,' she called after Enzo's rapidly disappearing frame.

Minutes later, she was downstairs and ready to take up babysitting duties. By the look on Caroline's face and the barely suppressed screams emanating from the depths of her being, it seemed to be not a moment too soon. Enzo had called a taxi and it was outside only a minute or so later, its purring engine competing with the whirring of the cicadas. As Enzo helped Caroline out towards it, she yelped again. Ruth grimaced in alarm; would the driver be happy about transporting such a passenger? Weren't they always supposed to be worried about waters breaking and ruining their upholstery? She held her breath as Caroline manoeuvred herself inside, Enzo hovering beside her, jumping anxiously from side to side in a manner so balletic it defied his stocky bulk.

Finally, they were both in and the driver pulled away, apparently unconcerned about what was occurring in the back seat. Overcome with relief, Ruth retreated back inside, shutting the door but not locking it from the inside. She assumed the couple wouldn't be back before morning but if they were, the last thing she wanted was them stuck on the doorstep with a newborn, trying to get into their own home.

Daniel, thankfully, had remained soundly asleep throughout the commotion. There was another bed in his room and Ruth lay down on that, hoping that the baby would be all right despite its early arrival. Caroline had been doing far too much, Ruth thought, working all hours, doing the laundry for their four rental apartments and carrying loads far too big. It was a relief that her parents would soon be here to help out, but Ruth knew that Caroline had said they were dreading the heat of mid-July.

'I really didn't time this one too well, did I?' she'd joked with Ruth and Ruth had had to agree, though she thought that Enzo should take at least fifty per cent of the blame.

After a fitful sleep, Ruth woke early and immediately checked her phone. There was the notification of a new text, but it was not from Enzo. Instead, Zak's name glowed on her screen.

Hope all well, the message read. *Looking forward to catching up when I'm back. x*

Ruth read it and then read it again. It didn't mean anything, she concluded. Or rather, she shouldn't read more into it than was really there. She should just take it at face value; Zak was a friend, they enjoyed each other's company and that was as far as it went. The kiss? Just a normal way to sign off a communication.

Hauling herself out of bed, she went to the kitchen to make coffee. Once she had a steaming mug in her hand, she read the message again. There was that kiss. Only one, but a kiss nevertheless. Perhaps she was being too negative about the whole thing. Perhaps Zak's kindness and friendliness and eagerness to spend time with her, for example taking her to the museum – were a sign he'd be interested in something more than just being mates.

Sighing, Ruth put the phone down and drank more coffee. She was overthinking all this so badly. What will be, will be, she told herself sternly, then added 'que sera, sera' and chuckled at her own wit. It was Italian, wasn't it? Or was it Spanish? Perhaps it was the same in both languages? Who knew.

The phone buzzed and she jumped out of her skin, then seized it up in a frenzy. This must be it, news of the baby. No. It was one of those communications from a phone company, cheerfully telling her she was now accessing Ital-Telecom and welcome! Everything was wonderful on this network and receiving texts would cost 50p, calls £2. Annoyed, she tossed the phone down onto the counter, before immediately picking it back up.

She must tell Zak the news.

> Excitement and drama here. Caroline in labour – I'll let you know as soon as there's any more news. Hope your father is bearing up. See you soon.

She read and re-read the message, then added a kiss. Just the one – a kiss for a kiss. No need to go overboard.

Daniel appeared as she was contemplating the screen, deep in thought. He looked at her, face screwed up in confusion.

'What are you doing here?' he asked. 'Where's mummy?'

Momentarily out of her depth, Ruth floundered for a moment. 'Um, well, she's fine, she's… well, she's having the baby. Your little brother or sister.'

Caroline had defied all Italian convention by refusing to know the baby's sex, wanting it to be a surprise.

'Oh,' answered Daniel, unimpressed. 'Can I have chocolate milk?'

As far as Ruth was concerned he could have anything he wanted if it kept him happy until his parents were back. She poured him a generous glass of his desired beverage and set it down on the table in front of him.

The phone buzzed and danced around on the table. She grabbed it up.

That's fantastic news! It was a reply from Zak. A very quick one. *A new baby is always a joyful thing. Keep me posted. I'm in and out of hospital appointments with dad – thank you for asking after him – so if I don't respond, that's why. But wishing everything well and missing you all. Back at the end of the week. xx*

Missing us? Two kisses? In an instant, Ruth rewrote the whole narrative of her and Zak. And then, just as she was thinking she could relax, another thought struck her. 'A new baby is always a joyful thing.' Zak had no children, and neither did Ruth. But where Zak had the option to have them if he wanted to, that opportunity had passed for Ruth.

At forty-five, her doctor had already told her she was perimenopausal and it was unlikely she would be able to get pregnant, let alone give birth to a healthy baby. Ruth knew so many women who had spent thousands of pounds and endured heartbreak after heartbreak trying to conceive through IVF, and others who had had to make terrible decisions about whether to go ahead with pregnancies after the baby had been diagnosed with chromosomal disorders. What to do in that situation was any woman's personal choice, but Ruth knew she wasn't capable of dealing with such a dilemma.

Would Zak not want to seek out someone who could give him the joy of fatherhood? He had indicated, when she had asked him, that he wished he had children. Ruth put down her coffee and ran her hands through her hair. However much she taunted herself, there was absolutely nothing she could do about this particular problem.

The next few hours passed unbearably slowly. By the time the clock had struck eleven, Ruth was starting to get anxious. Caroline should have had the baby by now, shouldn't she? It had been hours – twelve or more, depending on when exactly the labour had started. How long were second babies supposed to take?

Not wanting to stray too far from the house, she took Daniel into the garden where he played in the paddling pool while she sat with her feet in it, trying to keep cool, fanning herself ineffectively with her hands. She wondered where Enzo's mother was, but she was quite glad she hadn't showed up as she would inevitably only speak Italian and they'd be using a four-year-old as translator.

Eventually, she heard a noise at the door. Dragging Daniel out of the pool, she rushed towards the house, pulling him behind her. By the time she got there, Caroline was already over the threshold, Enzo hovering protectively behind her, and next to him a diminutive Italian *nonna* weighed down by a gigantic picnic hamper in both hands. In Caroline's arms was a tiny bundle wrapped in a snow white blanket. Instantly, Ruth slowed down, letting Daniel go ahead of her so that he could be reunited with his parents first.

Caroline bent down to her son, her face shining with love. 'Here's your baby sister,' she whispered. 'She's called Mia. Do you want to say hello?'

'Hello, Mia,' chirruped Daniel, happily. And then he turned away from her and did a complete circuit of the living room at top speed before dive bombing onto the sofa, seemingly overcome with the emotion of the moment.

Caroline introduced Ruth to Enzo's mum Giuliana, and when she had bustled off into the kitchen, Ruth tiptoed gingerly forwards and peeped into the swaddling wraps. Her heart turned over at the sight of the infant. She watched as the baby's tiny mouth quivered in an involuntary sucking motion.

'Gorgeous, gorgeous little girl,' she breathed. She felt an overwhelming desire to kiss her, to smother her in all the love she would never give to a child of her own.

Ruth sat on the sofa beside Caroline, and the new mother passed the bundle to her. Tentatively, she took the baby. As Ruth held tiny Mia close, reverentially stroking her silky smooth cheek, she thought of Majlinda, a child who had brought pure joy amidst the horror of war, but whose own father's injuries meant he could not even hold her.

Enzo made coffee and, once she'd handed the baby back, Ruth went upstairs and fetched a bottle of Prosecco she had in the fridge. They drank caffeine to keep themselves awake and wine to wet the baby's head, and Ruth felt a huge sense of relief descend upon them all.

It seemed that no ill harm had been done by Mia's early arrival.

'I, for one, could not be more grateful,' moaned Caroline, stretching her legs out before her. 'Getting rid of this huge bump I've been dragging around in forty degrees will be a godsend. She didn't come a moment too soon.'

'Look, you need to get some rest,' said Ruth. She looked from Caroline to Enzo, both of whom were white-faced with exhaustion, though also glowing with happiness. 'I can take Daniel if you like – but I don't want to intrude.' She glanced towards Giuliana, still busy in the kitchen, appearing to be having a massive cupboard clear out. Ruth wondered whether this was really the time, but kept it to herself.

Enzo laughed. 'You won't be. Mama won't rest until everything is stacked and stored precisely to her liking and she's taken a full inventory of what we've got in stock. Then she'll be off to the shops to buy another truckload of stuff. So if you don't mind having Daniel while I grab a couple of hours...'

'Of course,' replied Ruth. 'No problem.'

'I've postponed all today's boat trippers to other dates,' Enzo added, as he stifled a huge yawn. 'I reckon I can have one day off, the day I become a father to a daughter.'

Ruth smiled. 'That sounds perfectly reasonable to me.' She pulled her phone out of her pocket and gestured towards it. 'Can I have a picture of you both and Mia?'

'Of course,' Caroline and Enzo responded in unison. Ruth took her snap, then held the phone out for the couple to see. Almost as soon as she drew back her arm, a message came through. It was from Zak and comprised a row of question marks.

'Guys, Zak's dying to hear the news,' Ruth said. 'Shall I send him this or would you rather it came from you?' She didn't want to intrude.

'Zak! He made me swear to call him,' replied Caroline. 'But I've got my hands full right now.' Mia was stirring, fussing for milk. 'It would be lovely if you could tell him, and explain that I'll be in touch as soon as I can.'

'No sooner said than done,' responded Ruth, tapping out a message to go with the picture as she spoke, while Caroline settled the baby to feed.

'And Ruth, before you go,' Caroline added, once Mia was contentedly suckling. 'Sit down again a minute.' She waited until Ruth was settled once more on the sofa beside her. 'I just wanted to thank you so much for all your help. Your being here has made such a difference to me at what is frankly a crazy time to have a baby, when everyone we know is working all hours to make a living just like we are. You've been a marvel.'

Ruth shook her head. 'No,' she said, softly, 'no, not at all. I've done hardly anything, and everything I have done has been a pleasure. I'm so happy to have been able to help in your hour of need.'

Caroline reached out and took Ruth's hand in hers, squeezing her fingers. 'Well, just be aware how much I – we both – appreciate it. And – well – we'd love it if you'd consider yourself an honorary auntie to the children! Neither of us has siblings so they won't have anyone else to call *zia*.'

Ruth's mouth widened into a bashful grin. 'I'd love that! Zia Ruth! It sounds perfect.'

Daniel came into view, back from the kitchen where his *nonna* had been plying him with unsuitable snacks.

'What do you think, Daniel?' Ruth asked, catching him as he flew past and pulling him into a brief hug before setting him loose again. 'Zia Ruth. Do you like it?'

Daniel, his mouth full of biscuit crumbs, nodded enthusiastically before disappearing again.

'Well, that's settled then,' said Caroline, lifting Mia up and putting her over her shoulder to wind.

Ruth got up. She had nieces and nephews, the children of her own brother and sister. But all of them, as well as her friends' children, were growing up now. There were no babies in her sphere of existence anymore. And she felt

184

very close to this little Anglo-Italian family, even though she hadn't known them long.

'Good,' she agreed. 'I'll be off now. You make sure you get some rest.'

She hadn't needed to worry on that front. By the time she had gathered together the numerous items necessary for a trip to the beach with a young child – buckets, spades, sun cream, water, tissues, snacks, wet wipes, spare clothes etc – Caroline was fast asleep on the sofa, the baby snuffling softly in her carrycot beside her. Ruth crept out of the apartment as quietly as she could, making elaborate 'shushing' gestures to Daniel as she did so. Caroline needed all the sleep she could get.

A strange mix of emotions fought for supremacy within Ruth as she and the little boy took their familiar trek to the harbour steps and on to the beach. She could not stop her mind from dwelling on the miracle that was Mia, that was every baby. The years when she might have had children had passed her by in a flurry of ambition and busyness and what had she got to show for it? Every now and again, at moments like this or when reading of Sarah's Majlinda, she was filled with a sadness so profound she had no words to express it.

It nestled within her, an ache that would never be filled.

Chapter Twenty-One

Albania, 1943

He doesn't shoot.

Disgusted, the commandant pistol whips me across the face, and then a blow for Rezar, too. He calls his men together and they march towards the trucks, in a formation rather less rigid than before they'd quaffed a few bottles of rakia between them. The prisoners have been watching intently. I've got a feeling they want to clap, but am relieved when they don't. Humiliating the commander would be a sure way to renew his ire.

The engines start with a roar and a crack, and they are off, heavy tyres audible on the rock hard mud road until they are far into the distance.

Rezar and I are stunned, suffering too greatly from shock to celebrate our victory. Finally, once all trace of the convoy has vanished, my legs give way and crumple beneath me. I stagger to the benches that are still warm from German bodies, and sit down, my head between my hands. Hannelore comes over, puts her arms around my shoulders, congratulates me. She doesn't know where David is, what has happened. She just believes in me.

Eventually, I stir myself. I know I must get up, must get the Jewish people out of their hiding place. Must go into the copse to find David, to see if he made it there, to the hollow tree that the acorn should have guided him to. I have to do these things so that we can continue our journey. My father sent me on a mission to take the guests to the mountains and keep them safe. I'll have failed if I lose a single one.

But it takes me another fifteen minutes to regain the ability to move, to overcome the paralysis that has taken over my body.

When I eventually manage to get up, I go to release the Jews from their subterranean dungeon. As I open the door, I'm hit by the stench of fetid air, of bodies sweating in fear confined in a small space. Thirteen pairs of eyes are fixed upon me, shining with dread in the darkness. They don't know who I am; the blast of light after the hours in obscurity temporarily blinds them. They assume it is the Nazis, come to drag them to their trucks and incarceration. They are immobile with anxiety and terror.

And then Hannelore races in behind me, calling German greetings and healing words, words that are salve for their trepidation. Once nerves have been calmed and everyone extracted, I instruct Chaim and Moses to lead the group whilst I go to fetch David. God willing, we'll join them further along our route but they must not wait for us. They must proceed on their way at once; there is no time to lose.

The motley group turns its back on the roadside cafe and takes the first few steps onwards towards the mountains. Hannelore hangs back. She steps tentatively towards me, then suddenly is upon me, hugging and kissing me, sobbing until my shoulders are wet through. As I hold her, awkwardly, amidst all the unimaginable fear and trepidation I'm aware of the feel of her body against mine, so good that I groan inwardly. Eventually, the sensations surging inside me are too powerful and I have to push her away, making my excuse that we must get going, that we must put distance between this place and ourselves.

The Nazis could come back at any time.

The refugees set off, exhausted from a period of such heightened emotion, trudging through summer-parched fields, heads low, shoulders hunched. I detour to the wood and make my way to the oak tree through the dark created by the canopy overhead. I hope to God that David was able to find the tree again and that he is waiting there. I don't know how I would ever speak to Hannelore again if he is lost.

The way seems much longer than I remember it. Scuttlings and scurryings in the undergrowth remind me that I am not alone; there are rabbits and pinemartens and foxes all around me, unseen. I start to doubt my own sense of direction. If I can't find the oak tree, how on earth could David be expected to, who only saw it for the first time that very day? In the gathering dusk, every tall, thick-stemmed tree looks the same.

When finally I make out the silhouette of the oak tree two dozen metres ahead, I feel lightheaded with relief. I can barely keep up with the levels of emotion today has dished out; I'm shattered.

So as not to startle David by a sudden arrival, I make noise by kicking at the leaf mould and deliberately stepping on twigs that snap viciously in the dense stillness. When I am about five metres from the tree, I call out, a heightened whisper that carries weightlessly on the breathless air.

'David! It's me, Bekim. I'm alone. Are you there?'

For a few agonising seconds I wait, with nothing but silence ringing in my ears and my blood pulsing through my veins.

Then, a hesitant, wavering voice replies, 'I'm here,' and David emerges from the hole in the tree trunk that's like a open mouth set on end. He stumbles as he makes his way towards me, his eyes unused to the light after so long in the dark, his legs weak from so long spent motionless.

'David,' I say, 'thank God you're safe. Thank God.'

We give each other a hug that's uncomfortable in a completely different way to the one I exchanged with Hannelore. In Albania, men hug all the time but I don't think Austrians do because David is always self-conscious about physical contact.

I indicate to him to follow me and we retrace our steps to the path and, after an hour of fast walking, we catch up with the others. When I see Altin leading them, I almost faint with relief. For a short period, it won't all be down to me. Then I banish these shameful thoughts. And anyway, all I've been through seems worth it when I see Mr and Mrs Frankl's joy in being reunited with their son, who they can hardly believe is there, alive and well and in front of them. Hannelore, too, cries fresh tears of rejoicing at the sight of her brother.

I leave them to enjoy each other's presence and walk with Altin. He divulges nothing about the covert mission he's been on but his eyes are dark and wild and I feel sure that he has seen death today.

His praise for me is taut and restrained.

'You did well,' he murmurs, his eyes already fixed on the distant peaks that we're headed to. 'You have proved yourself worthy. It won't be long…' he adds, leaving the sentence unfinished.

My heart leaps in hope and desire. Won't be long... until I, too, can join the partisans?

–

Eventually, after many days on roads, donkey tracks and mule trails, we arrive at our mountain village. My boots fell apart not long after the incident at the roadside cafe, and I have made the rest of the journey barefoot. My feet are hard and calloused, heels thickened to a point where they no longer bleed. But even through the desensitised skin, I can still feel the warm glow of home, of stepping on earth that is my father's and my father's father's and so on through the generations.

The houses are empty as we stumble down the dusty main street, which is really nothing more than a narrow lane hemmed in by low, wooden houses with overhanging roofs for the winter snow. The women are out in the woods gathering herbs, or tending to their beehives or livestock, the men working in the fields and the children up on the high pastures with the flocks seeking out the lush grazing when the lower grasslands are bare and desiccated.

I used to worry so much about how Hannelore would react to the primitive conditions in our village, outside squat toilets, cold water from a well, rats, mice and innumerable insects as housemates, but now I see everything differently.

Now I am old enough to know that, after everything they've been through, Hannelore and all her kinsmen are just glad to be alive.

Summer is already turning to autumn by the time we arrive in the village, the changing colours of the trees and the increasingly stormy skies heralding the winter that's soon to come. We find accommodation for the Jewish people in various houses, a room here and a room there, and they readily help us to gather firewood in preparation for the cold. David proves himself to be master of the axe and chops as much wood in an hour as I do, then stacks it against the house walls like someone who was born to this life rather than to the comforts of a city apartment in gilded Vienna. I wonder how much he remembers of that cosy, padded childhood, how much he thinks about it, but I don't ask. Though our knowledge of the war is limited to hearsay and rumour, we are all aware that horror has spread across Europe like infection in a herd of cattle. It seems pointless to talk about the past. A past that it's clear will never come back.

A few days after our arrival, Altin reappears from a temporary absence and calls me to the privacy of an empty cow barn.

'I'm going, and I won't be back until…' he falters and then resumes. 'For a long time. Therefore, from now on all decisions are yours. Remember your *besa*, your obligation to lay down your own life for our guests.'

He hands me a rifle and ammunition – lots of ammunition.

'I taught you well when you were nothing more than a snip of a boy,' he says. 'But now you need to go into the woods and make sure your aim is true. It will need to be.'

With that, he's gone, melting into the parched, expectant landscape like a glossy stone sinking into a deep pool.

Though the harvest we bring in is a good one, there are many mouths to feed and, as the weeks pass, there's never enough to satisfy stomachs to the full. Everyone rallies round, and somehow the women manage to produce two small meals a day, even if it's only soup and rough maize bread, or a stew of carrots, potatoes and a little mutton.

When winter truly sets in, early in December, we are short of blankets and warm clothes, and I take the small amount of money I have – what's left of what my father gave me when we left Shkodra – to the nearest town on market day, hoping to find some bargains or barter good prices for what we need.

I arrive just as a crowd is gathering in the main square. Curiosity draws me to join in. At first, I can't make out what's going on. There are soldiers, shouting, tramping jackboots and muffled cries. I jostle to the front, pushing my way in between men, women and children. I get there just as the show starts. On a temporary scaffold, a man's body dangles, a black silhouette against a sky shrouded in grey. A shot rings out and, before I can stop myself, I've snapped my eyes in that direction. A corpse lies in a crumpled heap. Two blindfolded men, hands tied behind their backs, stand frozen in terror beside it. Another shot. Another body collapsing to the ground.

My belly clutches and clenches as the vomit spews forth from my mouth, barely missing my feet, and my eyes bulge in their sockets with the force of the nausea.

'Wh-what's going on,' I utter, to no one in particular, to myself, in astounded horror.

'Partisans,' grunts a man next to me, hardly opening his mouth as if unwilling to be spotted speaking. 'Government opponents, those the Nazis deem dangerous.'

With that, my reluctant interlocutor moves off, swallowed up by the throng. Dazed and shocked to my core, I resolve not to say a word about what I've witnessed to our guests. What good could come of them imagining the same fate for themselves? At the moment, the worst anyone fears – and this is bad enough – is being sent to a prison labour camp.

Somehow I manage to overcome my distress enough to buy some blankets, and some rough cloth and nails with which to cover the paneless windows of the village houses, to try to keep out the worst of the winter gales. But I return to the village with a heart heavier than it has ever been. There seems to be no hope, no possibility that all this is going to end, let alone end well.

Where are the Allies? The Russians?

More and more, I think of Altin and the partisans and I ache to join them – even now I know, have seen with my own eyes, what happens to those caught. But this plan is by necessity on hold, because my first duty is to do as Altin and my father have instructed me – to keep the Jewish people safe.

Partly in view of what I plan for the future, and partly because of the current and present danger, I practise assiduously with the rifle. I take David with me and show him how to hold the gun, how to go with the recoil, how to track a target and take aim.

'If anything happens to me,' I tell him, 'you must take over.'

He nods, and folds his arms across his chest.

'Your lives might depend upon it,' I insist, not sure that he's fully understood.

'I will do it, Bekim,' he replies. 'You can rely on me.'

Still only twelve years old, his eyes carry a weight of experience way beyond his years. Perhaps that is a trait that's common to all of us in these desperate times.

One day, when I'm out in the woods with the rifle, I get the opportunity to put the accuracy of my aim to the test. I spot a wild boar. He's huge and aged, with a hoary bearded chin and enormous yellow teeth. There's a scar down his right hand side that indicates a fight with a rival, or an escape from a previous encounter with a hunter, but he doesn't seem to have learnt anything from it. He's lumbering around without a clue that I'm there, silly old fool; he'll feed the entire village for a month. We really need this meat.

I raise the rifle, take aim and fire.

Killing a living thing shouldn't be that easy, I think, as the old pig drops to the ground without a shudder. I remember the Nazi slaughtering the chicken, the visceral fear that I would be next. The ease of butchery, of annihilation, when you have a gun; once you've done it once, you don't even think twice about doing it again.

That night, as the setting sun paints the sky in hues of purple, mauve and lilac, the whole village gets together. We've butchered the boar and hung the meat to dry, but we've kept a whole hindquarter for roasting over the fire we construct in what passes for the village square, which is really just the end of the street where the houses give way to the steeply rising slopes of the nearest mountain. There's freshly baked corn bread, and honey and apple pastries that the women have made with the last fruit from someone's orchard.

Rakia that's been carefully hoarded from last year's distillation is produced and the party soon gets going. After a glass or two, Chaim and Moses lead the entire village in a chaotic, rumbustious dance that leaves everyone in heaps on the floor, laughing uncontrollably.

As the new moon rises above us, and stars stud the darkened sky like all the lights of the city turned on at once, I find myself standing next to Hannelore. We don't spend time together anymore like we used to; I'm so busy attending to the things that need to be done, men's business, and she has to work with the women, in the fields and the home, doing the washing in the river, cooking and cleaning. I had forgotten how much more segregation between men and women there is in the countryside than in the city. Or perhaps I had not had cause to notice before now, or had not been old enough to understand.

But the truth is that it's not just happenstance; I'm consciously keeping my distance from Hannelore. Because every time I set eyes on her, a strange thrill channels through me and an ache begins, that starts in my belly and spreads to my groin and up into my throat, touching my soul along the way. I want to touch her, that beautiful chestnut hair, want to kiss those rosebud lips, to run my hands over her lovely form. I don't know how to control the urges I have; I just know that I must.

But now she's here beside me and she reaches out her hand and takes mine and squeezes it. She leans into me, resting her shoulder against mine. I look up at the night sky and think that I might be there amongst the stars, in heaven, an angel by my side. I clench her hand back, but mine are too rough, my grip too tight. I've become coarse with the manual work and the ways of men here, which are not Hannelore's ways.

She doesn't seem to notice.

'It's so beautiful tonight,' she sighs.

Beneath a crescent moon the mountains are dark and silent giants, guarding us, protecting us. A fleeting picture of the horrors occurring in the town, of the fate of captured partisans, passes behind my eyes. I dismiss it. But not before I've shivered at the memory, at the thought of Altin, of where he is and what he is doing.

Hannelore has cloaked herself in a blanket – one of the ones I brought back from town – and as she feels me shudder she wraps it also around me, so that her arm is around my waist and the edge of the blanket across my shoulders. Trying to move as little as possible so as not to risk breaking this spell, I put my arm around her, too. I pull her close, her slim body yielding beneath my strong forearm. I smell the woodsmoke in her hair and see how her long eyelashes flutter in the moonlight.

She raises her face towards mine. 'Bekim,' she says, in her faultless Albanian that sounds as if she's lived in our village for all eternity, not learnt it in the last few years. 'When we were children,' she continues, 'I didn't always know, or appreciate, what you were doing for us, not really. In the past, I might have used the word "brave" with no real understanding of what it meant. But now I know that it means you.'

She lifts her face a little higher still, and her lips are there, right before me, red and slightly parted and I cannot stop myself lowering my own and kissing her. The kiss goes on and on and if I wasn't in heaven before, I am now.

A voice calling my name, loud and insistent, followed by footsteps getting nearer and nearer make me jump away, disentangling myself from Hannelore's arms and the blanket.

'Bekim!' the sound comes again, along with, further away, a raised chorus of Chaim and Moses' singing. It's David, materialised in front of us, smiling and laughing. And then his expression changes and for one brief moment, a cloud of puzzlement crosses his face, and he opens his mouth as if to ask what's going on, what we're doing. But then the song resumes ever louder and David plunges forward and grabs both of our wrists, and he's dragging us back towards the fray, crying, 'What are you doing? Why aren't you dancing?'

As we approach the edge of the crowd he lets go of us and joins the song's refrain. It gives me my chance. I take Hannelore's hands. The rakia and the urgency of the situation make me bold. I need to tell her what I've thought and known and felt from the first day I met her but couldn't say because we were only children. Now we are adults – almost – and any day I might be off to join the partisans, as soon as Altin sends for me. I need to say it now.

'Hannelore, I lo—'

'Bekim!'

'Bekim the brave!'

Chaim and Moses are there, right beside us, laughing and joking and joshing, and almost falling over from the amount of rakia they've drunk. I drop Hannelore's hands as if they're burning. The lads are oblivious to the fact that they've interrupted something. They seize hold of Hannelore and pull her with them, tripping over their own legs and hers as they stumble back to the dance.

I stand and look after them, bearing away the girl I love. I should be cross, annoyed at them for spoiling the moment, for barging in. But instead I feel suddenly hopeless, deflated like the pierced bladder of a slaughtered goat.

It cannot be.

She and I are neither married nor promised to each other. And in the absence of my parents and with the compromised circumstances of hers, how could we be? Not now, not for a while. I'll have to be patient.

The next day, the first snow of winter falls, covering the landscape, capping the high limestone crags with a mantle of white, obscuring familiar landmarks under a thick opal blanket.

And so our world remains under harsh wraps for five long months.

Chapter Twenty-Two

Albania, 1944

*All non-Albanian citizens must report to Gestapo
Headquarters immediately.*
    *Penalty for non-compliance: imprisonment and
hard labour.*

Altin shoves the paper towards me, and I read the terrifying words.

'It's a lie,' he says.

His eyes are blacker and more piercing than usual, but
they are ringed with shadows. He seems inexpressibly
tired.

The partisans are fighting on more fronts than ever,
increasing the pressure on the enemy but also of course
on themselves. Long nights on the move or in combat,
sleepless days hiding out in perilous places waiting to go
through it all again, are taking their toll. The arm that he
broke three years ago is permanently bandaged now; he
says it helps with the ever-present pain, pain that he no
longer denies.

'What?' I ask, puzzled. 'It's a lie that they have to
register?'

'Tush!' Altin dismisses my question with an angry
hiss. 'No, that the punishment will be imprisonment and

hard labour. Anyone knows that what they really mean is death.'

My head reels. More danger, more jeopardy for our guests. I don't know how to tell them, what words I can use that will make it sound anything less than it is, i.e. another threat to their survival.

'What shall we do?' Even to my ears, my plea sounds weak and pathetic. But my mind has gone dead and I can't think of anything.

Altin flexes his arm backwards and forwards, clenching his teeth and letting his breath whistle out between them. He's had a few days off, been back to Shkodra to see Sarah, Majlinda and the new baby. He's told me that my parents and brothers are well, and that the baby boy, called Luan, is the spitting image of himself and walking already. That is how much time has passed since we left; we have seen out an entire autumn and winter here and are beginning to see the first signs of spring in the village's sheltered valley.

'I don't know.'

My mouth falls open in a wide O of disbelief. Shock ricochets through me. Altin has never been short of an answer, a plan, a scheme before. I gaze at him, at the deep weariness in his eyes, the exhaustion that's etched into the creases on his forehead.

I'm about to protest, to tell him that he must have some idea, but it's too late. Altin has turned away and is striding back to the house.

'I need to sleep,' he calls back, over his shoulder. 'You work it out.'

And he's right, I realise with a jolt of understanding. I'm fifteen now; if I want to prove I'm worthy of being a partisan, the least I should be able to do is look after our guests. If I don't, if I fail, I will have compromised the honour of the Albanian people and any one of my neighbours or acquaintances could launch a blood feud against me to avenge the disgrace. If that happened, my life wouldn't be worth living anyway.

I ponder the problem almost non-stop for the next few days. There are several options. One is to do as instructed and register the names of all the foreigners we have with us. Maybe that's safer than defying an order and taking the inevitable punishment if found out. But how do we know that the registration process isn't a trap, designed to make the Jewish people easy pickings whenever the army or the militia fancy rounding them up? Alternatively, we could just stay put and do nothing, relying on the village's remoteness and isolation, the distance from the nearest town of any size. But that seems dangerous, too.

Or there is one other possibility. We could retreat even further into the hills, to a cave complex high in the mountain where there is no chance of being discovered from one year's end to the next. The living there would be harsh in the extreme; we'd have to take everything with us, from clothes and firewood to pots and pans, carrying it all on our backs. Once there, all semblances of civilisation will disappear on the wind – no toilets at all, primitive or otherwise, water collected from the river or by melting snow, no cooking facilities bar an open fire made in the shelter of rocks where escaping smoke could not give us away.

But whatever hardship, we would be safe.

Whilst I'm contemplating the possibilities, mulling them over and churning them around, teasing apart the pros and cons in minute detail, something happens to make up my mind.

It's late afternoon and I'm mending a broken latch on the door of the house that the Albrechts are lodging in. Since the change in the season from winter to early spring, we've all been busy from dawn to dusk, and the village is quiet at this hour, even the youngest children having gone with the shepherds and goatherds out to the pastures.

Amidst the silence, I hear the sound of footsteps pounding along the track and look up to see one of the small village boys haring along as if being chased by the devil.

'What's the matter?' I ask, amused. He's my second cousin Arben, a scrawny little thing with a cheeky smile who reminds me a bit of myself at that age, full of brash bravado.

It's a moment before he's regained his breath enough to reply. 'Germans,' he finally manages to articulate. 'Coming, now.' He points agitatedly down the valley, towards the town and Tirana and the sea and the rest of the world that always seems so very, very far away from here.

But not far enough now. Not if the Nazis are on their way.

My mind springs into action. There's no one to go to for advice; Altin has melted into the hills once more and, as he made clear, I'm in charge.

'How far,' I ask Arben urgently, 'and how long?'

He shrugs and puts his hands on his hips, narrowing his eyes as if calculating time and distance. 'Thirty minutes,' he says, 'maybe less.'

Vehicles have to stick to the main track; Arben will have come cross-country. But if he is correct, it means that they are already at the crossroads in the valley below.

'How many?' I question. I need to know what we're up against, but I don't know to what end; it's one rifle and me against all of them, whatever way you look at it.

'Two trucks,' he replies, 'five or six men in each.'

That's what I call an uneven fight.

'OK,' I hiss, my mind made up. 'I've got a plan.'

There's nobody on the street when the German vehicles eventually roll into town. My heart trips over itself; it's too reminiscent of the roadside cafe incident. But I stand firm and strong, trying to give nothing away. The vehicles, adorned with those sinister swastikas all decent people abhor, rattle to a halt.

A soldier jumps out.

'We are making checks on unregistered foreigners,' he shouts, even though I'm only inches away from him.

'We don't have any here.' My answer is instant. Unequivocal.

'So we will check. I'm sure you don't mind.'

Minding clearly doesn't come into it. They will do as they wish.

I incline my head in tacit and disinterested consent. I walk up the street and stand outside the tallest building in the settlement, the one with the smallest door and narrowest windows, that has creaky wooden ladders leading up to the room on the second floor from where it is traditional to sit and wait and watch for the enemy.

The blood feud tower.

Tradition dictates that any violation of the Kanun, from murder to rape, from theft to failure to protect a guest, must be avenged by the community or the family involved. To avoid this, over the centuries men have fled to the sanctuary of the towers where they lock themselves in and sit tight until the matter is settled. Which could take years. During that time, they'd be brought food and water by women and children, who by the Kanun's moral code, could not be killed.

Now, the tower is being put to a different use, and the enemy being watched for is that of an occupying power. Inside, in that top storey room, are the Jewish people, each and every one of them, male and female, disguised as a Muslim woman, complete with headscarf.

I steel myself for the wait.

Eventually, having worked their way through every dwelling, however small and humble, the first small group of three soldiers is in front of me. They try to push past me, to elbow me out of the way. I stand firm.

'You can't go in there.'

'We have orders to enter every building in this village.'

'That may be,' I state, simply. 'But our women are in there. It is forbidden for a man who is not married or related to them to enter. If you go in, you defile innocent females and you debase our religion.'

Do the Germans even know that, up here in the mountains, not everyone is a Muslim? We have a Christian church in our village, its iron cross symbolising the word of Jesus. Please God – any God, I'm not fussy – let the Germans not know this.

I'm not just lying, I'm defying the orders of a German soldier – I could die for this. Inwardly I shrug, though my blood is cold in my veins and my hands are shaking. I've faced death before, when the officer had a gun to my temple, but unlike killing, which they say gets easier, contemplating your own end, I now know, does not.

The soldier who's been so insistent falters. At that moment, another set of three arrives beside us. There is a hurried conversation between them, accompanied by many glances up at the tiny window and over to me. I try not to give away how much of what they are saying I understand. I need to be a simple Albanian peasant boy, defending the women's honour.

After breathless minutes that seem like hours, the Germans click their heels and turn away. I watch, astounded, as they walk back down the street towards their trucks. I can't believe it. Surely it shouldn't be that simple? My heart seems to stop beating until the German engines fire into life and the trucks clatter away.

I enter the blood feud tower. Before going upstairs to release my captives, I drink a large swig of rakia. I think I deserve it. I know I need it.

This incident is all I need to make my decision about what we should do. It's clear that the village is no longer safe, and neither is non-registration a viable option. I tell the Jews that we are leaving, that they must take only what they can carry and that they should plan to be in hiding for some time. Though the news that simmers in the air is of Allied advances, who can tell? We can hope for the best, but must prepare for the worst.

It's the end of April and the nights in the high peaks are still cold. But I've decided that one of us must guard the cave entrance at all times. There's me, David, Chaim and Moses who are young and fit enough to do it. I'll take the nights and they can do the days. I give the two lads cursory lessons in using the rifle; they won't be anything like as skilled as me or even David, but it's the best I can do.

There is still snow on the ground up on the heights, and though one of the village women donated to me an old pair of boots that had belonged to her long-dead husband, they are so full of holes they are almost useless. This is a situation I've been in many times before in my life and I know what to do. I wrap my feet in cloth and then some thick hessian from an empty feed sack that I find in the animal shed. This must date from some forgotten boom time in the village for no one can usually afford to buy fodder for beasts. No matter; once I've managed to shove my feet back inside the boots the fabrics create a semblance of warmth and dryness.

The men walk ahead, the women behind, as it should be in rural Albania. Though the chances of encountering anyone are minimal, we must make sure that we call no attention to ourselves. For this reason the women also wear Muslim headscarves.

Hannelore looks, if anything, even more beautiful with a scarf. It draws attention to her deep brown eyes and perfect rosebud mouth, and to her flawless pale skin not yet weathered by age, sun and poverty like the local women. I hate to walk ahead of her when we have spent so many years, most of our childhood, walking side by side. But we have to do what is necessary.

Once we arrive at the cave complex, we settle in as best we can, assigning women's and men's sleeping areas, drawing up a rota for collecting water and firewood.

We have only been there a few days when weather takes a turn for the worse. This can happen at this altitude even this far into the new year. Rain follows the snowfall and quickly freezes, creating a hard layer that crackles and turns to ice underfoot. These are not conditions to be out in the elements but we are short of food. I must go hunting and hope to find a deer, or a rabbit foolish or hungry enough to break cover and forage in the open.

Hannelore, fed up and frustrated by being cooped up in such close quarters with the whole group, insists on accompanying me. We set out, my gun over my shoulder. Though a watery sun is shining, a brutal wind scythes down from the peaks and I see Hannelore shiver. None of us has quite enough warm clothing for the harsh conditions up here. At least we have come towards the end of the bad weather, rather than at the beginning.

We walk a long way before I spy two deer in the lee of a karst outcrop. Tension makes my arms stiff and my fingers, raw with cold, fumble at the trigger. Keyed up by the thought of how much we need this food, I shoot, and miss. The deer flee, leaping and bounding into the distance, disappearing from sight in seconds.

'Never mind,' consoles Hannelore. 'We'll get another one.'

'We better hope so,' I snap back. Irritation at my ineptness makes me short-tempered. I am responsible for everyone; feeding them is my most basic duty, and I am failing. My heart sinks at the thought of the months that lie ahead – how many we do not know – and whether I can fulfil the mission that Altin has given me.

We trudge on, but see neither sight nor sound of life. The stillness hangs around the mountains like a funeral pall. Disconsolate, I eventually admit defeat.

'Let's go back,' I say to Hannelore. It will be bone broth and potatoes for dinner again.

She looks at me, anxiety creasing her forehead.

'We'll try again tomorrow,' she replies, encouragingly.

'Maybe,' I pull my jacket tighter around me. The gun is heavy on my shoulder, the ache it sends through my muscles a constant reminder of my failure.

And then, when we are not more than fifteen minutes from the caves, I spot them. Not just one, but a pair of rabbits. They look lovely and plump and though I know that most of that is their winter coat, still it makes them worth the ammunition. Hannelore has seen them too, and I gesture to her to stay still. I take aim and fire and the largest rabbit falls, a red stain of blood spreading out over the pure white snow. The second rabbit runs, but it has strayed too far from the coppice where undergrowth would provide a hiding place. It darts in one direction and then another, panic-stricken, before pausing, frozen in fear. My aim is true and I get that one, too, with a shot straight to the head.

Hannelore races to collect the bounty; she carries one and I take the other. The sun is setting and the moon is already high in the sky as we turn once more towards the caves we now call home. A translucent, ghostly light bathes the mountain peaks and the valleys between as, one by one, the stars come out to guide us. Our pace has picked up now that we have been successful and it takes us only a few minutes to reach the small lake that lies not far from the cave entrance. It is still frozen solid, a black mirror to the sky.

'Bekim!' cries Hannelore, 'Come on! Let's skate.'

She lays down the rabbit she is carrying, steps onto the ice and begins to dance, a rhythmic, elegant waltz which she accompanies with a tuneful humming. Pretending she is on skates, she circles round and round, arms held out as if embracing an unseen suitor. She turns to me, and begins to laugh. 'I'm crazy, aren't I? But this is how the adults used to skate in Vienna, whilst we children ate toffee and slid around beside them.'

'You're not crazy,' I reply, shaking my head. Putting down my gun and the other rabbit, I step onto the ice to join her. 'Or maybe just a bit… but I like it.'

Hannelore throws back her head as she laughs again. Her milk-white skin is luminescent in the starlight and she glows as if lit from inside. I inch towards her, unsure of myself on the slippery surface; I've never experienced walking on ice before. Water rarely freezes on the Albanian coast.

'Be brave, Bekim,' she calls. She's further out towards the middle of the lake now. 'Bekim the brave! Isn't that your name?'

I blush despite the cold. Bravery is expected of me these days, but I would never boast about it. Not like I would have done when I was younger. Hannelore's not waiting for an answer, though. She whirls and twirls upon the lake's opalescent surface, laughing and spinning like a perfectly controlled top. I have just drawn level with her when I hear an ominous creaking sound, breaking through Hannelore's silvery laughter. The ice beneath my feet rises and falls like the earth tremors all Albanians are familiar with and I have the sudden sensation of the ground giving way.

The ice is breaking.

I scream, involuntarily, as one of my feet descends into the freezing water. My whole body is falling, my arms wheeling in a desperate attempt to balance, my heart pounding in my ears.

Barely have I hit the floor when Hannelore is beside me. She grabs one of my flailing arms and pulls with all her strength. The force sends me flying but it does the trick. Flat out on my stomach, my weight is distributed more evenly and the ice is thick enough to hold. I commando crawl to the lake's edge, only daring to stand fully upright once I've hauled myself onto the bank. Hannelore, lighter and smaller, slides along behind me.

I sit on the gentle rise that slopes up from the water's edge, my head in my hands. That was close. So close.

Hannelore kneels beside me. 'Bekim, are you all right?' Her voice is a whisper full of concern. It is a moment or two before I can respond. Eventually, I manage to nod my head.

'You were never going to die, Bekim,' Hannelore assures me. 'I wouldn't have let that happen. If you had gone in the water, I would have got you out.'

I look up and our eyes meet. I smile and nod once more. We get up; my backside is frozen and I can tell already that I'm going to have the most magnificent bruise. Chastened, we gather up the gun and the rabbits and set off for the cave in silence. I don't say as much to Hannelore, but I'm sure she knows. It was never my own death that I was worried about. It was the thought of what would happen to them all, the Frankls and the Albrechts, Chaim and Moses and the others, if I were no longer there to take care of them.

Hannelore and I never talk about the incident on the ice, and we don't go near the lake for the next few weeks. I go on more hunts to fulfil our constant need for food and Hannelore spends a lot of time with the three small children, entertaining them with games and stories. However much we attempt to find distracting pastimes, to laugh rather than to cry, there's no getting away from the fact that we're marking time. And marked time, as we all know, does not go at normal speed but creeps from minute to minute, day to day.

The night watch is time's slowest passing. Those long hours lying in the snow outside the cave with my rifle, alone under the stars, will stay in my memory forever. The wolves howl and the dogs that came with us from the village respond with anguished yowls and the wind plays games with my hearing, so that every crack becomes a jackboot on frozen ground and every susurration is the approach of whispering soldiers. The confidence I filled myself with when the Germans came to the blood feud tower deserts me.

Through the cold and fear of those lonely nights I look into my own soul and see how hard it is to be a human being.

If the Germans come, you stay and fight. If the Jews die, you die with them. Whilst you have breath in your body, you do not use it to run away.

My father's words revolve around my mind, and I bury my face in my sleeve and will that I can see it through.

Chapter Twenty-Three

Albania, 1944

Here in the mountains, spring is very short, often giving way to full-blown summer in one ostentatious, explosive burst. One day, there is snow on the ground, a nip in the breeze and tightly curled buds on the trees; the next, the snow has melted, the leaves unfurled, the blossom bloomed, and the wind is warm and dry. Multi-coloured wildflowers carpet the fields and meadows, bringing joy to souls that have been starved of light and hope for so long.

Against all the odds, we have survived the hard months; me, Hannelore, David and all the guests. It seems both incredible and mundane at the same time. I put my mixed feelings down to the exhaustion, the toll of hard living over long months.

Having spent weeks trapped in the cave due to snow, then rain, we are all desperate for fresh air and sunshine, and anything that might break up the monotony of the days and the diet, which for much of our sojourn has been limited to potatoes and corn bread, supplemented by any game I manage to kill.

People come up from the village now the paths are easily passable, bringing donkeys loaded with goods – wheat bread, spring greens and carrots, as well as apples that have been stored in cold barns over the winter. We haven't seen fruit for so long we fall upon it with undisguised relish. They also bring the flocks of sheep that will spend the next few months here, getting fat on the fresh, rich grass and herbs that flourish in the ever-strengthening sunshine. The villagers delight us with their fresh faces and conversations after so long in isolation, and they give us a few items of clean clothing and soap. I couldn't in all honesty say that I've ever spared soap so much as a second thought before – probably not even a first one – but even I am pleased at the thought of having a proper wash.

What the villagers do not bring, however, is the news we crave – that the war is over.

Nevertheless, we risk letting the Jewish children run with the village kids, the goats and sheep up in the high pastures; dressed in traditional clothing and having spent so long away from civilisation, there's little difference between them and the locals now.

The longer days give us all more energy and I don't spend so many hours sleeping off my night watch. Hannelore and I spend hours talking, discussing everything from philosophy to fairy tales. She learns all that she can from the adults in the group; it turns out that one of those who joined us as we left the city used to be a professor of theoretical physics at the University of Salzburg, and Hannelore greedily picks his brains for greater knowledge on this subject. I've never been much of a scholar but I hang around with them just to be with Hannelore. Though I long to hold her hand, to feel her hair, to kiss her lips like that one, beautiful time, it is never possible. We are never alone. Despite this, it's Hannelore's presence and Hannelore's spirit more than anything else that gives me the strength to carry on.

A couple of days after my birthday, momentous news reaches us, the news we have all been waiting for: on the sixth of June, the very day that I turned sixteen, the Allied forces landed in Normandy. But alongside the elation with which we greet this information is the continuing fear. The Germans in Albania are taking no notice of the increasing possibility that they may lose the war and, if anything, are becoming more brutal than ever. Captured partisans are shown no mercy, suspected communists likewise. Public executions and hangings, like the one I witnessed all those months ago, are ever more commonplace.

The word is that all those Jews who did obey the earlier order to register with the Nazis will be deported at any moment. Where they will be sent is not made clear. We have heard of the prison camps; they've been known about and feared since the war began. But now we are starting to hear of worse places, places where death comes in inexorable sweeps and where whole families are wiped out, men, women and children eradicated from the face of the earth. It's impossible to know what is truth and what is fiction, to tell fact from rumour.

All we know is that throughout Europe fear hangs heavy in the air.

On the rare occasions that we hear from Altin, he speaks of the Germans' last-ditch attempts at survival. The Russians are advancing on the countries of the Balkans, one by one, liberating first Rumania, then Bulgaria, then Yugoslavia. But the Nazis keep their desperate grip on Albania; apart from anything else, they need an escape route for their retreating troops. The fighting with the partisans is ongoing, constant spats and tit-for-tat engagements, a war of attrition that seems never-ending. The countrywide curfew is extended from early afternoon until dawn, the streets of towns and cities ring with gunfire, and grenades destroy roads, buildings and bridges.

We hear reports that there are many Jewish families still in Tirana and Vlore, living a nightmare, in constant terror of being discovered. There are units of Albanian soldiers who collaborate with the Germans, even forming a local platoon of the Waffen SS, so betrayal is possible. But they are the enemy and all true Albanians remain tight-lipped about our guests. Everyone knows who they are and who is sheltering them; no one tells. If anyone so much as tried to give the Jews away, they know that the penalty would be their neighbours tearing them limb from limb. All the same, it would only take one false move for the façades to fall and their true identities to be revealed.

Equally at risk are any households known to harbour or to be a base for a partisan. The Germans blow up such dwellings without ceremony. They do not take the time to evacuate the innocent, the uninvolved, first.

However, as the days pass, it becomes clear that we can finally return to the village; no soldiers have been seen in the vicinity for many months. It seems that the Nazis have more pressing problems to deal with in the bigger towns and cities, that preclude them from venturing this far off the beaten track. And so our disparate group of weary refugees troops back down the steep and treacherous path once more.

Hannelore, now aged fifteen, shepherds the younger ones, helping them over the rocky parts and carrying them across the many streams and rivulets that dissect the track. Everyone's clothes are worn thin with wear, patched and darned, ill-fitting and barely serviceable. The adults are skinnier and the children taller than when we left.

Hannelore and David, like all the others, long outgrew the shoes they came here with, so they, like me, are barefoot now. The much-mended boots I inherited from the old man's wife finally disintegrated weeks ago. I resolve to find some footwear for us all when I next go to town to sell fruit or milk or cheese.

'Where is Durrësi?' asks Hannelore, pausing for breath after a particularly steep descent. 'What direction?'

She has never learnt to orientate herself in the mountains and has no idea which way is north or south. I find her total lack of sense of direction both endearing and comical. I point into the distance, to where a hazy purple line denotes the horizon far across the green hills and valleys.

'That way,' I answer. 'Why do you want to know?'

Hannelore shrugs. 'My mother and father still talk of getting there, of how we could try again to take a boat to Italy and then the US. Maybe not right now, but soon, once the Allies have advanced further.'

She makes as if to start walking again but I am blocking her way and I cannot move. A sudden rush of nausea paralyses me and I reach out for the rocky side of the bank beside us, steadying myself and taking deep breaths to quell the dizziness.

'Are you all right?' Hannelore puts her hand upon mine. 'Do you feel unwell?' Her voice is full of concern. 'Here, have some water.' She thrusts a clay bottle towards me and I drink a long slug of the soft spring water it contains.

'Fine,' I say, brushing off the incident, furious that I've shown vulnerability. We walk on in silence for a while, me in front, Hannelore behind.

When we next pause to rest and wait for the older women to catch up, she speaks again.

'What's the matter, Bekim?'

For one split second, I consider lying. What good will the truth do? But then I can't hide it anymore, am sick and fed up with deception and concealment.

'You must know that I don't want you to leave.'

The words are out and I can't take them back. They hang between us like unexploded grenades.

She runs the back of her hand across her forehead and then through the stands of her hair that have escaped from the headscarf.

'I know,' she says finally, and I can taste and smell the longing in her voice as clearly as I can hear it. 'And I don't want to leave, either. Not really.' There's a long pause and then it comes. 'But…'

She leaves the sentence unfinished, floating upon the unconquerable ocean of reality and inevitability. Of course the Frankls will want to leave Albania, to go somewhere modern and advanced and cultivated – somewhere like them. But if I could just prove to Hannelore that I'm worthy, show her that I could give her the life that she deserves… perhaps then there'd be a chance.

Chapter Twenty-Four

Italy, 2019

When the phone rang, Ruth was lost in the world of the 1940s, in the love between Bekim and Hannelore that had blossomed throughout their long years together, during Hannelore's exile from her homeland and Bekim's enforced role as protector-in-chief. The discordant jangling of the ringtone cut through the still heaviness of the afternoon silence. Ruth grabbed it up. It was Zak. She hesitated for a moment before answering.

'Hi there,' she said. 'How are you?'

Just keep it neutral, she told herself. But nevertheless, her heart lurched in her chest and beat a little faster at the sound of his voice.

'Well,' Zak replied, 'I'm fine. And dad is holding up, but it's one appointment after another and he gets confused or doesn't understand what the doctors are telling him, so I'm going to have to hang on here for a little while longer.'

Ruth's stomach contracted. 'Oh, I'm sorry to hear that,' she commiserated. 'Sounds like it's a good thing you're there.' *Is your father the only reason?*, a treacherous voice whispered in her ear. *Shut up*, Ruth rudely told it, at the same time as trying to listen to what Zak was saying.

'Thank you so much for the news about Mia and the picture. Caroline and Enzo look so happy.'

'Oh yes,' agreed Ruth. 'The baby's utterly gorgeous. I don't think they're getting much sleep, though.' She'd heard Mia wailing a few times in the night, filtering up through the open windows.

'Well, that's babies for you, I guess,' responded Zak. 'Anyway, it was lucky that you were there to help out. They'd have had to take Daniel with them to the hospital otherwise.'

'I suppose they would.' Ruth recalled Enzo's panic and the anxious wait before the couple's triumphal return with their precious new arrival. 'All's well that ends well though. Now I'm looking forward to going shopping – a chance to buy all those delectable baby girl clothes and toys the stores are full of.'

A silence fell. Ruth's heart flipped over as she imagined what Zak might be thinking. How much he might have liked to purchase special items for his own child. 'But tell me more about your father,' she interjected, trying to quell her doubts. 'What is the prognosis?'

Though she had never met him, she felt she knew Bekim. The book had brought him to life and Ruth could picture him in her imagination, cheeky smile and all. Albeit the actual man was now nearly eighty years older than the one she was reading about.

'It's not great, in all honesty,' sighed Zak. 'The lung cancer is advanced. Stage four. It would be too dangerous to operate, even if dad were younger and less frail. We knew it was bad, but perhaps not quite this bad. The main thing now is to keep his spirits up and make sure he's comfortable.'

Another silence fell, this one bordering on the awkward.

'Zak…'

'Ruth…'

They both spoke at once.

'I was just going to say that I'm so sorry to hear that. But you go ahead,' Ruth said, hastily. 'Carry on.'

'Thank you.' There was another long pause. 'Ruth, there's something I need to talk to you about,' said Zak, suddenly serious. 'Something important.'

Ruth's mind spun out in a whir of possibilities. He was going to tell her about another woman, clarify that he was in a relationship, that things had changed during his stay in Albania. But then she snapped herself back to reality. He would say no such thing because he had no need to. The last person he was obliged to explain himself to was Ruth. And he didn't need to point out that he couldn't have a relationship with her because such a thing had never even been on the cards or remotely likely.

'My dad. Bekim.' Zak was talking and Ruth, absorbed in her own thoughts, had hardly been listening. 'He knows he hasn't got long left. He's suddenly started to talk voluntarily about the past, which he's never done before. All of the material in the book – well, it was blood out of a stone really. But now he's remembered something, some artefacts that were hidden long ago and that he needs to find. He's hazy about the details, what exactly these things are and, more importantly, where they are, but he seems to feel guilty about them, as if there's something he should have done that he hasn't. I'm trying to get more out of him but it's not easy.'

'OK,' responded Ruth, slowly. 'That does sound mysterious.' It did, but she had no idea what it had to do with her.

'And,' Zak continued, hesitant now, 'there's another thing he wants. Hannelore. After all these years, he's suddenly desperate to find Hannelore.'

Ruth looked out at the garden, at the trees hung with glossy fruit, and the heat haze in the distance. 'Right. I see.' She felt a strange disappointment in finding out what she had suspected, but wished not to be true. That Bekim and Hannelore didn't live happily ever after. Of course they hadn't. How could two people from such diverse backgrounds have stayed together? Ruth's stomach curdled at the realisation that their love had been torn asunder, even as she forced out of her mind the thought that she and Zak were in a similar position. Brits and Albanians were poles apart in so many ways – culture, religion, background. It was crazy to think she and Zak had a future.

'So – she's still alive?' It suddenly felt like a matter of urgency to know. 'Hannelore?'

'We don't know,' Zak answered, then paused, coughed, cleared his throat. 'But I hope so. My dad hopes so. And I was wondering… Look, it's a big ask. But you said that you had time on your hands. And that research is your thing.'

Oh yes, she'd told him about the driveway and hearing aid scams.

'So I thought maybe you could help. I just don't have time at the moment, what with dad's appointments at the hospital and supporting my mother etc. etc. Would you… would you be able to do some searching online, delve into some archives, I don't know? See if you can find her. I'll email you all the details I have for her once I'm back home later today.'

Ruth smiled. Regardless of her uncertain situation with Zak, she would not hesitate to do whatever she could to help his father, an old man who had done so much for others during his lifetime. 'Of course,' she affirmed. 'Of course I will. I'd love to help and as you say, this is right up my street.'

Zak let out a short chuckle of relief. 'I thought as much. But only do it if you really don't mind.'

'Far from not minding, I absolutely want to.' Ruth paused. 'Just one question, though: when did they last see each other? Did they have any time, once the war was over, to enjoy a love affair like they would have had in normal times?' There was a hopeful inflection at the end of her sentence that indicated the need she had for a response. Zak declined to oblige.

'I'm still saying nothing!' he laughed, and then stopped abruptly, his voice taking on a worried, serious tone. 'But thank you. I'm so grateful. The only thing is – well, we might not have much time. Dad's condition is serious and he really, really wants this sorted before...' Zak halted, unable to continue. Ruth could hear the emotion in his voice that sounded near to tears. He was so close to his father. She resolved to spare no effort in her quest to bring peace to an elderly hero at the end of his life.

'Don't worry,' Ruth said, softly. 'I understand. I'll do everything I can to help. I'll start straightaway.'

Once she put the phone down it occurred to her that she had been so wrapped up in the idea of finding Hannelore that she had forgotten to go back to the subject of the artefacts. Zak had indicated that he neither knew what or where they were; Bekim had not yet provided this information. Ruth wondered why these things had had to be concealed, whatever they were. Was it to do with their value? The Nazis were known to have looted all sorts of treasures from homes and businesses, museums and galleries across Europe, pilfering whatever they wanted. People were still trying to get such possessions back.

Intrigued by the mystery, she began googling, and soon found out that there were stories of precious items such as prayer books left behind by the Jews with their Albanian rescuers. Instead of the few years they had all thought that these things would be held in safe-keeping, it had ended up being many decades, due to the complete isolation of the country during the communist era. Ruth felt a thrill of excitement at reading this news. What fresh revelations did Bekim's story still have in store?

As a child, she had loved stories about intrepid adventures involving buried booty, poring over the maps in books that showed on some desert island somewhere, beneath a lone palm tree, wooden chests overflowing with gold doubloons, silver jewellery, diamonds, rubies, emeralds and sapphires. 'X' marks the spot the treasure hunters would be told, by a white-bearded mariner with gnarled fingers and skin burnt to the shade of burnished oak from a lifetime sailing the high seas. And off they would set, braving stormy oceans and nefarious pirates, seeking their fortune. A shiver ran through Ruth as she recalled the thrill these buccaneering tales had induced in her. And here she was, aged forty-five, with her very own treasure hunt to pursue.

Sitting back in her chair, she tried to focus. The artefacts were fascinating, but she needed a bit more to go on. She had no chart with a convenient search location already marked upon it so she was reliant on Zak being able to pump Bekim for more details. The search for Hannelore could begin as soon as Zak had sent the email he'd promised. In the meantime, she just had to wait.

Suddenly impatient and too full of pent-up emotion to sit still, Ruth leapt from her chair. She'd go into Leuca and look for a present for baby Mia, and when she got back she'd see if Daniel wanted to come for a swim. The late afternoon had become Ruth's favourite time on the beach, when the crowds had started to disperse and the sun had lost some of its infernal heat.

Walking to the marina to fetch the car, that sun was sweltering. The air pulsed with its brilliance and the cicadas hidden in the shrubs and flowering plants that lined the road thrummed at full volume. Though the sun could sometimes feel punishing, at the same time Ruth relished the warmth, feeling her skin soaking it up, eager for vitamins. Her whole body felt invigorated and reenergised by rest and sunshine and she thought with dread about returning home, to the grey drizzle and rampaging winds of the east coast of England.

She dreaded, too, the return to work which, though she had no idea what form it would take, would have to happen. Her savings would not last forever. In the past, she had spent nearly all her life indoors, in wintertime barely seeing daylight, going to the TV station when it was still dark to do the programme, then working on the following day's edition, leaving only once dusk had fallen again. Even though she'd consigned her ideas of living off the land to the dustbin, Ruth did hope that she might find something to do that didn't involve being indoors staring at a screen all day.

Wasn't there some woman who'd become a shepherdess, written a book about it and made herself famous into the bargain? Ruth wasn't seeking fame and fortune – though she had to admit there was a small part of her that had enjoyed the modicum of recognition she'd gained as a TV newsreader – but there was something wildly romantic and carefree about the idea of tripping over green meadows, shepherd's hook in hand, guiding her flock.

Oh gosh, that makes me sound like a vicar, it occurred to her, a smile breaking out on her face at the idea. She definitely didn't have a vocation; of that she was certain. And she was probably only thinking about sheep because of Bekim's story and the mental picture she had of the children running wild in the hills, delighting in their freedom after long months of confinement in a dark cave. That was the thing about all of these farming jobs: they were fine in summer, horrendous in winter. No, yet again, she'd have to come up with something else.

The inside of the car was like entering the fires of hell. As soon as the engine had started, Ruth ramped the air conditioning to the max. It was three thirty in the afternoon so by the time she got into town, the shops would be open again. She managed to nab a parking space in the same spot as before and set off into the town's small commercial centre. How much more lovely it was to shop in emporiums housed in the ground floors of ancient stone buildings, all individual and idiosyncratic in their own way, than to visit one of England's bland out-of-town malls. Ruth wondered amongst the boutiques, fingering clothes made of beautiful Italian linens and silks, lifting jewel-coloured bars of artisan soap to her nose to inhale the myriad fragrances, all of which sung of the land around: lavender and thyme, orange and grapefruit, bergamot and sage. Perhaps she could do that?

Sell handmade soap and candles… Or maybe not. Jo Malone and her ilk had already cornered that market.

Eventually, Ruth came upon a baby shop, its window full of exquisite goods: cotton and cashmere blankets, wooden teething rings and toys, cute outfits adorned with sheep – she couldn't get away from those animals today! – and llamas. Funny how South American quadrupeds often featured on baby clothes, Ruth mused. The bell tinkled as she pushed the door open and went inside.

Twenty-five minutes later, and after much deliberation, she had made her choice. A beautiful plain white soft wool blanket that, though Mia didn't need it right now, would come into its own as soon as the season changed, and a cuddly elephant that Ruth simply couldn't resist. As she stepped back out into the heat, her phone rang. It was Zak.

In a panic, Ruth fumbled to press the accept call button. She'd only spoken to him an hour or so earlier. Had something happened to Bekim to make him ring again so soon?

'What's up? Is anything wrong?' She couldn't keep the anxiety out of her voice.

There was a brief pause and then Zak's familiar chuckle. 'Nothing wrong. Nothing wrong at all.'

'Oh, phew,' replied Ruth, relieved. 'Sorry, that was a bit of an abrupt greeting, wasn't it? Just with what you said about your father earlier…'

'I understand.' Zak sounded preoccupied. In the background, Ruth could hear voices.

'Where are you?' she asked. 'It sounds busy.' She moved into the shade of a restaurant awning as she spoke.

'At home,' Zak said. 'Appointments done for the day. My sister's gone back to the house in the village, so it's just me now. That's the neighbours talking to my mum you can hear; they always want to be kept abreast of everything that's going on. They're such a support for my parents when I'm not here.'

'How wonderful to have such a community around you.'

Zak gave a snort of laughter. 'Yes – though, be warned, you cannot keep secrets about anything around here. Everyone knows your business. It can be a bit wearing, if I'm honest.'

Ruth laughed. 'I understand. Still… it's good that there are people looking out for your mum and dad when you're not there.'

'What are you doing anyway?' Zak questioned. 'It doesn't sound like the beach – no children's high-pitched squeals and shrieks!'

'You're right. I came into Leuca to buy Mia a present and have a mosey round the shops. It's been really nice, actually. I'm going to have a coffee in one of the cafes before going home, try to imagine myself as one of the cosmopolitan travelling set.' Ruth ended with a laugh to show this latter was intended as a self-deprecating joke. She didn't know why, but she felt that she could say anything to Zak and he would understand it exactly as she intended. It was a nice feeling.

'Sounds great,' responded Zak. 'I was phoning to say I'm about to sit down and bash out that email with everything I've got on Hannelore. It's going to take me a bit of time to go through it all and put it into intelligible form, but you should have it within the next hour or so.'

'Perfect,' said Ruth. Perhaps she'd put off the swim to another day. All she wanted to do was get started on the search.

Chapter Twenty-Five

Albania, 1944-45

My chance to prove myself worthy of Hannelore comes in October.

Altin materialises in the village. For the first time, he is not alone but with a band of men, each as tired-looking and haggard as he is. Their uniforms are no longer smart as Altin's was back in the early days of the partisan struggle; now the collars and cuffs are frayed, the fabric worn thin in places. But they walk tall, because the partisans are winning.

We slaughter a spring lamb to celebrate their successes and once we've eaten, Altin calls me over.

'It's the final push now, Bekim,' he says, cupping a match with his tanned, muscular hands and lighting his cigarette. He hands the packet to me and I tap one out; I had to force myself at first, but I enjoy smoking now. We draw on our cigarettes, and blow smoke clouds into the still air.

'We need all the men we can get.' He looks straight at me, meeting my eyes with his and holding them. 'You will come.'

I nod, affecting an insouciance I do not feel. I've been waiting for this for so long. Expecting it. Hoping for it. Excitement leaps within me.

'But what about our guests?' I ask, not by way of excuse but out of my duty towards them.

'David and the other lads can cope. We'll leave weapons for them, ammunition, everything they need. They won't have to use them, though. The Germans are fighting with every man they've got to hold the towns; they haven't got manpower to spare for an insignificant place like this.'

Later, when I tell Hannelore, a dark cloud of fear and apprehension crosses her lovely face, but she does not flinch.

'Yes,' she says simply, 'it's right that you should go.'

–

In Tirana, everything is in chaos. Perhaps I've been too long in the hills, away from people and crowds and vehicles and noise. But when we first arrive I'm utterly disorientated. As I pull on the boots that Altin has given me as part of my uniform, it occurs to me that I haven't even told my parents. I've had so little communication with them over the last year that they've become shadows in my memory, and Lefter and Fatos, too. Suddenly I want to see them all with a desperation that is like a physical pain, a twisting in my gut that will not ease off.

Altin hands me my gun, a German revolver, purloined from a raid. I take it, check it and roll the cylinder, drawing reassurance from the firm, cool, smooth feel of the metal, its solidity. The understanding sears through me that there'll be no visits home until this battle is won or lost, no hugs and kisses for cry-baby Bekim.

If I haven't grown up yet, I will now.

Altin introduces me to the rest of his band of fighters. Chief amongst them are Edip, whose left hand is missing two fingers but who can still wield a gun or a knife with his right; Fatbard with a mane of black hair and a haunted look in his eyes that Altin tells me has been there ever since his village was razed to the ground by the German army on the hunt for partisans such as him; and Dalmat whose name derives from the ancient Illyrian tribe that once inhabited this land.

They are ferocious and fearless, these men, fighting as if they have nothing left to lose. Which, in all cases except Altin's, is true. Edip's betrothed died of pneumonia in the winter of '43, Fatbard's family perished in the fire the Nazis started, and Dalmat lost his parents to a bomb blast. They wear their anger on battle-hardened countenances, their desire for revenge in their fingers that twitch to pull the trigger on the enemy.

One early morning, Altin and I go out on a recce through the streets of the capital, lurking in the shadows between buildings, always conscious of who is before us, or behind. The Germans are constantly moving position and there are more and more troops every day as whole battalions are driven towards the Mediterranean in front of the advancing armies. We quickly establish the new red zones and, having procured food from a street vendor, retreat back to base, the cellar of a rickety old building that I'm sure will collapse if someone so much as leans on it, let alone drops a bomb on it.

We perform these reconnaissance missions regularly for a few days. In that time I learn about fear, the true nature of it, and what it means to be brave. I realise that it is all a pretence. You pretend to not be frightened and you pretend to be brave and, as time passes, it stops being an act and becomes reality. I also learn that the thing that gets you through, apart from the human instinct to survive, is camaraderie. Never have I felt closer to people I barely know than during those weeks spent with rough and rugged partisans in that cellar in Tirana, playing cards, drinking rakia, and waiting. Waiting for the fighting to start.

It doesn't take long. The tension swells until suddenly it breaks and the action starts. In every street and square, the partisans engage in hand-to-hand combat with the Germans, a fight to the death that each side is determined to win. I want desperately to take part, but Altin refuses. I'm deemed too green to participate in this part of the struggle.

'I have another job for you, Bekim,' he tells me, his voice even lower and more gravelly than ever in its seriousness. 'An important one, that I can trust you to do well.'

There's no point in arguing; Altin is the boss and his word goes. I have to accept and hope that I can do him – and myself – justice, and that his faith in me will be rewarded.

I'm sent to a field behind a factory to man an old Italian machine gun emplacement that's been regained from the militia. For a few days, this is nothing other than tedious.

But on the fifth day, the fighting explodes, quite literally, in front of me. A German truck speeds past; I take aim and fire but it comes on me too suddenly and is travelling too fast for my bullets to do more than nip and graze at the back wheels. The soldiers on board, however, have time to throw grenades; two or three of them at least.

The impact of each grenade is like an earthquake, throwing up hard sods and clods that rain down on me. If that had been the extent of it, I would have been fine. But one hits a ramshackle shed, and a huge wooden post with a metal rivet hanging from it is torn from its rickety foundations and sent flying to land on my legs. As the rivet pierces my skin and chisels into my bone, I scream and, for the first and only time in this hellish war, tears of pure physical agony pour down my cheeks. I twist my head to the side and they soak into the scuffed earth beneath my face, turning soil to mud as if the ground is absorbing all the pain and heartache and misery of the world.

I lie, defeated. My legs are pinioned to the ground, preventing me from moving, and as the blood drains out of me, I drift in and out of consciousness. I have no way to keep track of time but I know it must be getting late when the light fades and dusk begins to fall. Thirst grips my throat and I fantasise about liquid, about drinking a long, cool slug of pure mountain spring water. At some point I must fall asleep, because when I open my eyes, Hannelore is there, kneeling over me, wiping my brow and uttering soothing sounds in her mellifluous voice.

'Where am I?' I ask, overcome by confusion. 'What's happening?' And then, with an increasing sense of panic. 'Why can't I move my legs?' I try to sit up but Hannelore gently pushes me back down.

'Shush,' she whispers. 'Don't try to move. They'll come for you soon, the partisans. They know you're here. Just lie still until they get here.'

I let my head sink back down onto the hard ground and momentarily close my eyes. Hannelore is here; everything will be all right. The thirst returns, lashing at my throat.

'Water,' I mutter. 'Do you have any water for me?'

'Soon,' Hannelore murmurs, 'soon.' Her hand sweeps slowly and deliberately across my brow and I have a sudden recollection of my mother's cool touch when suffering some childhood illness, chickenpox or measles.

'Thanks for coming, Hannelore,' I mutter. My eyes close again; I can't seem to keep them open. How much time passes I have no idea, but when they flicker open again, I can't see Hannelore anymore. I reach out for her, seeking her warmth and comfort, her revivifying presence. But though I can still smell the scent of her, of olive soap and sunshine, she is gone, melted away into the growing darkness.

A half-sigh, half-groan rises from the depths of my being. The pain has been largely absent up to now, but suddenly it wells up, assailing me. I groan again, try to thrash around, remember I can't move. Why has Hannelore left?

The tears form again, pricking at my eyes before they begin to trickle down my cheeks. In an acute moment of realisation, I get it. Hannelore is not here and never was. I have been hallucinating. My desire for her, to see her, conjured her up before me like the mirage of an oasis in a desert appears before a desperate traveller.

I'm going to die, I think. I will die here in this muddy field. It seems fine, at that moment. My life will end defending my country and my people, and who can wish for more than that? It's an insult in our country to say a man died in his bed. Mine will be a noble death; my kinsmen will be proud of me.

The next thing I know, Altin is there. I know he really is there – not just a fantasy like Hannelore – because in the moments that follow he has hefted the post off my legs with his bear-like strength, lifted me up and deposited me unceremoniously in the back of an army truck. The pain of being moved is so intense I black out. The last thing I'm aware of is Altin leaping into the passenger seat and shouting at the driver.

'*Shko!*' he yells. 'Go as fast as you can. My nephew must be saved.'

–

When I wake up I'm in hospital, in a ward crowded with other men. The smell of the place hits me first, a mixture of disinfectant and sweat, stale body odour and well-worn boots.

The realisation descends upon me that I'm not going to be my country's saviour, that I haven't earned a medal or become a hero, and the tears prick behind my eyes once more. So much for being the brave, unyielding partisan fighter, saving Europe from the darkness of fascism. I lasted less than a week.

The nurse who comes to check my bandages and take my temperature confirms what I fear.

'You'll recover,' she says briskly, 'but not before the war ends. It's going to take four months or so for that leg to heal. It's broken in three places.' Her smile, despite her brusque manner, is sympathetic. So my fighting career is over before it has truly begun. A slam of resignation sinks deep inside my stomach.

'You're one of the younger ones we've seen. Your family will be proud of you.'

I don't know what to say. They'll be glad I'm alive, I'm sure. And proud, probably. But there's only one person whose opinion really matters. No, two actually. Altin's and Hannelore's. Though when I'll get to see either of them is anyone's guess. It's too dangerous for Hannelore to venture anywhere near the capital, and Altin will be fully occupied fighting for his and all of our lives.

Outside, the inferno rages on. By the end of October, the battle with the Nazis is all but over. In the final days, the British air force bombards the retreating army. I lie in my bed and hear the roar of the engines and feel the reverberations that resound around the ruined city as the bombs drop, smell the cordite and the fire. In an instant I am taken back to the bombing of the harbour at Durrësi, all those years ago.

This war has gone on and on and on. But the news we hear, told in ever more excited voices by the nurses, orderlies and doctors, is that it finally seems as if it might be over. German resistance is faltering; they know the end is nigh. Even before the official surrender, more and more of them are laying down their arms and holding their hands up high.

The partisans are heading for victory.

Chapter Twenty-Six

Albania, 1944-45

The Germans give in. By early November, all have left Albania.

Rather than go out and celebrate with everyone else, I'm stuck in that hospital ward and will be for several months. My left leg, entombed in plaster, means I'm more or less immobile. I hear reports from the staff about the partying, the all-night drinking and dancing in the streets and I'm filled with envy. Interminable boredom, I soon find out, is far worse a result of injury than pain.

Infuriatingly slowly, 1944 turns to 1945. One day, I'm sitting up in my bed reading the newspaper when the nurse comes.

'You have a visitor,' she says.

I've been reunited with my mother, father and brothers; all four came to visit and stayed for several days. But as far as I know, they've returned to Shkodra, anxious not to neglect the business for too long in such uncertain times; looters abound where the bombing has destroyed buildings, and thieves are everywhere. Nevertheless, I look around, wondering if perhaps they've come back to see me again after all, or sent a relative or friend with food to relieve the monotony of the hospital's limited menu.

But the person I see is someone completely different.

It's Hannelore, wearing a man's winter coat that's much too big for her and a knitted scarf wrapped round and round her neck and head. I'm in full possession of my faculties now, and I know for certain she's not a mirage. Shock and delight render me momentarily speechless. When I'm able to say something, it's not what I want.

'Wh-what are you doing here?' I stutter.

She laughs, a gentle sound like a mountain river running over smooth-worn pebbles. 'That's nice!' she teases. 'Just the sort of welcome I expected.'

She looks around her for somewhere to sit down, and sees a rickety chair on the opposite side of the ward. She gets it and places it beside my bed. Her face is worn and tired, thinner than I remember, or perhaps it's been too long since I've had a chance to look at her properly.

'How did you find me? How did you know where I was?'

Hannelore reaches out and puts her hand upon my arm. 'Altin told us.' She pauses and takes a deep breath before continuing. 'Everything has changed, Bekim, in ways none of us expected. We waited a while after the Germans left before we felt it was safe to travel. A week or so ago, we came down from the mountains to Tirana. We couldn't believe the devastation – almost all the buildings are damaged – but nevertheless, we have found some-where to lodge, only one room in an apartment for the four of us, but it has an electricity supply and water… sometimes. It's enough.'

I think of how happy she will be to have such luxuries, albeit intermittent, after so long without. No more priva-tions, no more kitchens and bathrooms infested with rats as big as cats, and cockroaches and spiders.

'We're hoping to get our travel visas soon,' she continues. 'That's why we had to get here, to Tirana and the embassy. But there's no sign of any documents yet. In Europe the war is still raging and I don't think we'll be able to do anything until it's finally done with. But Bekim, though the Nazis have left Albania there's terror on the streets. The Communists are arresting people left, right and centre, men are disappearing in the night never to be seen again.'

I nod. I've heard as much from Altin, who visits often, and from the other men on the ward. Anyone suspected of collaborating with the Italians or the Germans is at risk. A new regime is trying to embed its power as quickly as it can and those in charge will let no one and nothing get in their way. In place of fighting the Nazis, Albanians are fighting each other.

Perhaps the battle wasn't so glorious after all.

It's hardly surprising that the Frankls want to get out as soon as possible. But still, my heart sinks as I listen to her words. I remember how happy I was all those years ago when the Italians invaded because it meant that her family would have to stay here a little longer. I was only thinking of myself and how much I wanted to keep hold of Hannelore.

Now, so many years older and a little bit wiser, I understand that it isn't that simple and never was.

–

Hannelore visits regularly over the next few weeks until I'm discharged from hospital. When they do tell me I can go, I'm not sure where I should go to. Back to Shkodra? I can't help in the shop or cafe as I'm not mobile enough yet. I'd just be a burden on the family and anyway, I don't even know how I could get there. The thought of hours on the bus or in the back of a cart makes me feel nauseous.

But then Hannelore comes up with the solution. The occupant of one of the other rooms in her family's apartment has left hurriedly in the night and there's no sign he's ever coming back. Whether a collaborator, an anticommunist or a royalist, nobody knows and it doesn't pay to ask too many questions. So there's a spare room and a bed if I wish to take it, and the Frankls will take care of me, if I'll accept that, too.

'Please, let us, Bekim,' pleads Hannelore, as she lays out the plan before me. 'After everything you've done for us and the others – all the lives you've saved – we can at least do this for you in return. And anyway,' she adds, 'I'm so bored. Cooking and cleaning for you will give me something to do!'

Mr and Mrs Frankl are out all day trying to earn money; they've taken on a market stall and they get up early in the morning to go to the outskirts of the city to buy produce from the country people. They bring it into the centre of town to sell on at a small profit. They make hardly anything but at least we can all live on the fruit and vegetables that are too old or over-ripe to sell.

Hannelore spends the days making soups and broths and anything you can concoct from water and a few bits of turnip and potato. Somehow, she makes it tasty, however little she has. During this time, David teaches me to play chess and we spend hours in increasingly competitive matches. As my leg heals, I'm keen to get back to fitness and David helps me devise fiendish exercise routines that he completes with me. He is a fine, strapping teenager and hates the confinement of the apartment, but it's not safe to spend too much time out and about. There is hardship and worry and despair during those weeks and months, but I remember them as some of the happiest of my life.

Of course it cannot last.

One day, Mr Frankl comes back with a radio. I've no idea how he got hold of it but it's better than if he'd returned with a nugget of pure gold. We listen avidly to the news broadcasts, and we all cheer at the top of our voices when we hear that Germany has capitulated. All the joy, however, is rapidly swept away over the following days as we learn more and more about the horror that occurred across Europe under the Nazis. We had had no idea about the concentration camps, about the death marches and the systematic extermination of those like the Frankls. It only makes the family more determined to get out of Albania, of Europe, so tainted by this genocide, as soon as possible. They are desperate to reach America, where relatives settled before the war and are waiting for the Frankls to join them.

Initially, the Albanians refuse to let anyone out of the country. But I know it is only a matter of time until this changes. And indeed, so it turns out. A typhoid epidemic provides the catalyst that forces the authorities to issue exit permits to all who want them. All that remains is to wait for the British boat to leave for Brindisi.

'Look at my mother and father,' Hannelore says, one day when we are alone together. 'See how they've aged, how difficult they find it to cope.'

I know she is right. My parents had brought a photograph with them when they visited us recently. I have no idea when it was taken as I have no recollection of it, but it captures the Frankls and me not long after they first arrived and I'd got to know them all. Of course, us children are utterly transformed, in height and maturity. But what shocked me more when I saw it was how different Mr and Mrs Frankl look. Immeasurably older now, and sadder, their cheeks shrunken around jaws that now miss so many teeth, their hair white, their skin grey and wrinkled from poor nutrition and worry.

'I have to go with them, they can't manage alone. And David… he needs me, too,' utters Hannelore, her voice and eager eyes in her upturned face imploring me to understand.

We're sitting by the window of the apartment's kitchen, which looks out over the rubble of the ruined city and towards the sea. The sun is setting and the sky is pink and purple and rose and orange and it's like the colour of my bruised heart, knowing that I'm going to lose her.

'Yes,' I respond, simply. What words can you use when you have no words?

'There's something I have to ask you,' Hannelore says.

My heart leaps. Really?

'We don't know exactly where we're going,' she continues, 'or when we'll get there. So Papa wants to know, would you look after his sacred things, just until we're settled? Once we have a permanent address, you can send them to us. Or even better, as soon as I can leave Mutti and Vati, I will come and collect them.'

The words land more heavily than any German bomb. The truth is like a body blow. The Frankls are going and Hannelore with them. It had been ridiculous of me to even think, to even begin to imagine, that Hannelore's parents would allow her to throw in her lot with a penniless Albanian boy. That *she* would ever want this.

Though their world is in pieces – has been for seven long years – before the devastation, it used to be a world of comfort and plenty. And it is back to such a world that they are heading, to a world where, with the help and support of their family members in America, they will once again find safety and security. The daily rigours and privations that are the way of life for the Shehus and our ilk will no longer trouble them. In my stupid sixteen-year-old naivety and gullibility, I had thought that joining the partisans, becoming a fighter, might persuade Hannelore to stay with me. But that dream is over now, just like all the other dreams this war and its aftermath have buried.

I look at Hannelore, who is waiting patiently for my reply. I must rise to the occasion, do the right thing, however much it hurts, however hard it is.

'Of course I'll look after them,' I tell her, my voice breaking as I choke back my tears. 'Anything you want – just leave it with me. You'll get it all back as soon as possible, I promise. You have my *besa* on that.'

She moves towards me and instinctively I open my arms and we hug and hug until there's no breath left in either of us and we're both crying though most of the tears are hers, I'm sure.

'Thank you, Bekim,' she sobs, her cheeks wet, sodden strands of her chestnut hair plastered against her pale skin. 'Thank you so much. I know I can trust you.'

Not long after, I go with the Frankls and the other Jewish families back to Durrësi, my old hometown, and see them onto the boat. They will be housed in a Displaced Persons camp in the heel of Italy until they are able to continue their journey to America. I stand in that harbour, that like our country is bombed but not beaten, and wave until the tiny black speck disappears over the horizon, taking Hannelore to a new life. I look at my watch, the family watch, passed down from my grandfather to my father to me. It won't go to children that Hannelore and I have now. For the first time, I know that for a fact, and I have to confront it as a certainty. The thought brings new tears to my eyes which I beat back, angrily.

As I leave the place where it all began, I know that I must make a new life, too.

Chapter Twenty-Seven

Italy, 2019

Ruth's eyes filled with tears as she read Bekim's words of sad farewell to his youthful dreams and fantasies. The war had forced people to grow up so young, so fast. The thought of this brave man, now old and ailing, desperate to gain closure on long unfinished business, provided Ruth with the impetus she needed to push on with the job Zak had enlisted her help with.

Zak had managed to elicit some more valuable information from Bekim about the objects, namely that they were indeed things belonging to the Jewish family, just as had been described in her Google searches. Where and how they could be found remained a mystery – as did the whereabouts of Hannelore. The determination that had habitually taken over Ruth when she still had a job and was given a story to research came back to her now. She threw herself at the task and was so busy she barely noticed the passing days.

And then, one day, about ten days after he'd left, Zak came back as promised. He sent her a message, asking if she was free to meet him at the *osteria* for dinner. Ruth was ridiculously pleased, both with the invitation and with the thought of seeing him.

That evening, under the restaurant's twinkling fairy lights, Zak greeted her as politely and courteously as ever but before she'd even sat down, he was asking, 'Did you find anything?' In his voice, hope mingled with desperation.

Ruth shook her head ruefully. 'Not so far. But I will. I've never failed an assignment yet.'

Zak nodded. 'Thank you. I know you're doing your best. I just can't help but worry…'

Ruth wanted so much to hold out her hand, take his, provide the solace of touch. She remembered the deft, firm grip of his hand in hers as he'd helped her out of the water and onto Enzo's boat when they'd gone to the grottoes. That seemed ages ago now, before Bekim's condition worsened, before Mia's birth. Before he asked her to find Hannelore.

'I've got to spend some time at work; I've neglected it, not been on top of what's going on there,' Zak was saying, and Ruth knew the moment to reach out to him was lost. 'But at the end of the week, I'm going back to Albania again. To find those objects dad is obsessing about, amongst other things.'

Ruth nodded. Of course, Zak would have to spend a lot of time back home at a time such as this.

'I understand,' she said, quietly.

Zak fiddled with his wine glass, lining it up with his plate.

'Would you like to come?'

The question came out of the blue. Ruth stared at him in surprise.

'I mean, if you are interested. If you'd like to.'

The chance to see Albania, this country she had read so much about, was far too good to turn down. She couldn't believe Zak was inviting her.

'I'd love to,' she responded simply. 'What an adventure!'

In the days that followed before their departure, Ruth redoubled her efforts to find Hannelore and the rest of the Frankl family. The fact that the trip would inevitably pause her research propelled her to work harder than ever, spending hours glued to her laptop, snatching snacks and drinks and consuming them whilst still poring over online documents and files. Bekim's story had captivated her from the very first word but since then it had become something so much more than entertainment or the opportunity to learn a bit of history.

Zak's request for help had given her the chance to make a difference, to achieve something far more important than a workplace award. Ruth had never won a gong for any of the many 'TV News Programme of the Year' prizes and had always longed to. Now, that no longer seemed to matter. Probably no one but Bekim and his family, and hopefully Hannelore and hers, would ever know if they were successful, but Ruth didn't care. Her perspective on almost everything had changed and she had begun to realise, for the first time ever, that it really was true that doing things for others was so much more fulfilling than doing them for yourself.

From the manuscript, she knew that the Frankls had definitely numbered amongst those in the Displaced Persons camps in the small towns and villages in the region, so she turned her attention to local archives as well as those in the US that she had previously been focusing on. She even went back to the museum she and Zak had visited but the director was away on holiday and there was no one else who could authorise access to the archives, so she returned empty handed.

Her concentration was not helped by the fact that overnight the helicopters were hovering once more. Woken, Ruth hoped that this wasn't making things even worse for Caroline. Parents of newborns got little enough sleep as it was. Concerned, she popped in to see Caroline and the baby every day. But now she was no longer pregnant and despite the broken nights, Caroline had renewed energy, even feeling able to put Mia in her sling and take her and Daniel down to the beach. And Caroline's parents had arrived, having moved their flights forward. Their presence, along with tidal waves of love and presents, was clearly a huge support for the new mum.

Ruth felt guilty about the relief she experienced that she no longer needed to help out. Not that it had ever been a chore. Far from it. Even before she became Zia Ruth, she had loved the time she'd spent with Daniel. But she was glad to be off the hook now, so that she could get on with her task of locating the elusive Hannelore. Leads led her to Tel Aviv, to New York, to Los Angeles and even, somewhat unexpectedly, to Madrid. But all fell through and, by the eve of their departure to Albania, Ruth was still no nearer to the end of her quest.

Zak had arranged for them to take the overnight ferry from Bari to Durrësi. There were no flights available for several days to either Tirana or Podgorica in Montenegro, so the boat would get them there sooner. After a surprisingly good sleep in her comfortable cabin, Ruth went up onto the deck the next morning to watch as they docked. She had such a vivid picture of the port from the descriptions in Bekim's book. Although it had been hugely expanded since the war, the number of moorings increased and the equipment modernised, she could still picture the Jewish refugees as they stepped ashore, tired and disorientated, seeing with disbelieving eyes the primitive country they had come to, a world apart from the sophistication and wealth of their cities of origin: Vienna, Hamburg, Berlin.

Disembarking, Ruth half-expected them to still be there, that jaded bunch of weary travellers, making their way in a very foreign land. Instead, aside from the port officials, the first Albanians she and Zak encountered as they set off for Shkodra was a herd of goats, lethargically watched over by a floppy-eared dog and meandering casually along the verges of the immaculately surfaced EU-funded highway that led away along the coast. The landscape was not dissimilar to Italy, parched at the height of summer, olive and pomegranate trees studding the brown fields, with shrunken, scrubby bushes forming minimal barriers along the roadside.

A stone directly ahead of them caught Ruth's attention and she pointed it out to Zak. 'Careful,' she said, 'you don't want to blow a tyre.' But almost immediately, she saw what it really was: a tortoise making tortuously slow progress across four lanes of admittedly very light traffic.

Zak swerved generously to avoid it.

'I hope it makes it,' mused Ruth, thinking of Bekim proudly showing Hannelore the tortoises' hang out.

After a while, the two lanes became one and, not long after that, they hit the outskirts of Shkodra, the empty pastures and occasional dusty village replaced by low-built concrete buildings, well-laid out fruit orchards and commercial enterprises. As they got closer to the centre, it increasingly resembled Bekim's descriptions of a busy and vibrant city. Shops crowded together along every street, selling everything from brooms to coffins, fruit and veg to building supplies, hot rotisserie chickens to cheap rucksacks and bags.

A cacophony of noise surrounded them: car horns, bicycle bells, blaring music and the rhythmic clopping of horses' hooves. Every mode of transport seemed to be in use, from pony and trap to pick-up truck, from car to coach. Amidst the vehicles, numerous cyclists serenely wended their way to their destinations, proceeding in any direction, either with or against the flow of traffic, and at any speed, apparently heedless to anything going on around them. A horse and cart was stationary in the centre of a roundabout, the driver talking on his mobile phone, the animal munching contentedly on the contents of one of the planters that surrounded the central stone structure. An air of disorganised but functioning chaos suffused the hectic scene.

Zak navigated it all with his usual cool efficiency and they soon pulled up outside a high concrete wall. Opening a door in the gate, he led Ruth through to an attractive courtyard full of potted plants that burst with colour and vibrancy.

'What do you think so far?' asked Zak, as they waited for his mother to answer the door.

'I'm overwhelmed,' answered Ruth. 'It's all so different and… well, I've never been anywhere like this before. You have to understand that I've led a very sheltered life,' she added, jokingly. 'My holidays normally take place in the south of France or the Costa del Sol. This as near to the Wild West as I've ever got!'

Zak laughed. 'It's OK,' he teased. 'We're quite tame really. Most of us, anyway.'

Zak's parents, Bekim and Drita, were bright and welcoming. Though their tanned faces were lined and wrinkled, both looked far younger than their true years. As Zak introduced Ruth to them, they exchanged quick glances that Ruth couldn't quite fathom, and smiled smiles that verged on being smirks.

'So you are the beautiful young lady our son has told us so much about,' Bekim exclaimed to Ruth, clasping her hand with a grip that belied his ill-health. Zak translated his Albanian into English for Ruth and, as he did so, she noticed a very slight reddening of his cheeks. Parents never lose the ability to embarrass us, she thought, with a wry inward smile.

Drita was the sprightliest eighty-year-old Ruth had ever met. She bustled around her old-fashioned kitchen preparing endless meals and snacks, slicing delicious home-grown fruits, grilling vegetables from the garden, baking bread and serving it with honey from the beehives in the mountain village. To accompany everything was rough red wine from the family's own vines, and home distilled quince rakia, a drink often better and more accurately known as firewater. It was so strong it burnt Ruth's throat and stomach and the tiniest sip sufficed.

Once they'd been fed and watered up to their eyeballs, Zak took Ruth to see some of the sights. First, they headed for the Marubi Photography museum where, as well as photos of the redoubtable Edwardian English lady traveller and Balkan hero Edith Durham, the many characters from Zak's manuscript came to life before Ruth's eyes. The collection included everything from a study of traditional haystacks to groups of adults and children from all over the country in national dress. Men and boys sported elaborately embroidered waistcoats and tight white breeches, while women and girls wore many layered skirts and curious hats that were a mixture between a fez and a beret. The men almost always had a weapon, a gun or a knife, or both.

Ruth thought of Bekim's precious knife, lost in his quest to get hold of the ID cards. Poor Bekim.

Zak gestured to her that he wanted to show her something. He pointed to a picture of a man and a woman. The woman was dressed for winter in a thick, checked coat tightly belted at the waist. She was looking into the lens with a clear, frank gaze. Next to her, half-turned towards the camera, was a man, tall, slim and proud in military uniform, his hand clasped around the handle of his rifle, his expression one of determined defiance. The caption proclaimed them as partisans, members of the 27th Assault Brigade, a unit formed in Shkodra.

'The guy looks just as I imagine Altin,' remarked Ruth, unable to take her eyes from the striking image. Bekim's uncle would have stood strong like this, utterly unbowed in the face of an enemy so much greater, so much more powerful than the small band of fighters in the hills.

Zak smiled a slow, wistful smile. 'That's because it is Altin,' he said, simply.

'No!' exclaimed Ruth, her voice startlingly loud in the hush of the almost empty museum.

'I know,' agreed Zak. 'It's a coincidence, isn't it? But nevertheless, here he is, great-uncle Altin.'

Ruth wanted to reach out and touch him, run her fingers over his bold form.

'Who is the woman?' she asked. 'Not Sarah? She was not a partisan, was she?'

'She was not. And no, that is not Sarah.' They both contemplated the photo in silence for a while.

'They look as if they were close,' ventured Ruth. 'Altin and this… and his companion.'

Zak shrugged. 'They probably were. Who knows what liaisons were fostered when these young people were far from home, facing danger every day? I don't think we can judge them for it.'

'Definitely not,' agreed Ruth, emphatically. 'No judging here, I can assure you.'

Nearby hung another image, this one of a young boy wearing dungarees much too big for him so that the bib came up almost to his chin.

'And this reminds me of the child Bekim,' laughed Ruth, pointing at the cheeky-looking imp. His chest was puffed out with pride at being the subject of something so rare and glamorous as a photograph, just as Ruth could imagine Bekim would have been.

'I know what you mean,' chuckled Zak. 'My dad has definitely always had a mischievous side.'

They went up to the castle next, with its stupendous views over Lake Shkodra, and then back into the town for an aperitif. Outdoor seating areas ranged along the middle of a pedestrianised street, each one belonging to one of the many bars and restaurants that lined the road. Sitting there in such pleasant and convivial surroundings, enjoying a glass of surprisingly good Albanian wine, Ruth was forced to reassess all her preconceived ideas about Albania as a wild and untamed land. Here was the height of relaxed Mediterranean living – and all at a fraction of the price of Italy, or the UK for that matter.

'I think I'm going to have to start a one-woman marketing campaign for your country,' she said to Zak.

'Huh!' snorted Zak. 'Well, I guess it could do with a boost. But don't be too deceived. The bad stuff is still out there, unfortunately.'

Ruth shrugged. 'You could say the same for anywhere, I suppose.'

'Umm,' uttered Zak, in a non-committal way. 'But look,' he went on, abruptly changing the subject. 'My next mission is a trip to the mountains. Dad's revealed that the missing artefacts are up there somewhere and given me an idea where we might find them. I still don't know what they are, though.'

'Ah!' interjected Ruth. 'I might be able to help you there. I've read stories of other families who kept precious things such as prayer books for the departing Jewish families. Do you think it could be something like that? I even wondered,' she paused, hoping she wasn't leaping ahead of herself, 'if that candlestick that is mentioned in the manuscript could be one of them? It sounds like the kind of treasured item the Frankls might have wanted to leave for safe keeping, until they were settled.'

Zak stared at her in open-mouthed surprise. 'Yes,' he suddenly cried, alarming the waiter who was standing nearby, taking an order from another table. 'Yes, of course, that must be it. Mustn't it?' His voice fell as doubt set in. And then another thought struck him. 'I can see why it would matter so much. It would be a matter of honour to get such things back to their rightful owner.'

Ruth nodded.

'So,' continued Zak, 'How do you fancy it? A trip to the hills…'

He left the sentence hanging and Ruth wasted no time. 'Of course! I wouldn't miss that for anything.'

Zak smiled and it looked as if a weight had fallen from his shoulders. 'It will be a three-day trip, if that's OK. Dad's next appointment isn't until Monday, so we can take the long – and most scenic – route; a boat across the lake, a night in Valbone, and then a hike along a mountain trail over the peaks to my family's village. My sister, Albana, is there now, and so is my jeep so we'll be able to drive back down when we're ready. And you'll have seen a bit more of the country.'

'That sounds fabulous,' Ruth said, 'I'd love it.'

Zak refilled their glasses from the bottle of wine he'd bought.

'It's really nice,' Ruth said, taking a sip. 'Unexpectedly so. Before now, if someone had asked me what I thought of Albanian wine, a) I wouldn't have known and b) I would have assumed it to be pretty ropy. But I would have been wrong.'

Zak nodded. 'Yes, it's certainly coming along. Actually, I must confess that our diminutive neighbour Montenegro has even better ones, but little of it is exported. They prefer to keep the good stuff for themselves.'

Ruth giggled. 'And who can blame them?' she said. She leant back and lifted her hair from her neck to cool it; it was still hot, even though the sun had set long ago. It was so extraordinarily lovely, sitting here with Zak, feeling so relaxed in his company. Though it was such a tough time for him, he had the knowledge that he was doing everything he could for his beloved father. Ruth hoped that was a comfort to him.

'Ruth.' Zak's voice broke across her thoughts. 'I really appreciate you being here,' he said, quietly. 'Having someone to share this with makes such a difference. I mean, I know I've got my sister but sometimes family are just too close, aren't they? Her anxiety is as strong as mine and that makes it hard to talk to her about it all.'

Ruth's heart went out to him. 'Whatever I can do,' she replied, simply.

'I always loved my dad,' Zak went on, his eyes roving over the blue-black sky above. 'He was a wonderful father; even during the tough times, of which there were many, he always remained optimistic, never losing that spirit that comes across so vividly in the manuscript. But because I left Albania when I was still young and self-obsessed, as men in their twenties are wont to be, I really had no idea of everything he endured in the war, all he did for others. I never even thought about asking, to be honest, and he didn't mention it due to the risk of such a conversation. Anyone could be accused of past crimes of collaboration, of supporting the wrong group, of foreign contamination. It was best to keep quiet, even within your own family.'

'You've made up for it now, though,' replied Ruth, gently. She understood this to be the remorse, however misplaced, that so many people feel as their parents reach the end of their lives. The feeling that whatever you did, it could have been more – you could have done better. 'You can't rewrite the past,' she continued, 'and any omissions in what you discussed, or how much you were or were not allowed to delve into the past, were the fault of Enver Hoxha, not you.'

Zak pulled a face of resignation. 'Yes, you're right. You're so wise. You always know the right thing to say.'

The words hovered between them, gradually settling onto the table as if they were familiar objects that belonged there.

'I'm not sure about that,' said Ruth eventually, smiling modestly.

Zak looked at her, his gaze steady upon her. 'I am,' he stated, definitively. And then, as the emotion fizzed between them, he stood up. 'We better get back. It's an early start in the morning.'

Chapter Twenty-Eight

Albania, 2019

By six thirty the next morning, Ruth and Zak were aboard the public minibus to Lake Komani. The driver clearly took his role as apprentice to Lewis Hamilton seriously, flinging the vehicle around bends and curves, twists and turns, as if participating in a time trial and approaching potholes as if the vehicle's worn tyres were impervious to them. Which, Ruth concluded not long into the drive, they most certainly weren't.

'Nearly there now,' said Zak, as they entered a long, dark tunnel.

Ruth nodded. The stained tunnel walls flashed by, the driver still proceeding at a fair lick despite the numerous speed limit signs. She blinked as they emerged from the obscurity into the bright, white light of day, then braced herself against the seat in front as the driver slammed on the brakes. Just inches ahead of them lay a vast expanse of sparkling water; they were on the dockside already.

Ruth looked warily back in the direction they had come from. No, it wasn't a dream. The tunnel disgorged travellers directly onto the quay, making Ruth wonder how many ended up going over the edge every year, finding themselves unexpectedly in the lake rather than beside it.

With relief, Ruth climbed down from the minibus and followed Zak to join the small throng of passengers waiting for the ferry. There was a smattering of tourists amongst them, but the majority were local people, each one of them surrounded by a quite amazing amount of luggage. There were bags, packages, boxes and crates, containing everything from beer to flour, from clothing to shoes. One man had a string of lively goats that took some time to corral onto the boat when it arrived.

Ruth managed to find some space for her feet in amongst the stuff that was quickly loaded and piled up all over the deck. She leant against the railings as they set sail, watching as the lake opened up in front of them, wide and utterly flat, painted in colours of aquamarine. It was staggeringly beautiful. Sheer cliffs soared up directly from the water itself, iron–grey karst studded with scrubby green shrubs and plants that clung on for dear life. From dark fissures in the rocks narrow waterfalls tumbled down-wards, catching the brilliant light like shimmering ribbons of liquid platinum. At times it seemed as if the boat were headed straight for the rock walls themselves, and then suddenly a narrow passage would open up, a twisting bend in the age-old valley that had been flooded over three decades ago to provide hydroelectric power.

There were no obvious stopping places, just a system of waving from on shore or clapping from on board that indicated to the boatman that someone wanted to get on or off. Pulling into the most unlikely nooks in the valley wall, there would often be several generations of a family waiting with donkeys, mules and strong arms to unload the supplies that had been brought back from the city. Ruth saw little sign of the villages, hamlets or homesteads where these people must live; apart from the odd low–built farmhouse, they were completely invisible, hidden in the folds of the hills. Roads, telegraph poles and electricity cables were all similarly absent.

'It feels like time has hardly moved on since the events in the manuscript,' Ruth commented to Zak, watching as an elderly woman, dressed all in black, gamely shouldered a crate of beer and set off up a narrow, twisting path with ease, soon disappearing behind a rocky outcrop. The goats had also disembarked at this stop, along with their moustached owner. He unleashed them from the rope that bound them and they too melted away into the hillside in a flurry of dust and bleating.

'It's hard to imagine, isn't it?' he agreed, 'how life in some parts of Europe still appears barely touched by the twenty-first century.'

Arriving in the small settlement of Fierze, they boarded another bus which would convey them to Valbone via towns and villages where pigs roamed the streets and hawkers offered baklava and fruit from trays balanced on rickety stands in the shade. Ruth drank in the sights, sounds and scents, revelling in them whilst at the same time aware that, had she come on her own, it would all feel quite frighteningly foreign. But with Zak by her side to guide and advise, as well as translate, she could indulge herself and simply enjoy the moment and the delicious pastries and freshly squeezed juices that Zak had brought along for lunch. They ate during one of the bus's halts, sitting in the shade of a Judas tree, surrounded by the clamour of bustling villagers going about their business.

Valbone, which they finally reached after a journey that totalled six hours, was a welcome sight, a cluster of Alpine style wooden houses and chalets set amidst lush pastures and shimmering beech woods, and ringed by towering mountains. Ruth was sad to find out from Donna, the guesthouse owner, about the myriad threats the region was under, such as the companies that wanted to frack and mine and exploit its natural resources in any way possible. The impression derived from the journey, of an isolated land lost in the past, untouched by modernity, was perhaps not quite the full picture.

'What about tourists?' asked Ruth. 'Do the local residents want more of us? Or are they resentful at the intrusion?'

'Oh no, not resentful at all,' exclaimed Donna. 'Attracting visitors from all over the world is what we hope will save us!'

She explained that, notwithstanding its own complications and occasional negative impact, tourism was seen as a possible way for everyone – locals and government – to make enough money to be in a position to reject the demands of multinational corporations.

That night, alone in her room and getting ready for bed, Ruth heard wolves howl in the darkness. She went to the window but could not see the animals; they must be far away, hiding out in the Accursed Mountains that she felt she knew so well from Bekim's manuscript. A huge moon hung in the navy sky, bathing the landscape in ethereal white light. Of course, Valbone was connected to the outside world, by the internet if not by fast roads, but Ruth could not escape the sense of having stepped into a bygone age where wild beasts still roamed and people lived by the sun, to a large extent, going to bed at dusk and getting up at dawn. She already believed herself more than a little in love with this remote, beautiful place.

The next day, fortified by a breakfast of bread, honey and yoghurt, Ruth and Zak set off on the half-day hike to his ancestral village. At first, the trail followed the river, and then gradually wound up and up through ever more spectacular landscapes of undulating countryside and high peaks. At the top of the path lay a pass that divided two valleys and from there the view opened out in all directions. Pine studded slopes fell away beneath pointed mountaintops; all looked pristine, entirely untouched by human hand.

At this highest point, the pair stopped for a break and some water. Zak appeared lost in thought and wandered off to stare out at the distant horizon. Ruth stood, captivated by the magnificence of the scene. It was akin to looking at creation in all its majesty and awe, as it had been for hundreds and thousands of years. On distant mountain peaks, snow still nestled in rocky nooks like white linen in a baby's cradle.

Majlinda's cradle, or Mia's, thought Ruth. Never mine. Never my own child's.

Melancholy descended upon Ruth for a brief moment. And then the sun emerged from behind a cloud, and a flush of brilliant light flooded the world. Bekim's words from the manuscript flashed through her mind. '*I must make a new life, too.*' Bekim had had that reality thrust upon him, at a time of huge upheaval, emotional distress and uncertainty about the future. But he had done it. He had lost the love of his life but found a new path to follow. If he had been able to rise to that challenge, at less than half Ruth's age and with none of her education and resources, then so could she.

Sunshine gleamed all around, soaking into the depths of Ruth's being. Deep within herself, she felt something shift, some indefinable change taking place in what she had come to believe was the truth. Suddenly, she understood that she didn't need a baby to be happy, or a partner. All she needed was to come to terms with the choices she had made, to own them, and to do her best to live a good life. The revelation was both profound and profoundly simple and Ruth could hardly believe it had never occurred to her before.

As they struck out again across the pass, Ruth realised she would never look at life the same way again. Reading Bekim's story, being given the chance to help out by finding Hannelore for him, had changed everything. It felt like a second chance and she would grasp it with both hands.

Chapter Twenty-Nine

It was an easy walk downhill from the pass to the village, which basked in all its breathtaking loveliness under the summer sun. Everything was green and burgeoning with fecundity: tall maize stems already heavy with cobs, wheat ripening in sun-dappled fields, knobbly emerald apples clustered on low-hanging branches of ancient fruit trees. Between the houses, washing fluttered on lines and chickens pecked at the grass.

Aged villagers, to all of whom Zak called out a greeting, stooped low over their crops, weeding and gathering or working the soil with hoes and trowels, while songbirds flitted by overhead, darting from branch to branch, descending every now and again to pluck a morsel from the turned earth. Haystacks of various shapes and sizes dotted the meadows, reminding Ruth of the photos in the Marubi museum. With their peculiarities and idiosyncrasies, they were like residents in their own right and as such, Ruth felt they should have names. A tall thin one with a lopsided top was definitely an Alfie, whilst a pair of smaller ones beside him must be Susan and Sukie…

She was jolted back to reality by Zak coming to a halt and pointing at a gorgeous ancient stone cottage that looked as old as the hills surrounding it.

'We're home,' he said simply, and even though Ruth knew it never had been his home as he'd never actually lived there, she understood completely what he meant.

Inside, the thick walls kept out the heat and it was welcomingly cool. Ruth happily divested herself of both her rucksack and her walking boots, and slipped on a pair of flip-flops, always her favourite form of footwear. Zak's sister was not around, either off visiting a neighbour or working in their veg patch located a short walk away in a field that led down to the river.

'You'll meet Albana later. In the meantime, I'll show you around the village,' Zak suggested.

They both had a long drink of cool water that, Zak said, came from their very own spring, before venturing back out into the heat. On every path, behind every wall, grinning down from every tree, Ruth felt that she could see Zak's dad, the young Bekim, grinning cheekily at them, full of life and energy, unaware of the trouble on the horizon, the traumas war would throw at them all. They went first to the tiny church, its steeple dwarfed by the soaring mountain peaks rising up behind it.

'I hadn't realised that some Albanians are Christian,' mused Ruth. 'If I'd ever thought about it at all, I would have believed the whole country to be Muslim.'

'Well, most people are,' agreed Zak. 'But that's because of the long Turkish occupation of the country centuries ago. In the more populated areas, people converted to Islam. But up here, many didn't bother to change and no one bothered to make them. These mountain villages were too remote to matter. Hence a legacy of Christianity still remains.'

Next, they went to the blood feud tower, its small, high window at the very top the only way for its long-gone inhabitants to keep in touch with the outside world.

'Just imagine being incarcerated here for five, ten years or more,' breathed Ruth, after they'd climbed the steep, winding staircase to the tiny living quarters.

Zak shook his head. 'I can't. But these feuds – they still exist. There are over fifty families in the Shkodra region alone where people are living "in blood". Many of them are children who must be prisoners in their homes for fear of going out. They cannot attend school, and their parents cannot work. It's truly shocking.'

Ruth sighed. 'You've told me about the ancient lores of the Kanun and it seems noble, valiant and proud somehow. But the reality is quite different, of course.'

'We should always keep our ancestral moral values,' responded Zak. 'But during the communist years, when the Kanun was suppressed, the correct interpretation of its codes was lost, and since its revival aspects of it have become anarchic. In my opinion, a modern state should live by modern laws and the Kanun belongs in the archives.'

Leading the way down the staircase, Ruth was glad to get back out into the open. They walked down to the river which cut a silver course through the valley floor, its pure, gleaming ripples reflecting the blazing sun, and Ruth soon forgot about the bloodthirsty elements of Albania's past and present. It was hard to imagine anything sullying the beauty and tranquillity that reigned here. They sat down in the shade of a lone beech tree and listened to the water burbling by.

'*I forgot about the rest of the world, and there seemed no reason why I should ever return,*' Ruth said, quoting the words of the formidable Edith Durham on one of her sojourns into the Accursed Mountains. Looking around her, at this place that seemed to exist in some parallel universe to the real world, she added, 'Now I understand exactly what she meant.'

She felt sleepy after the last couple of days of travelling and the hiking, lulled into a trance by the singing of the river, the bees buzzing past, the soporific heat. Her eyelids gently closed.

Ruth wasn't sure if she had dozed off for seconds or minutes when a gentle pat upon her shoulder woke her.

'Come,' said Zak, his voice full of solicitous kindness. 'We should get you back to the house where you can rest properly. It's been a tiring couple of days.' He stood, and held his arms out towards her. 'Here, let me help you up.'

His hands were dry and firm as he guided her to her feet. Holding them, Ruth felt grounded, secure. Once she was upright, he released her left hand but, just for a moment longer than was necessary, retained her right.

'Albana will probably be home by now,' Zak said, as they made their way along the dusty track back to the house. 'So get ready to do some serious eating – my sister is as much of a feeder as my mother is!'

Ruth uttered a playful groan. 'Honestly, thank goodness I brought my running shoes with me. I'm going to have to seriously get back on my exercise wagon or the consequences of this trip are not going to be pretty, at least as far as my waistline is concerned.'

Zak laughed. 'You have nothing to worry about,' he said. 'And I promise you that you won't be able to resist Albana's spinach and cheese pastries. They are second to none.'

Albana, like Zak's parents, was not only delightful but delighted to see her brother and Ruth. She showered them with questions that came so fast Ruth didn't have time to answer them and Zak couldn't keep up with the translation.

They ate supper at a table in the garden, surrounded by rampant buddleia and oleander bushes. The air fizzed with insects and Ruth was transported to a long-ago childhood in rural Norfolk, before widespread pesticide use and monoculture in crop growing reduced Britain's bug population to a fraction of what it had been.

Zak explained that few villagers stuck out the winter at this altitude anymore. Most retreated to Shkodra or Tirana, only returning in the spring to plant their crops, repair their houses, and cater for the embryonic tourist trade. Before the first snows, those who intended to stay stockpiled everything they'd need, from socks to cigarettes, and hoped they'd last until the thaw came in four, five or sometimes even six months' time.

When the meal was over, Zak poured them all a small glass of home-distilled rakia. 'Fortification,' he joked, as they toasted each other and downed the fiery liquid in one, as tradition dictated.

'For what?' asked Ruth, almost choking at the strength of the alcohol.

'For tomorrow,' answered Zak. 'I've got some news – I was keeping it until after the walk because I didn't want to hurry. I just wanted us to enjoy it at a leisurely pace.'

'Well, go on then!' exclaimed Ruth. 'Don't keep me in suspense.'

Albana laughed in a way that told Ruth she was in on the secret. Though she didn't speak much English, she understood a lot of what she heard.

Zak drummed his fingers on the table as if searching for the right words. 'It's the artefacts,' he revealed, eventually. 'Dad remembered the missing information. He still can't recall exactly *what* the objects are – but he knows *where* they are. And that is in the caves.'

'The caves?' repeated Ruth, incredulous. 'But why? What on earth are they doing there?'

'Because of the political situation, my father was unable to return the items to the Frankls,' explained Zak, in a calm and measured voice that belied the emotion he felt. 'No communication with the outside world was allowed, and even to possess the address of someone foreign could have you imprisoned as an agent of propaganda, a spy or traitor. The items remained stashed in the family home until Hoxha banned religion of any kind. At that moment, it became too dangerous for the artefacts to stay where they were, due to their religious nature. But of course getting rid of them couldn't be countenanced. So Bekim came here, to the village, and then went on up to the caves and buried them there. He's given me an idea of the location. So, at daybreak tomorrow, I'm going to fetch them.'

He reached across the table and laid his hand upon Ruth's. For a moment she felt ridiculously self-conscious. Apart from anything else, Albana was watching. But after only a few seconds, the feeling subsided and it came to feel natural. Normal.

'Will you join me? Another sojourn into the wilderness, if you haven't had enough already.'

'Of course not!' The words blurted out before Ruth realised how they sounded. 'I mean, of course I haven't had enough. I'll definitely come. Try stopping me.'

They all laughed and Ruth felt so at home, so comfortable in the presence of Zak and Albana, here beneath the wide Albanian sky where the stars shone so brightly.

That night, Ruth lay under the eaves in her attic bedroom, and thought of Bekim. So much responsibility was thrust upon him when he was still so young, bringing the refugees here and making sure they were kept fed even when resources were stretched so thin as to be barely there. And then, when even this remote village became too dangerous, escorting them further up into the mountains, lying outside the cave night after night whilst wolves prowled the snow-covered expanses of emptiness, and waiting for the soldiers to come.

He must have been so scared, Ruth imagined, and so desperately lonely. For despite being surrounded by people, he had to raise himself above them, their vulnerability and terror, and make himself invincible. That was a big ask for anyone, let alone a teenage boy with minimal education.

It was a wonder that he had done it and that they had all survived.

Chapter Thirty

Before going to sleep, Ruth had used the weak internet connection to check her emails, and she briefly did so again upon waking. She'd followed up so many leads and searched more and more remote corners of the web in her attempts to track Hannelore down. She knew that, if Hannelore was out there still, she would find her eventually. But Bekim's time was limited, his lung cancer advancing mercilessly day by day. Ruth was constantly plagued by fears that her efforts would not come to fruition in time – and her latest trawls did nothing to allay those fears. There was still no news.

Dressing quickly, Ruth tried to stop herself worrying about where she should look for Hannelore next. She and Zak had something else to track down today: the artefacts. Zak had already been up for an hour, and when he took Ruth outside after a swift breakfast, she saw why. Tethered to the fence, tails swinging, manes blowing in the breeze, were two chestnut horses that Zak had already fetched from a neighbour.

'What!' Ruth baulked at the sight; she'd never been near a horse in her entire life, let alone actually sat on top of one.

Zak took one look at her face and burst out laughing. 'Honestly, it'll be fine,' he assured her. 'These nags are docile as anything. But it's a long way and we have to get there and back during daylight. This is the best method of transport, I promise you.'

After an undignified scramble to get into the saddle, which required a hefty leg up from Zak, Ruth found herself precariously seated on her mount. Gingerly, she picked up the reins the way Zak showed her.

'What do I do now?' she wailed, helplessly. This was ridiculous. What on earth was she doing in the Albanian Alps, miles from anywhere that might remotely be described as civilisation, let alone anywhere that might contain anything useful like a hospital or even a doctor, on a horse of all things? 'Zak, help!'

But Zak was still chortling away as if this was the best joke ever, and when Ruth caught his eye she couldn't help but laugh too. What better place to be on an August morning but here in this glorious place, surrounded by beauty and breathing the fresh mountain air, free as a bird?

'OK,' she said. 'You win. I'm going to channel my inner Calamity Jane and I'll be fine. Whip crack away!'

Zak gently urged his mount forwards. 'Mine is called Oli by the way, and yours is Pepi – she'll just follow us. There's nothing to worry about at all. Just don't sing – that might frighten the horses!'

'You beast!' called out Ruth as Pepi stepped out behind Oli. 'You've never even heard me sing. I might be Norfolk's answer to Taylor Swift for all you know.'

They were both still bellowing with laughter when they passed the last village house and began to follow the river's course to the head of the valley. It took two hours of steady upward toil to reach the caves and Ruth was heartily grateful that it was Pepi taking the strain and not her. They moved through a majestic landscape of magnificent karst mountains studded with gargantuan limestone boulders. Wild grasses rippled in the gentle breeze like waves across a green sea and wispy clouds hung in an azure sky. They passed a lake, shrunk back from its edges now at the height of summer but still darkly deep, their stately progress reflected on its glassy surface.

'Is that the lake where Bekim fell through the ice?' asked Ruth, excitedly.

'The very same,' concurred Zak. 'I shudder to think about what could have happened. My dad has nine lives but he definitely lost one of them then.'

Soon after, they emerged from a narrow gully into a sheltered dip fringed by high peaks. Zak stopped his horse and Pepi obediently halted next to him.

'Here we are,' said Zak.

Ruth looked around her. There was absolutely nothing to be seen, no sign of anywhere that could house a party of refugees through an alpine winter.

Zak flicked his head. 'Come on. I'll show you.'

He dismounted and came over to help Ruth down. Her legs wobbled as her feet hit the ground and she felt the ache in her knees and buttocks, but other than that she seemed to have survived the ride. Zak took a stake from his saddlebag and tethered the horses, then looked at her expectantly. 'So, where do you think the cave is?'

Ruth shook her head and raised her arms helplessly. 'I've got absolutely no idea. Are you sure we're in the right place?'

Laughing, Zak took her hand and led her forwards. Surprised, and trying not to feel self-conscious, Ruth folded her fingers around his palm. His grasp was firm, keeping her upright as she stumbled over rocks that protruded at various heights across the valley floor. Still there was nothing to reveal the cave's whereabouts.

Until suddenly, there it was right in front of them, the entrance a stark gash in the rock, a fissure beyond which darkness lay.

Zak pulled a torch out of his pocket and turned it on. As they entered the cave, Ruth gripped his hand a little tighter and stayed as close behind him as she could. A short passageway opened out into a large cavern, the torch's narrow beam of light sending shadows leaping in the blackness beyond.

'He said it was here somewhere,' Zak murmured, throwing the torchlight into a corner behind a jutting piece of rock. 'The place where he buried the objects.'

Ruth strained her eyes in the darkness. She could hardly make anything out. 'I hope he got it right,' muttered Zak, the contours of his face exaggerated by the sparse illumination of the torchlight. 'He's been very vague all along. It was so long ago, after all. He's riven with guilt that he forgot about the items, that he didn't make attempts to return them as soon as he could, as soon as Hoxha was ousted. He promised Hannelore he'd look after them, you see. He'd given her his *besa*.'

Despite the dim light, Ruth saw tears shimmering in Zak's eyes. She remembered what he had told her about *besa*, about how dedication to the bonds it entailed ran deep in Albanian veins. No wonder Bekim cared so much about finding the artefacts; he could not go peacefully to the next life without having fulfilled his promise. It spoke of the power of this ancient tradition, and also of the profundity of the relationship between him and Hannelore. He had loved her so much, thought Ruth, a love beyond measure.

The torchlight flickered on a spot tucked between the curves of the cave walls.

'My father tried to erase the very existence of the items from his memory during the time when even knowing about them was dangerous. Then, when it was all right again, he couldn't quite get the memory back. But it's hardly surprising, given what happened to...' He faltered, unable to carry on.

'After what happened to who?' questioned Ruth gently, sensing that this was going to be one of Zak's greatest revelations.

Zak heaved a huge, shuddering sigh. 'Altin and my grandfather Gezim, Bekim's father, were both executed by the regime. Summary justice, the death penalty without trial. We still don't know what they were accused of. We'll never know.' It was as if the blank obscurity of the cave had enabled Zak to articulate something that daylight would not allow him to. 'They survived the war, taught my father to be a man, and then they were brutally slain by evil rulers who made a mockery of everything they had ever fought for or believed in.'

Ruth was stunned, too shocked to speak. This was the truth that Zak had come so close to revealing before, at the museum and right back during their first meal. He had been unable to say the words then and, now that he had, the tears were flowing down his cheeks. Ruth's fell too, in commiseration. She wanted to take him in her arms and hug him close to assuage the pain that he clearly felt so keenly. No wonder he was committed to doing everything he could for Bekim before he, too, was lost to him forever.

'I'm so sorry,' she whispered. 'I had no idea. Though I knew Hoxha was a tyrant, I didn't realise the extent of the brutality.'

Zak wiped the back of his hand roughly across his face. 'It's OK. Why would you know? But thank you for caring.' He raised the torch, which he had let drop, and refocused it on a patch of earthy soil amongst the rocky ground. 'Right,' he said, his voice achieving a tone of forced efficiency. 'I think it might be here.'

Pulling a trowel from his back pocket, he knelt down and began to dig.

'Here,' said Ruth, 'let me hold the torch. And I can take over if you get tired.'

She directed the beam to Zak's hands as he dug and dug. She didn't know whether to go back to the subject of the executions but thought that surely there must be a way to find out the truth.

'Were no records kept?' she asked tentatively, as she watched his even, rhythmic movements. 'Nothing opened up once Hoxha had died? And what did he die of, anyway?' she added, the thought suddenly occurring to her.

Zak paused for a moment, sitting back on his heels. It was cool inside the cave but perspiration glimmered on his forehead.

'There was no great Ceauşescu moment – our dictator died of diabetes. And yes, there are files, those of the Sigurimi, the secret police. But they have only recently been opened and much information is missing so we don't hold out a lot of hope of finding their bodies or knowing exactly what happened to them. Many, many people – thousands – died in the labour camps or were murdered.'

With these words, Zak fell silent. Ruth couldn't think of anything to say. Words seemed inadequate, irrelevant. She hoped Zak could feel the sympathy she had for him and his forebears.

Zak resumed his digging. Eventually, the point of the metal trowel hit something hard.

'It's either a rock — or it's what we're looking for,' he breathed, clearing the soil away with his hands. Reaching down, he fastened his grip around the object and wrenched it out. After a few heaves, it came free of its muddy hiding place. Zak placed it onto the cave floor and it sat there between them, an old, pockmarked wooden box, chipped and worn at the edges.

'Let's take it outside,' he said curtly. The weight of expectation was clearly taking a toll on his nerves.

On the threshold of the cave they paused, pupils contracting with the sudden hit of fierce sunlight. Once their eyes had adjusted to the brightness, they ventured forth. Zak placed the box on top of a large, flat stone and contemplated it for a moment.

'Here goes,' he said, his voice heavy with emotion. He lifted the wooden lid, which opened surprisingly easily given how old it was and how long it had remained buried in the damp earth. After so many decades, the mystery of the artefacts was about to be revealed.

Slowly and carefully, Zak lifted out an object wrapped in a cloth that frayed into fragments as he disturbed it. Within its folds was a book, the Torah or Hebrew Bible, riddled with damp and age, the paper pages stuck together with damp, the ink smudged to illegibility. But still there, still recognisable. Next were the remnants of a tallit, or prayer shawl. It had disintegrated to almost nothing, just a few strands of thread remaining. Last, and the only item still intact, was a silver Menorah, tarnished black through lack of use and polish.

'A Hanukkah candlestick,' breathed Ruth. 'A beautiful one. I thought this might be one of the treasures.'

'It's in the book, isn't it?' murmured Zak. 'How Bekim spent Hanukkah with the Frankls, saw the candles lit, participated in their rituals. He would have known how much it meant to the family.'

Ruth smiled and laid her hand on his sympathetically. 'We'll get it back to them, whoever still remains. I promise I won't give up until I've found Hannelore or her relatives. I give you my *besa*.'

Zak picked up her hand and squeezed it, then raised it to his mouth and planted a kiss upon it. His lips were cool and firm against her skin and his touch sent tingles down her spine. Ruth was suddenly conscious of how close they were, and how she had just shared a momentous occasion with him. For a moment, there was silence, just the sun glinting off the pale rock upon which the ancient objects lay, and the air heavy and still with expectation.

And then one of the horses whinnied and a gust of wind sent fragments of the prayer shawl flying and Zak let go of Ruth's hand as he dashed to pick up the pieces. Ruth realised she'd been holding her breath in anticipation – but of what, exactly? She couldn't say. She knew in her heart of hearts that there was nothing more than friendship between her and Zak, and that she was kidding herself to imagine anything more. And yet… Increasingly she had begun to think – maybe. Maybe he had some of the same feelings for her that she had for him.

Carefully, Zak picked everything up and put it back in the box. He'd brought a small backpack to carry anything they found back home. Stowing the box inside it, he hefted it onto his shoulders, and together he and Ruth walked to the horses and untethered them.

They rode home without talking, arriving in the village just as the sun was beginning its slow descent behind the mountains. Leaving the animals with their owner, Vjosa, they walked the short way back to the house, Ruth determinedly trying not to show how much her thighs, calves, knees and bottom ached. But of course, Zak noticed.

'Are you all right?' he questioned her with a smile, nodding down at her lower limbs.

Ruth grimaced. 'Not really. I mean, I've never ridden a horse before and today I've done it for five hours, using muscles I didn't know I possessed. What I wouldn't give for a hot bath with some essential oils.'

Zak laughed. 'I can offer you a brisk swim in a very cold river,' he rejoined, 'but a bath I cannot do. But seriously, I hope you're not too sore?'

Ruth shook her head. 'No, I'm fine. Just exaggerating to attract sympathy. A shower and a stiff drink will do me fine.'

But as they approached the house, Albana came flying out, hands raised in distress. 'Zak,' she cried. 'I've had a call from mum. Dad's taken a turn for the worse. We need to get back down to Shkodra as soon as possible.'

Ruth's blood ran cold in her veins at the sight of Zak's face. Fear was etched in his furrowed brow and narrowed eyes, and in the ghostly pallor that instantly settled upon his tanned complexion.

Over a quick cup of tea while Zak and Albana gathered together what they'd need, it was arranged that Ruth would stay in the village to feed the chickens, shut them up at night and collect the eggs while they were gone.

'One or both of us will be back on Thursday anyway,' Zak told her. 'Albana's arranged to sort out something important with the bees then, so she has to be here. And you really don't want to come to Shkodra; we'll just be in the hospital or at various appointments, and you've seen all the sites.'

Ruth agreed. 'I'd much rather stay here,' she said. 'I'll feel that I'm helping out if I do that. In Shkodra I'd just be in the way. Plus, I don't want you worrying about me when you've got your dad to think about.'

'If you need anything, just go see VJ at the place we borrowed the horses,' called Zak, as he and Albana got into the jeep. Ruth waved as they sped off down the stony, unmade road, then she went back to the garden with a glass of wine and her book. She tried to read but couldn't settle, feeling nervous about what they would encounter in Shkodra or on their drive to get there. It would be getting dark soon, and she'd heard that the road was bad, potholed, narrow and hazardous, precipitous drops on all sides...

Stop worrying, she told herself sternly. Zak's done the journey countless times. He'll be fine.

Chapter Thirty-One

Next morning, Ruth was surprised to find that it was nine o'clock by the time she woke up. The ride and the mountain air, combined with the emotion of the day before, had exhausted her. She groaned as she stretched out her stiff legs and massaged her thighs. Going for a run was the last thing she really wanted to do right then but she couldn't bear to sit around the house with nothing to do but worry about Bekim. Later, she would continue the search for Hannelore but she had hours on her own to do that. She should go out now, before it got too hot, and get it over and done with.

Throwing back the sheet, she climbed out of bed and pulled on her running gear. Outside, it was a glorious day, the village basking lazily in the low sun, the freshness of the mountain air invigorating and revivifying. Ruth fed the chickens and let them out of their coop. Nestled in the straw of their nests, she found three white eggs, still warm. Gathering them up, she took them back to the house.

The eggs in the large earthenware bowl on the sideboard were all marked with their laying date and Ruth didn't want to break the system. Placing her finds by the sink, she poked around on the sideboard for a marker pen, picking up various bits of paper, an old newspaper and an envelope or two, in her search before finding one. Having successfully dated them, she added the eggs to the bowl and went over the whole chicken-keeping thing again. Maybe she could remould herself as an earth mother, after all.

She couldn't resist a quick check of her emails, but nothing new had arrived overnight. Trying not to feel despondent, Ruth drank a quick glass of water as she adjusted the laces of her running shoes. Forcing herself away from the laptop, she went out of the house and shut the door behind her. It felt strange not locking the door but apparently nobody did and in fact Zak hadn't even given her a key.

It's good for you, she told herself sternly, as she set off on her run, muscles protesting loudly. She took the route along the track that edged the river, her feet slipping slightly on the stones and pebbles. The beauty of the scenery took her mind off her aches and pains and eventually she got into her rhythm and began to enjoy her run. Though she had not intended to go far, she did not want to stop and kept pushing herself onwards. The goal of the half-marathon hung before her, spurring her to run further, providing the incentive to keep going. If she could manage thirteen miles here, in these mountains, she could surely do it anywhere.

She pressed on, feet flying over sun-hardened mud tracks, sweat pouring down her back. Eventually, beginning to get tired, she stopped for a breather. Ahead of her lay a pine wood that shrouded the lower slopes of a peak that rose majestically up behind the trees' green canopies. Keen for some shade, Ruth took a path that led under the sheltering branches. Here, the scent of pine needles suffused the air, along with the insistent singing of songbirds.

The winding path meandered and rambled, often crossing with others, gradually getting narrower and narrower. It traversed narrow streams and rivulets that sometimes Ruth had to jump across but over some of which had been laid planks or logs to serve as make-shift bridges. After a while, Ruth realised she'd gone much further than she had intended. Looking around, the trees seemed to close in before and behind her, leaving her unsure about exactly which way she had come. Her breathing quickened as anxiety rose within her. For a few moments, she felt panicked, tears smarting in her eyes. Clenching her fists and forcing herself to keep calm, she continued onwards. She must surely reach a village or a house soon.

She didn't.

Instead, the footpath just ran on and on, ever upwards. It must lead somewhere, Ruth thought, as it was clearly in regular usage, the undergrowth and tree branches cut back for ease of movement. Every now and again, the imprint of a small hoof in the mud bore testament to regular use by pack animals, as did the occasional pile of dung swarming with flies. But there was absolutely no sign of human life.

In the distance, a dog barked and Ruth's heart leapt. A domesticated animal might mean a settlement, or at least an owner, a person she could get directions from. But then the bark turned into a warning bay, long and guttural, and Ruth shuddered. A guard dog? It sounded far away, but how far? She glanced over her shoulder, terrified it might be about to leap out of the bushes and attack her for invading its territory. And if not a dog, maybe a wolf – she'd heard them already, in Valbone. Or a bear. Ruth really didn't want to meet either. She ploughed on, more slowly and cautiously now, on her guard.

And then suddenly, without warning, the woodland abruptly ended and opened out into a clearing. Ruth's eyes contracted in the bright sunlight. Once they'd grown accustomed to the glare, she looked around. She was on the edge of a large field that was thickly planted with large, luscious plants that, judging by their health and vigour, were well tended for. She took a step forward. And then stopped short, realisation gradually dawning. This was not any old crop, not wheat or potatoes or maize. Ruth knew exactly what these were.

Cannabis plants.

Hundreds of them, robustly tall and lush and strong in the blazing sun.

Fear plucked at Ruth's belly and sweat broke out on her brow. She had forgotten her running cap and the beating sun broiled her brains. This wasn't some cottage industry; this was cannabis cultivation on an industrial scale, which, as Zak had explained to her, back in the cosy safety of Santa Maria del Mare, apparently was rife in the hidden nooks and crannies of the mountains.

Dumbfounded, as if drawn by some hidden force, Ruth stepped towards the plants, reaching out her hand to finger their flamboyant leaves, her gaze scanning the full extent of the plantation. The thought ran through her mind that it was like that scene in *The Beach*, when the backpackers find themselves face-to-face with both the cannabis and the trigger-happy guards. Ruth gulped. Her breath was coming fast and sharp, catching at her throat. She forced herself to take long, slow, calming draws of air; she was being stupid and melodramatic.

Retreating a few paces, she noticed a pile of jerry cans heaped up under the trees and dark stains of water around the base of the plants. It was clear that they had been recently watered. Someone was putting a lot of work into this crop, that much was plain. And plain also was the fact that they would be unlikely to welcome her presence here.

A noise, like the sharp snap of a broken branch, set her heart beating piston-like against her chest. An animal? But what kind? Terror seared through Ruth's veins and she waited, poised to run if she heard it again.

But there was only silence. It banged in her ears, loud as a musical crescendo.

Cautiously, wishing herself invisible, Ruth crept back towards the sheltering canopy of the trees. Every footstep, every rustle of fallen leaves beneath her feet, was loud as a drum roll. She could feel her own pulse, her blood pumping furiously around her body, preparing for fight or flight.

Another sound, deafening, sharp and harsh, rent the air.

For a second, Ruth couldn't think what it was, couldn't place the noise. Thunder? A storm? And then it came again, the crack of an explosion, shattering the tension all around. Ruth's heart skipped a beat.

Gunshot.

Her legs were liquid, shaking and weak. She fell against a lichened tree trunk, hugging it for stability and support. She had to get out of here – and fast. Struggling to collect herself, she thrust herself through a clearing in the undergrowth, found the path and fled. She ran, as fast as she could, her breath coming in great, heaving sobs. Eventually, lungs on fire, she could run no further. Stumbling to a halt, she sank to her knees, retching and whimpering, exhausted and terrified.

The realisation struck her with full force. She had wandered off the path, Red Riding Hood or Hansel and

Gretel style, and come across not a wolf or a wicked witch but something bad, something evil. Someone had used a gun to warn her off, might even have been trying to shoot her. They would probably follow her; they might be behind her right now.

And she had no idea how to get home. Dragging herself to her feet, summoning all her energy, Ruth ran on, continuing downhill, hoping that eventually she would arrive somewhere recognisable. Emerging from the wood, she looked around her. Nothing seemed familiar and she didn't have time to stop and get her bearings; the people guarding the cannabis fields might be right behind her.

Striking out, she chose a direction at random. Anything was better than staying still, making herself a sitting target. Out of the corner of her eye, she saw a movement. Gazing intently towards it, a flush of relief suffused her body. A small group was approaching, a few people along with donkeys or mules, pack animals loaded down with luggage. They must be tourists on some 'wild camping' trek, Ruth assumed, and paused, panting for breath, waiting for them.

She could ask the way back to the village, perhaps beg them for some water, because stupidly she had brought none with her and was desperately thirsty. Running her tongue around her dry mouth she cursed her lack of foresight. Where did she think she was? In the benign lanes of Norfolk, or the harsh Albanian Alps? They weren't called the Accursed Mountains for nothing. She narrowed her eyes to scrutinise the group more clearly. But instead of continuing towards her, the procession had halted, and snippets of an animated conversation – or a row – drifted towards Ruth in the still air.

Wondering what was going on, she deliberated for a moment. Should she approach or wait for them to draw nearer to her? Eventually, as their argument showed no sign of abating, she decided on the former and started off at a slow jog. She was a few metres away when one of the darkly dressed figures detached itself from the others and stood, blocking her path. For a moment, Ruth thought his approach was friendly. And then, with a hideous jolt of shock, she saw what he had in his hands and what he was now pointing at her.

A gun. A big one, a rifle or some sort of hunting weapon.

Ruth faltered, stumbled, almost fell. Her heart was in her mouth at the same time as her mind seemed unable to fully take in what was happening. The man advanced, shouting, waving the gun, making a wild gesture with his arm that indicated that Ruth should clear off, and fast.

Paralysed, Ruth's mouth goldfished helplessly. She wanted to say that she was sorry, that she'd go, but please don't shoot. But no words would come out. And even if they had, the man probably would not have understood.

Finally, she came to her senses, her limbs obeying her instructions to flee. She ran. With no idea where she was going and her pulse racing out of control, she ran as far and as fast as she could. When the man had raised his gun at her, he definitely hadn't been joking.

A jumble of emotions swirled around her mind. Gradually, a piece of Zak's information crystallised. He had said that, as well as infiltrating Italy, another way the drug runners got their goods into Europe was via Montenegro, using little-known, hardly used mule trails over the mountains. The animals she had seen had been heavily laden and the men accompanying them rough and tough-looking individuals. A drug smuggling gang? It seemed highly likely.

Shit, shit, shit, thought Ruth, her heart pounding, her breath now coming in uneven rasps with the exertion. She'd definitely never run as fast as this before, nor as far, she reflected ironically. Contemplating when it might be safe to slow down a bit, she glanced over her shoulder. The group was no longer in sight. Immediately, her pace reduced and she was about to stop when, in a matter of moments, the ground came up to hit her.

Winded, Ruth lay sprawled on the stony path, dazed by the suddenness and impact of her fall. She blinked, trying to clear her head and then cried out loud as a sharp, savage jolt of pain shuddered through her body. Trying to move, she was floored by another jag of agony which brought her out in a cold sweat.

Bloody hell, bloody, bloody hell. She'd twisted her ankle, maybe broken it. Not paying attention to the uneven surface, she'd caught her toe on a protruding rock and gone head over heels. Inspecting her arms, she saw that her right elbow was shredded, the skin ripped right off, blood seeping forth. Her knees too, were clearly cut, but she couldn't see them properly as she was lying on her front and it hurt too much to move. Folding one hand across the other, she let her forehead rest upon them and emitted a long, low groan.

Here she was, alone and injured, in the Accursed Mountains, which were now well and truly living up to their name, far from anywhere. To make matters even worse; no one – least of all herself – knew where she was. Fumbling in the phone pocket in the side of her running shorts, she pulled out her mobile. This was her only chance of being found. Praying for a signal, Ruth pressed the home button. The screen went from black to the familiar picture on her home page, herself on an assignment for her news programme. As she felt for the emergency call button, her eyes registered something terrible. The battery symbol was red, the number reading one per cent. Shit! It hadn't charged up last night; she'd plugged it into the charger but it clearly hadn't had power and was now all but dead. Frantically, she pressed the button. For a brief moment, the phone indicated that it was dialling. And then it went dead, the screen darkening, the phone dying in her hand.

Ruth let it drop to the ground and lay her head back down. She was done for. It was all over. She was here, far from anywhere, unable to move, with neither food nor water, the hot sun burning into her skin. The horrific but perfectly plausible fact that she would die here drifted across her mind. And there was nothing she could do about it.

Chapter Thirty-Two

A tiny trickle of water crept over a bed of white stones. Ruth cupped her hands and attempted to scoop some up. Capturing a small handful, she raised it to her mouth and gulped it down, desperation erasing all thoughts of hygiene or contamination from her mind. She repeated the motion multiple times until her thirst was somewhat slaked. The water didn't look clean and there was barely any of it. But it might be the difference between life and death.

Somehow, groaning and wincing in agony, Ruth had dragged herself onwards, commando crawling, until she found both the minuscule brook and a tree to provide some shade. Now she'd stopped again, her ankle burnt and throbbed with excruciating pain that radiated upwards and through her entire body. She knew she should continue, keep going until perhaps she happened across someone working in the fields, a shepherd guarding a flock, perhaps even a farmhouse. But looking around her, seeing the emptiness that lay in all directions, she didn't hold out much hope for any of these. And if she pressed on, made herself even more exhausted and riddled with agony, would she have achieved anything?

As if all of this wasn't enough, there were still the drug-smugglers to contend with. What if they returned? What if they sent someone to find her, the foreigner who'd intercepted them, the person who might talk? Tears pricking behind her eyes, Ruth forced herself to be strong. She could not afford to give in to self-pity, to give up. She knew, had read in numerous stories of triumph over disaster, that the thing that kept people going in the direst circumstances was hope. It was what had spurred Bekim on when facing so many challenges. It was what she needed to cultivate and to rely upon.

But hope was hard to find as the sun climbed ever higher in the sky and the heat intensified. At first, Ruth had been hungry, but now thirst overrode everything. She lapped at some more of the muddy water. God knew what disease she was going to catch from it, but if it kept her going for a little longer, it was worth the risk.

Eventually, appalled by her lack of action, Ruth attempted to crawl on. But the pain was so intense that she could not continue. Think of that man who cut his own leg off with a penknife and kept going, she railed at herself. But it was no good. She was not that strong, not that tough, not that resilient.

If she stayed where she was, she had this tiny amount of water, and the shade of the tree. It didn't seem wise to leave these and end up completely in the open. She took her phone out, tried to turn it on again in the vain hope that it had somehow regained some battery life, but it was stone dead.

Hours passed. At times Ruth felt positive that someone would find her, at others, despairing. But most of the time she just blamed herself for being so unutterably stupid as to run so far, taking nothing useful with her and telling no one where she was going. Admittedly, there'd been no one to tell. But she could have passed by VJ's house and asked him to keep an eye out for her return. As soon as she thought this, Ruth scoffed at herself. She would never had done that; it would have made her feel ridiculous, like a child unable to look after herself.

'But you can't look after yourself,' the internal voice chided her. 'You're a bloody stupid idiot who doesn't deserve to be rescued after acting so foolishly.'

As the heat of the afternoon built, Ruth's remaining energy evaporated. Despite the unrelenting throbbing of her ankle and the aching of her knees and elbow, she slept.

When her eyes flickered open, it was to the gathering dusk, the sky above a deep shade of purple tinged with umber. A whole day had passed, and now it was early evening. She wondered if Zak would have tried calling her. She was sure he would have. Apart from anything else, he'd have known that she'd be waiting to hear about Bekim. And he would probably have wanted to find out if she'd got anywhere nearer to finding Hannelore. Plus, Albana would be fretting about the chickens and whether she was looking after them properly. At this thought, Ruth groaned anew. The chickens! She'd let them out but wasn't there to put them back in the coop. They'd probably all have been eaten by a fox by the time anyone found them. Albana's precious brood, destroyed because of Ruth's idiocy.

Suddenly it was all too much to bear and Ruth began to cry, fat, salty tears streaming over her hot, sunburnt cheeks. If she wasn't crying for herself, she was crying for Albana's chickens. She thought of her mother, back home in Norfolk, with no idea of what was happening to her daughter. In the haste of leaving and amidst the search for Hannelore, Ruth had completely neglected to inform her mother that she was visiting Albania; her mother thought she was safe and sound having a nice holiday in Puglia.

Not lying at death's door on a remote mountainside, surrounded by cannabis plantations and drug smugglers.

Ruth's sobs intensified.

She cried and cried until she was utterly spent, wrung out and exhausted. Starving hungry and desperately thirsty despite the river water, she drifted off again, fitful nightmares plaguing her attempts at slumber.

At one point, she jolted awake, sure that someone or something was watching her. Opening her eyes, she was confronted by the sight of another pair, glowing gold under the sparse light of a new moon. A fox, staring her out in the darkness.

Oh God, thought Ruth. *It's not Albana's chickens that are in danger of being devoured, it's me.*

She and the fox played an uneasy game of 'who blinks first' until suddenly, the fox dropped its tail, turned away and sloped off into the shadows. Once it was gone, Ruth almost felt regret. At least the creature had been company, proof that she wasn't the only thing alive out here.

Though in the middle of the bleak and shadowy night, that was scant comfort.

Chapter Thirty-Three

Morning dawned, the sky flushing pink and gradually turning to blue. There was a wind today, and white clouds scudded past. Ruth's eyelids fluttered but she could hardly open her eyes. She'd left her contact lenses in, for if she'd taken them out she'd have been additionally disabled by not being able to see her hand in front of her face. But the inevitable consequence was that her lids were gummed together, sore and painful, joining the soreness and pain of her ankle, knees and elbow, in fact the whole of her body, complaining loudly from both its injuries and the discomfort of a night lying on hard, stony ground.

Eventually, Ruth managed to coax her eyes open, rubbing a few drips of water into them and blinking in the milky light of sunrise. Her ankle pulsed unremittingly and her cuts stung. Uncleaned, they were probably getting infected. *I'll die of sepsis*, she thought, *if not of thirst and starvation*. She gave up trying to move and merely lay, inert and motionless.

The sun rose higher, its scorching rays relentlessly drenching the world. Minutes passed, or maybe hours, Ruth didn't know. She dozed, but thirst tearing at her throat and hunger gnawing at her stomach prevailed against true sleep. Time passed, but Ruth had no idea how much of it, no inkling about how long she'd lain there, helpless and hopeless. Until suddenly she became aware of the light dimming as if a shadow had passed before the sun. Was there someone there?

Before she'd mustered the strength to look up, a cacophony of voices shouting in Albanian was suddenly surrounding her. The drug farmers. The smugglers. They'd found her. She'd known they would. She ignored them. They could do what they liked with her. She could muster neither the energy nor the will to stop them.

And then someone was beside her, crouching down, laying a hand on her shoulder and saying, gently but insistently, 'Ruth. Ruth, are you OK? Ruth, speak to me. What happened?'

It took a second or two before Ruth's dehydrated, starved and terrified mind registered who the voice belonged to.

Zak. It was Zak, come to rescue her.

'Oh, God,' she muttered, her voice hoarse, her throat so dry she could hardly form the words. 'Zak, thank God you're here.' And then she stopped, unable to carry on.

Zak's voice again, speaking urgently and insistently in Albanian. She heard scuffling, and felt the ground vibrating with many footsteps. She should open her eyes, raise her head and see what was happening. But she couldn't be bothered.

'Ruth.' Zak again, in English. 'VJ is here. He's not a doctor but he's used to dealing with injuries. Where are you hurt?'

'Right ankle,' Ruth murmured. 'I think it's broken.'

'OK,' replied Zak, speaking slowly and cautiously. 'Ruth, this is going to hurt because we don't have any strong pain killers. Here's some water and some ibuprofen. It's the best we can do. And then VJ is going to strap the ankle to stabilise it until we can get you to a doctor.'

Ruth nodded, as much as she could with her head still lying on her hands. She fumbled in Zak's fingers for the painkillers and the water. As soon as she started to drink, her thirst kicked in, and she drank and drank, draining the bottle. When she'd finished, Zak took it from her.

'More,' she pleaded, feebly.

'Not now,' answered Zak. 'It'll make you sick if you drink too much in one go.' He said something in Albanian and Ruth was aware of someone else moving nearer. As VJ worked, she sweated and yelped with pain but she let him get on with it. He might not have been a doctor, but his touch was sure and firm, his hands working quickly and deftly. By the time he'd finished, the ibuprofen had kicked in and her head, courtesy of the water, begun to clear.

'Do you think you can try to sit up now?' asked Zak.

In reply, Ruth lifted her head and pushed herself up with her hands. They'd gone numb from being in the same position for so long and she shook them out as pins and needles assailed her. She rolled herself over and managed to sit.

'Oh dear,' said Zak, with a commiserating smile. 'You are a sorry sight.'

Ruth gave a short, ironic laugh. 'Thanks.' She sniffed and wiped her nose with her hand, rubbing off the grit and dirt that seemed to have lodged on her face, stuck to her dried tears of last night. 'But I'm sure you're right.'

'OK, so now we need to get you back down to the village. You obviously can't walk – so Toto is going to help you.'

'Who the hell is Toto?' asked Ruth. 'Pardon my French.'

Zak laughed. 'Over there,' he pointed.

Ruth's eyes followed the direction of his finger. 'You are joking, aren't you,' she exclaimed, as her gaze fell upon a stubborn-looking four-legged animal with a weird saddle contraption on its back. 'Do I not even merit a horse these days, just a donkey?'

Zak smothered a smile. 'It's a deluxe version!' he protested. 'A mule, not a donkey. Unfortunately, the horses are out on a five-day trek and Toto is all VJ had. But he'll get you home and the saddle means you don't have to put your ankle to the pain of sitting astride. It's an old one, designed especially for grand ladies such as yourself.'

At this, Ruth could not help but emit a feeble laugh. 'This is utterly ludicrous,' she said, in between fits of hysterical laughter. 'I nearly died out here and now I've got to ride home. Where's the bloody ambulance? What kind of country is this?'

Zak shook his head. 'If we'd known where you were, I would have called the Air Ambulance from Tirana, or even from Podgorica. But we had to find you first.'

'How did you do that?' Ruth questioned, wonderingly. 'I was beginning to doubt I'd ever be found.'

Zak gestured around him with a wide sweep of his arm that took in the band of amassed villagers. 'The community. Everyone young and fit enough for the walk downed tools and set out to help.'

Ruth sighed and reached out for his hand. 'Thank you so much for doing that. Thank everyone for me, please. I'm so grateful. And,' she added, mustering a brief smile, 'I'm joking about the mule. I don't care how I get home, as long as I get there. I'm just so glad you're here.'

Zak's fingers encircled her palm. 'I'm glad too,' he said softly. 'I can't even begin to tell you how worried I've been.'

The moment was palpable, the air still as their eyes locked.

'Help me up then,' interjected Ruth, to break the tension. 'I don't think I can do it on my own.'

Over the journey, Zak filled her in on how he'd tried calling and how, when by four o'clock in the morning he still hadn't managed to get through, he'd begun to panic. Bekim had stabilised under his doctor's care and was no longer considered to be in immediate danger, so Zak had woken Albana and they'd driven at the highest speed possible back to the village. Arriving to find the house empty and the chickens out – alive, thank goodness – Zak had put the search party into place.

As they arrived back in the village, the road was lined with a handful of residents, mostly octogenarians not able to go out with the rescuers, all waiting eagerly for the safe return of this hapless foreigner. They clapped as the little procession arrived and Ruth blushed under her sunburn.

She gave the onlookers a grateful wave. 'A triumphal return on an ass,' she quipped to Zak, walking beside her, a moment's playfulness emerging from her exhaustion.

'It's been done before,' rejoined Zak, swift as lightning.

And then he burst out laughing, Ruth joining in with some feeble chuckles that were all she had energy for.

Chapter Thirty-Four

Back at the house, Ruth managed to get a wash and brush up. She fell upon the meal Albana had prepared, feasting on eggs and homemade bread, pastries and fruit. Once they'd eaten, Zak gave her more painkillers and helped her gather together her stuff before helping her into the jeep.

'You lie down in the back,' he said. 'It'll be more comfortable for your ankle like that. I'm going to take you straight to the hospital. If it's broken, it'll need to be set and it might even need an operation. There's plenty of time for your food to go down though – it's a three-hour drive at the best of times, but it'll take us more like four as I'll have to go slow to spare you from some of the pain. And then there'll be the wait to see a doctor when we get there.'

'I hope it's not broken,' said Ruth.

Zak tutted reprovingly. 'We'll see what the doctors say, apart from, "what were you doing going out running on your own in such inhospitable terrain?"'

'Don't worry, Zak,' replied Ruth, wryly. 'They can't possibly say anything I haven't already chastised myself for.'

As they followed the road down, Ruth pondered her extreme good fortune at having been rescued, wincing at every switchback turn and bump over the potholed surface. From her prone position on the back seat, she could see white puffs of cloud hanging motionless in the midday sky. Every now and again they passed through a sparsely populated village, the sharply peaked Alpine roofs of farmhouses flashing by. At one point, Zak slowed to a near halt. Pushing herself up on her elbows, Ruth saw the obstruction: a herd of hardy, shaggy goats around which a mean-looking dog patrolled. The goatherd hove into view, eyes narrowed against the sun's glare, following his flock to new pastures. He took no notice of the jeep or its passengers.

Sinking back down, another wave of relief swept over Ruth. Thank goodness she was with Zak, who knew this road and these mountains like the back of his hand. She was safe. Eventually, she fell asleep, completely exhausted by the pain, the night spent out in the open, and her gratitude at being alive.

She woke up as they were pulling into the hospital car park.

'I thought I'd seen enough of this place for a while,' commented Zak drily, as he helped Ruth out.

'Sorry, sorry and sorry again,' sighed Ruth. 'I really am terribly sorry.'

Zak grinned at her. 'Don't worry, I'll cope. For you – nothing is too much trouble.'

Inside, the wait to see the doctor was not as bad as Ruth had feared.

'It's broken,' pronounced the doctor, displaying the X-rays on the light box. 'A small fracture, a bad sprain and a lot of swelling. It will heal itself – no need to operate – but you'll have to wear a cast and to rest it as much as possible for the next few days.'

'Thank you so much,' Ruth said. 'That's a huge relief.'

As they left the hospital, Zak turned to Ruth.

'I know you're tired,' he said, 'but I think I should take you back to Italy. Dad's all right for the moment, and you've probably had enough of Albania for a while.'

Ruth smiled gratefully. 'I actually would really like to get back there. I need my own space and if I stay with your parents, they'll feel that they have to look after me, and the last thing I want is to impose on them.' She hobbled on, working hard to get to grips with the crutch she'd been given. She thought of Bekim, whose ill-fated stint with the partisans had ended with a terribly damaged leg, and thanked her lucky stars that her injury was nowhere near as bad. It still had implications, though. 'But hang on a minute,' she ventured, worry making her voice tight and high, 'how will I manage the steps to the apartment with this?' She raised her booted foot and gave it a tiny waggle, the most she could manage with the pain and the boot's unwieldiness.

Zak frowned. 'I had thought of that,' he said. 'And I wondered if… I mean what I thought was… you could stay at my place? It's all on one level, just along the road from Caroline's, with a veranda overlooking the sea. Remember I showed it to you when we walked back from the marina. You could make yourself comfortable there. I promise I wouldn't intrude on your personal space; I'm out a lot of the time, anyway, at work, which will be busier than usual after I've been away for so long,' he added.

All sorts of ideas flashed through Ruth's mind on hearing Zak's suggestion. But above all else, it provided the perfect solution to her current dilemma. She didn't want to go home to the UK; she still had three weeks of her holiday left and she wanted to absorb the sunshine – once her current sunburn had subsided – and enjoy *la dolce vita* for a bit longer. When she went back to dreary

England, she had no idea what she was going to do so she wanted to put it off as long as possible.

'It's a deal,' she said simply. 'I'd love that.'

Zak booked an overnight passage on the ferry and once more, when Ruth was in her cabin, she fell fast asleep. Her experience had drained her. She was conscious of the fact that she still hadn't told Zak about the cannabis plantation and the sinister people she'd encountered on the mountainside. It all seemed too much effort just now. She'd do it when they got back.

But once they were sitting on Zak's veranda, drinking fresh lemonade and eating pizza, another distraction prevented Ruth from telling Zak the full story of her accident. She opened her laptop to find a new email in her inbox. As she began to read it she immediately let out a gasp.

'Oh my God,' she breathed. 'It's her, Zak. It's really her. I've found Hannelore!'

In a nanosecond, Zak was up and by her side, pulling up a chair to sit right next to her. Ruth expanded the email so that the words were large and easily readable on the small screen.

Dear Ruth, the email began.

> *This is Miriam Rosen here, Hannelore Rosen's daughter. I'm answering on her behalf as she's not very tech savvy and, at the age of eighty-eight, sometimes gets confused. But I can confirm that she is the person you're looking for. She was born Hannelore Frankl in Vienna in 1931 and fled to Albania with her parents and brother, David, in 1939, a short while after Kristallnacht.*
>
> *During my childhood, my mother spoke often of the Albanian family who sheltered them during*

their time in that country. She desperately wanted to contact Mr and Mrs Shehu, and especially their son Bekim, who she said had been such a special friend to her, as well a protector to them all. But it took a long time for them to get permission to leave Southern Italy and receive permits to enter America. When they finally got here, it was too late. Albania had closed down, and no communication was possible.

Over the years, my mother has frequently expressed regret about the lack of contact. I tried, two decades or so ago, after the fall of Hoxha's regime, to find out more. But by then Hannelore had forgotten all the Albanian she had ever known and we drew a blank. My father died around this time and at that point my mother lost heart for the search. Her brother, David, was also dead so it was only Hannelore left who remembered anything of that period and it gradually faded from her mind.

However, perhaps some greater force is at work because very recently my mother started asking about Bekim again. She said she had had a premonition that he was unwell, and there wasn't much time left. She told me that there were things still remaining in Albania that her father had left there and that she needed to fetch so that she could hand them on to me and my sister, and to our cousins, sacred heirlooms that were part of our family history.

And then, as if by some miracle, I received your email, forwarded on to me from the Jewish organisation that you contacted in Baltimore.

Please, do get back to me by phone or email whenever you are able to. And I hope I'm not being presumptuous, but I would like to ask you something: could I bring my mother to Albania, to meet Bekim and to collect these items — if, of course, he still has them after all this time? I'll understand if that is not the case, but we would still like to come, whilst Hannelore is fit enough to travel.

Kind regards and hoping for a positive answer,
Miriam Rosen

Zak read in silence, and then read again.

'That's incredible,' he uttered, still staring at the screen as if afraid that, if he took his eyes away, the email would dissolve and disappear. 'Absolutely amazing. I can't believe it. It's too good to be true.'

He turned to Ruth. 'We need to do it, straightaway. There's no time to lose.' He checked his watch. 'It's six a.m. there now. Is that too early to call?'

Ruth burst out laughing. 'I think it is! Plus, it's a Sunday; we should let her have a bit of a weekend lie-in.'

Zak slumped back into his chair and let out a hefty sigh. 'All right,' he conceded. 'But we'll phone in two hours, at eight. OK?'

'Deal.' Ruth got up and hobbled to the kitchen. 'Do you mind if I make coffee? For some inexplicable reason, I still feel tired. And,' she said, meeting Zak's gaze, 'I need to tell you something.'

Zak smiled nervously. 'OK.'

Ruth made the coffee and brought the mugs to the table. She fingered the glossy leaves of the lemon tree that stood in a pot beside the table, searching for the right words.

'Fire away,' Zak said, encouragingly, as soon as Ruth was sitting back down. He appeared as unruffled as ever, but Ruth thought she detected a wariness in his eyes.

'When I was on my run' she began, 'I came across something... well, something I didn't expect. A huge field of cannabis plants. Whilst I was trying to take it in...' she faltered, paused, rallied herself to carry on 'I couldn't see anyone but someone fired a gun. I ran away, but almost immediately, I came across some rather unsavoury characters. They had donkeys, or mules, whatever, loaded down with cargo of some kind. Drugs, I assume. They weren't very pleased to see me.' Her heart was thumping in her chest at the recollection of events on the mountain. 'They threatened me, and one had a rifle, which he pointed right at me. It was... well, I was scared. Terrified.'

'That's dreadful, Ruth.' His forehead was creased in anguish and his eyes narrowed in consternation. 'I can only imagine how frightened you must have been.'

'That's why I ran so fast that I fell and did my ankle in. Do you think they were drug smugglers? And do you think, when they know I saw them, that they'll come after me?'

Zak got up and went to lean on the veranda rail. The sea stretched out, the same impossible blue as ever. 'Firstly, I'm sure your suspicions that they were trafficking cannabis is correct – absolutely sure of it – but as to how much danger you were, or are, in? It probably wouldn't have been much consolation at the time, even if you had known, but as a European, they would have thought twice before harming you because of the likely consequences. And as to whether they would bother to try to find you again, of that I'm convinced there's no chance whatsoever. They will have forgotten you already, and they won't be worried about you finding them. No doubt they have some police in their pocket for protection in case anyone starts to investigate.'

Ruth shuddered. 'Well, that's good to know,' she breathed, with a heartfelt sigh of relief. 'As in, that there is unlikely to be a hit squad tracking me down.'

Zak turned to face her. 'I feel responsible, Ruth. I took you there and I exposed you to the risk. It just wasn't one I thought you were ever going to face.'

Ruth grimaced. 'No, Zak. Bumping into those guys was my fault and my fault alone.' She drank her coffee, thankful for its heat as chills broke out on her skin at the memory of their pursuit.

'I'm sorry for what you went through,' said Zak. 'I hope it won't put you off Albania for life.'

'Oh no, not at all!' cried Ruth. 'Just… well, it's good to have shared what happened. To have shared it with you.'

She paused, drank coffee, raised her eyes to Zak's. He held her in his steady gaze.

'I'm glad about that.' Zak's voice was weighty with emotion. 'Because I'm going to live there. I've made the decision to take early retirement from the factory and go back. To go home.'

'Gosh!' Ruth struggled not to gape open-mouthed at this revelation. 'What are you going to do there?' The answer to the question mattered, and Ruth wasn't entirely sure why. Except that she liked Zak being here in Italy. Being somewhere familiar, where she could easily stay in touch with him. Because more and more, and especially since the rescue, she simply couldn't suppress the feelings she had for him. The truth was that, throughout her sojourn in Italy and Albania, she had been slowly falling in love with Zak, the kind, caring, handsome man who was such good company and had, quite possibly, saved her life. Because if he hadn't found her on that hillside, she wasn't sure she would have made it.

'That's easy,' replied Zak, a dreamy, faraway look in his eyes. 'I'm moving to the village, to restore the house and the outbuildings and set up a tourism business. More and more people are coming to the area, attracted by the pristine environment, the lakes and waterfalls and treks over the mountains. I won't be doing it to get rich. I'll be doing it for myself, my parents and for Albania.'

Ruth's eyes had widened in envy. 'Oh wow,' she enthused. 'That sounds absolutely amazing. Can I come?'

As soon as the words were out, she slapped her hand to her mouth in horror. What had she said?

'Joking,' she spluttered hastily. 'Just joking, obvs. I'll be going home to Norfolk, back to the grey skies and bitter winds.'

Zak smiled. 'There are plenty of those in the winter in Albania, I promise you. But perhaps it's true that we have better summers. And more sunshine, generally.' He gestured towards her. 'Come here.'

Slowly, Ruth got up and, limping, went to stand beside him. Zak held out his arms and took her hands in his. He pulled her towards him, deliberately, never taking his eyes off her face. And then his arms were around her and his lips on hers and they were kissing, and it was so long since Ruth had been kissed that, for a moment, she was worried that she'd forgotten how to do it. But then, as the kiss continued, she forgot such doubts, forgot anything and everything except the here and now, her and Zak on the veranda, under the hot Italian sun.

When they finally released each other, Zak smiled down at her. 'I can't think of anything I'd like more than for you to come to Albania with me. I would love that.'

They stood for a moment, holding each other as time stood still and the cicadas thrummed. Ruth felt all her doubts fall away. Her worries over whether she should trust Zak seemed crazy, delusional. He was the most trustworthy person she'd ever met; nobody could be less like the mendacious Simon.

'I'm sorry it's taken so long for me to be honest with you about my feelings,' murmured Zak. 'I... well, you know how it is. Most people have been disappointed in love at some point or another, haven't they? But when you've been betrayed, it can be difficult to trust again.'

Ruth's head lay against Zak's chest. She could hear the beating of his heart. So his reticence, the distance she had sometimes felt he had put between them, had been self-preservation. It hadn't even occurred to her that he could have been through something similar to what she had.

'What happened?' she asked, simply.

'Ahhh,' he sighed. 'It's all in the past now and I hate that it can still raise its ugly head and affect the way I treat people, the way I've treated you.'

Ruth lifted her head to look him in the eye.

'It was someone I met at work,' explained Zak. 'She wasn't my employee, I hasten to add. A consultant who came in to help us develop a new product. Her name was Cristina. I fell for her, big time. But she was just passing the time whilst she was down in the South. It turned out she had a fiancé in Milan; I was a mere dalliance. It was Aurora who saw through her and uncovered the truth.'

Ruth remembered the immaculate Aurora. She had thought her behaviour a bit odd, bordering on hostility, and now she understood the reason. Aurora had been looking out for Zak, wary of anyone who might prove as bad for him as the adulterous Cristina.

'Poor you,' she sympathised. 'Perhaps it's our age; we've been knocking around for long enough to have been through it all.'

She told him about Simon; a confidence for a confidence.

'We can forget about both of them now, can't we?' said Zak, once she'd finished her story. 'Put them behind us where they belong.'

There was a pause and then he looked at his watch.

'It's well after eight on the East Coast. Do you think we can make that call now?'

'I think we can,' agreed Ruth. 'No reason to delay.'

They stood, looking at each other. Neither moved.

'Yes,' muttered Zak. 'I mean no – no reason at all to delay.' He sounded suddenly and uncharacteristically nervous. Ruth knew how much this mattered to him. 'You do it,' he said. 'She knows you from the email and… well, I might get too emotional.'

And so Ruth picked up the phone and made the call. It was emotional, inspirational, joyous. And by the end of it, an arrangement had been made for Miriam to bring Hannelore to Tirana at the beginning of October, when the weather would be cooler but the winter rains not yet begun, to finally meet Bekim again after an absence of over seventy years.

Chapter Thirty-Five

Albania, October 2019

On a shimmering autumn day, Ruth and Zak stood impatiently waiting for Hannelore and Miriam to emerge from customs control. Ruth had made a sign which she held up alongside all the others on display from taxi drivers, tour guides and hoteliers. No one was sure that Bekim, who'd insisted on also coming to the airport despite his increasing frailty, would still recognise his childhood sweetheart.

But when two women materialised from the crowd arrivals, one grey-haired and one chestnut, Bekim cried out with joy. 'There she is,' he called. 'There's Hannelore.' Though so many years had passed, he still knew her, could still tell her face and her smile from all the others in Tirana International airport that day.

Over the next couple of days, the old people talked and talked, Zak translating. After all this time, the only language the pair now had in common was a few words of Italian. But what they shared was something that did not need to be spoken. It was the love that had endured a seventy-four-year separation, brutal repression, new lives and new families, a deep, pure love that nothing could destroy.

'Do you think Drita is all right?' asked Ruth, at the end of the first day. 'It might be hard for her, to see Bekim and Hannelore so close.'

Zak shook his head. 'She's fine. She understands and she knows how much it means for my dad to have this opportunity.' They went on a trip, taking Hannelore to Durrësi and a little way into the mountains. It was not possible to go all the way to the village or the caves; the journey would have been too much for Bekim and Hannelore, and Zak didn't want his dad to be too far away from the hospital. He had rallied with Hannelore's visit, but they were all aware that it was only a matter of weeks now before his illness would take over.

Hannelore and Miriam marvelled at everything: at the boulder-strewn, potholed roads; the poverty of the many dusty villages they passed through; the horses and carts that still provided transportation in the countryside.

'I expected everything to be so different,' Hannelore murmured, as two elderly men guiding donkeys through a roadside hamlet waved at them. 'But I still recognise it all.'

More than anything else, the two Americans wondered at the warm welcome they received everywhere, the generous hospitality, just as had been the case all those years ago. Walking by the side of Lake Shkodra, the towering walls of Rozafa Castle on the hillside above them, Hannelore cried with delight at the sight of a Dalmatian pelican rising from the water, wings making a calligraphic V against the vivid blue sky.

'Do you remember when you almost fell through the ice?' Hannelore asked as they drank coffee in a lakeside cafe.

'Oh yes,' laughed Bekim, his face suddenly lit up by the memory. 'I was nearly a goner, then. Thank goodness I was strong enough to pull myself out.'

A frown crossed Hannelore's face. 'But that's not what happened at all,' she retorted, her indignation undimmed by age. 'I hauled you out. It took every ounce of my strength to do so. Goodness knows how you managed to be so heavy when none of us ever had enough to eat.'

Bekim chuckled, his filmy eyes twinkling. 'I'm teasing,' he said. 'Of course it was you who rescued me. All these decades years later, I'm finally able to admit that a girl saved my life.'

Hannelore stared at him in astonishment for a moment, and then began to laugh, a thin, reedy sound that came in fits and starts but that was, undeniably, the sound of happiness.

'You always were incorrigible,' she chuckled. 'And you still are.'

Ruth and Zak, enjoying the old people's banter, smiled conspiratorially at each other. It had been exactly the right thing to do, to make this trip happen. Bekim had been flagging before Hannelore's arrival; now he had rallied and was displaying glimmers of his old self.

'You taught me to ride a bicycle,' Bekim continued. 'Do you remember?'

'And you taught me to swim,' rejoined Hannelore. 'And you showed me the tortoises and explained why I couldn't take one home with me. You had so much wisdom, alongside your boastful nonsense.'

'Boastful nonsense!' Bekim repeated, his reedy voice filled with mock annoyance. There was a short pause. 'Well, maybe just a bit.'

They all laughed and Ruth felt her heart melting anew. Bekim, though so old and ill, still had character in spades. Hannelore, too, retained her ability to be supercilious and self-deprecating all at the same time.

'The first thing you ever explained to me was Kristallnacht.' Bekim's eyes were focused far in the distance, over the expanse of the lake. 'You told me what it meant, what had happened, but I didn't really understand.'

Another silence descended. The five people around the table, Hannelore, Bekim, Miriam, Ruth and Zak were momentarily lost in contemplation of the horrors of the past.

'So much of those years we spent together were filled with fear, rife with hunger and danger,' Bekim recalled, his voice raspy with weariness now. 'But somehow, these days, I find that it's the good times I recall. The fun we had. The adventures we shared.'

Hannelore nodded, her mouth quivering with age, her grey hair blowing wispily around her still-beautiful face. 'Good trumps evil in the end,' she whispered. 'Who would ever have thought we'd live to tell the tale, that we'd both be sitting here now? Survivors, that's what we are.'

Bekim nodded. 'I suppose we are,' he murmured. 'I suppose you're right about that.'

Over the next couple of days, they stayed at home, Hannelore and Bekim passing the time reminiscing.

'It's so funny, isn't it,' mused Ruth. 'This current generation would be poring over albums or going through the photos on their phones or Facebook pages. Hannelore and Bekim have nothing but the pictures that still exist in their minds.'

Zak smiled a bittersweet smile. 'It seems to keep them going, though,' he said. 'Now I know what these conference interpreters have to go through: one language coming in one ear and another in the other!'

Ruth gave him a brief, encouraging hug. 'You're doing a great job. You can see how they're loving it.'

By the end of the visit, both Hannelore and Bekim were tired. But there was one final thing to do, the most important of all: the handing over of the objects. As Hannelore took the silver Menorah, the bible swollen with damp and the remnants of the prayer shawl, she looked straight into Bekim's eyes.

'You told me the very first time I met you that your name meant "blessing",' she said. 'I think you were most disgruntled that I seemed unimpressed by this information.'

She paused to gently run her arthritic hands over the carved silver of the candlestick. 'But it wasn't long before I started to see the relevance of that name. You were a blessing to us. We've been circling around the issue but now the truth must be told. With your courage and your indomitable spirit and, it must be said, your bare-faced cheek, you saved us, not just once, but over again. These objects you have returned to me now are merely a representation of what you did, of what you were prepared to sacrifice.'

Bekim, tears streaming down his cheeks, intervened. 'It was nothing special,' he said, shaking his head. 'Only what anyone would have done. Any Albanian.'

'But still,' broke in Hannelore, 'I must thank you from the bottom of my heart, for everything. You made a promise... and you kept it.' Bekim smiled and gently laid his hand on top of Hannelore's. The faraway look in his eyes contained all the recollections of times long past, some discussed, some still to be recalled, some lost forever.

'Of course, Hannelore,' he said.

Tilting his head downwards, his gaze rested on his friend and his face lit up, as if he were seeing not the elderly, grey-haired lady but the beautiful, terrified but trusting girl with whom he had fallen so deeply in love eight decades earlier.

'I had no idea it would take this long, but I was always going to get them back to you, sometime, somehow.' He sighed deeply, a sigh of age and memory and the knowledge that life rarely happens the way you think it will.

'I gave you my word. I gave you my *besa*.'

Chapter Thirty-Six

Albania, December 2019

The silence in the damp-laden air was broken only by the soft sigh of closing prayer books. Reluctantly, the mourners turned away from the graveside and made their way to their waiting vehicles. Zak was weeping and though Ruth had tried to hold her tears back so that she could comfort him, now Bekim was buried she wept, too. Throughout the short ceremony, Zak had clutched in his hand the watch that Bekim had received from Gezim and which now belonged to him. Ruth could hardly bear to watch him stroking the smooth watch face and the soft, well-worn leather strap as he said his last goodbyes to his father.

Between them, Zak, Ruth and Albana helped Drita into the car and back home for the wake. After Hannelore's visit, Bekim had faded fast and finally passed away on a bright December morning. Twenty-four hours later, the funeral had taken place under drastically altered skies that had now fully shouldered the mantle of winter.

In the house, once all the guests had gone, Zak drew the curtains. On the windowsill was a Menorah, gifted by Miriam and Hannelore to remind Bekim of all the years he had watched the candles lit and taken part in a ceremony which, though nothing to do with his religion, had everything to do with the woman that he loved and her family. Bekim had lived long enough to see seven candles lit this year. Silently, Zak lit the eighth and final one.

When they had all finished crying again, Albana took Drita to bed. Zak and Ruth, both desperate for a breath of fresh air after spending so long in a fug of cigarette smoke, went to stand outside in the town house's small garden, bundled up in coats and scarves. Zak put an arm around Ruth and drew her to him.

'I'm so glad you're here,' he said.

Ruth nodded. 'Of course. I'm glad I'm here too. I wouldn't have wanted to be anywhere else.'

Zak looked up to the dark sky. 'Under communism, when I was a small boy,' he murmured, 'you could see every star so brightly and so clearly. There was no street lighting and most homes were without electricity. So there was absolutely no light pollution at all.'

A motorbike backfired and then roared past in the street outside. A steady hum of traffic from the main thoroughfare beyond intruded on the night's peace.

'And it was so quiet. Unbelievably quiet. In the centre of Tirana, at six o'clock in the evening, you could have heard a pin drop. There were no cars, no traffic, no vehicles. The few people who were allowed in from outside marvelled at it; they couldn't believe it. We hated it. It was the silence of oppression, of imprisonment. To think that this was the reward for Bekim and all those who fought so hard and believed so strongly in freedom.'

Ruth's heart went out to Zak, her lover and her friend, whose own heart was aching for the father he had loved so dearly.

'It was awful, what happened. But at least he lived to see the end of that terrible regime.'

'Huh,' snorted Zak. 'Unlike Altin and my grandfather.'

Ruth squeezed his hand. 'Don't dwell on the bad things now,' she urged. 'This is the time to remember the beautiful things, the amazingly brave, selfless things all your family did. Let's focus on the good, not the bad. Remember what Bekim said: that at the end of his life, instead of the hard times and the pain, he recalled the joy and the laughter.'

Zak sighed. 'You're right.'

They were silent for a moment, contemplating the night sky, the sprinkling of stars and the crescent moon that hung there, a slither of silver in a cloth of navy.

'Do you think Bekim came to terms with the loss of Hannelore?' asked Ruth.

There was a long pause before Zak replied. 'Yes,' he said, 'but it took time. A very long time. That's why he married so late, why he was forty-one when he had me and forty-three when Albana was born. But he always said that when he met my mother, he knew it was meant to be, that she was the one. And my mother never, ever resented the fact that he'd had a past love. She understood. She still does. You saw how she welcomed Hannelore and Miriam to her house. She bore no bitterness.'

'That's good,' said Ruth, simply. 'She's a good woman. They are all good people.'

Zak smiled down at her and planted a kiss on the top of her head. 'And they both went on to live good lives, Bekim and Hannelore. They were happy and loved, and that's all any of us wants, isn't it?'

Ruth nodded. She pictured the two young people, clinging on to each other as their last days together approached, knowing that the agony of war and its after-math were about to tear them apart. She snuggled a little closer to Zak's warm bulk.

'Edith Durham reported that Albanians are "the race with about the worst reputation in Europe",' she mused. 'Not that she agreed. And I have to say, apart from the drug gangs and the smugglers, neither do I.'

Zak laughed. 'I'm glad about that,' he said. 'Though it's probably true. But maybe if people knew that Albanians saved the lives of nearly every single Jewish person in the country, and the scores who fled here, they'd think differently.'

Ruth turned to him and wrapped her arms around him, resting her head against his chest. 'I'm sure they would,' she murmured, her words muffled by his thick coat. 'I feel so privileged to know the story.'

A light in an upstairs window flicked off and suddenly the darkness became even more intense, and the stars brighter.

'I'm so glad that Bekim had the chance to meet Hannelore again before he died, and give her the precious objects,' Ruth sighed. 'It's wonderful that you unearthed them in time – literally!'

Zak smiled and nodded, slowly and thoughtfully. 'They're the second best thing I've ever found,' he agreed.

Now it was Ruth's turn to smile. 'That's my line!' she interjected, referring back to their very first dinner together, and grateful for a momentary release from the emotion that fizzled between them. 'So – I have to ask – what's the first best?' She lifted her head and looked up to meet his gaze as she waited for his answer.

'That's easy.' Zak raised his hand and brushed a stray lock of hair from Ruth's cheek. 'You. You're the first best thing I've ever found.'

A rush of feeling so strong it rocked her very foundations swept over Ruth. Involuntarily, her arms tightened around Zak's waist as she used his solidity to steady herself.

'Ruth,' continued Zak, his voice low and solemn. 'It's a long time since I've said this to anyone. But I want you to know... what I mean is... you've come to mean so much to me, even over such a short time. And... well, the thing is that... I love you. I really love you.'

Tears sprang to Ruth's eyes, of joy rather than the sadness of earlier.

'Oh Zak,' she responded, voice thick with crying, 'I love you, too.'

Looking at him with misty eyes, Ruth saw herself reflected in his black pupils.

He placed a gentle hand on her head and ran his fingers through her hair. 'Would you... will you come to Albania with me, to the village, like you said in Italy?'

Ruth's breath caught in her throat. 'Yes. Yes, please. I really, really want to.' She thought back to how she had felt at the beginning of her 'mid-life crisis' holiday, how she had been searching for a meaning, for a new path, a fresh direction. Had she found the answers? Maybe, and maybe not. But she now understood that it didn't matter. Having the answers wasn't the point. Ultimately, life was about living, making the most of every day. And that, Ruth decided in a flash, was what she was going to do from now on.

Ruth nodded and dropped her gaze. Her hand reached to Zak's wrist, fingers grazing the watch strapped there, the family heirloom passed down from father to son that had become a symbol of honour and pride.

'Do you mind that I can't give you children? That you won't have a son to pass the watch to.'

Zak groaned and rubbed his forehead against her hair. 'No, Ruth, of course I don't mind. Albana's daughter will have the watch and she'll start a new tradition, of handing on to the girls. It's about time this family got with the twenty-first century.'

Ruth laughed, all the tension suddenly dispelled.

Zak put his hands to her cheeks and lifted her face to his. 'You don't have to worry about anything. I'll love you faithfully and for always, Ruth. I give you my promise. I give you my *besa*.'

Afterword

The story of the Albanians who sheltered Jews was little known until late in the last century. As the shadows of communism lifted, so the tales of bravery, resourcefulness and sheer, unadulterated kindness gradually began to emerge into the light.

Over time, many amazing tales emerged. Yad Vashem, the Holocaust museum in Jerusalem, now lists seventy-five Albanians in its Righteous Amongst Nations, the title given to those who risked their own lives to save Jews. Because of the length of time when Albania was a closed country, most of the awards were given posthumously, collected by sons, daughters, cousins. You can read more here, but have a box of tissues handy because the stories are certainly tearjerkers:

https://www.yadvashem.org/yv/en/exhibitions/besa/index.asp

Each one of those people who guarded and fed and watched over Jewish refugees during those long years of war put their own personal safety and that of their families on the line to do it. They were people who, for the most part, had very little themselves, but shared their bread, their homes, their friendship. It is an example of true altruism: the Albanian hosts had nothing to gain, and everything to lose, by their actions.

In the troubled times that we now inhabit, it's reassuring to recognise the goodness that can preside in the human heart.

Acknowledgements

This book has been a very long time in the writing, and has seen many previous iterations before arriving at this one. Thanks are owed to my agent, Megan Carroll of Watson, Little, who has stuck with it throughout and, far from giving up on it – and me – has helped me to get it to this point of publication. In addition, I've always had a tendency to over-complicate things and it was my editor, Emily Bedford at Canelo, who helped me see the way to simplicity. I'm so delighted with the way the book has turned out, but I couldn't have done it alone.

Thanks also to Yad Vashem, who provided me with many original documents and testimonies relating to the Albanian 'Righteous amongst nations'; it was this information that proved invaluable in creating the story of Bekim and his family.

My family were with me on our first trip to Albania, which I hope will be followed by many more when we are all allowed to travel again. In the meantime, I have to thank all of them for bearing with me whilst I try to write, hold down a full time job as a teacher and be a mother to three amazing teenagers.

I hope that readers enjoy the book and hearing this little known story of Albania and its Jewish refugees.